the unmasking

Also By Lynn C. Miller

Novels

The Fool's Journey
Death of a Department Chair
The Day after Death

Nonfiction

Coauthor, with Lisa Lenard Cook, *Find Your Story, Write Your Memoir*

the unmasking

A NOVEL

LYNN C. MILLER

University of New Mexico Press | Albuquerque

Library of Congress Cataloging-in-Publication Data
Names: Miller, Lynn, 1951– author.
Title: The unmasking: a novel / Lynn C. Miller.
Description: Albuquerque: University of New Mexico Press, [2020]
Identifiers: LCCN 2020014427 (print) | LCCN 2020014428 (e-book) |
    ISBN 9780826361714 (paperback) | ISBN 9780826361721 (e-book)
Subjects: LCSH: College stories. | Chautauquas—Fiction. |
    Silver City (N.M.)—Fiction. | LCGFT: Campus fiction. |
    Detective and mystery fiction. | Novels.
Classification: LCC PS3613.I544 U56 2020 (print) | LCC PS3613.I544 (e-book) |
    DDC 813/.6—dc23
LC record available at https://lccn.loc.gov/2020014427
LC e-book record available at https://lccn.loc.gov/2020014428

Cover illustration courtesy of Design Cuts
Designed by Felicia Cedillos
Composed in Dante 10.65/14.65

In memory of
Christie Logan
luminous spirit, incomparable friend

Author's Note

This book is a work of fiction. Although some of its buildings share a resemblance to those of a famous research university, Austin University does not exist. All characters, colleges, departments, events, and places in *The Unmasking,* including Fresno University and the Oso Grande Lodge in Silver City, are entirely creations of the author's imagination.

One

I am no longer young. A tug in Bettina Graf's chest underscored this simple truth. Her students filed past her on their way to the door, earbuds engaged, midriffs blooming from the confines of snug jeans. A few pairs of eyes glanced her way respectfully, but most gazed past her as if she were ground rather than figure, a grain of sand on the beach rather than the sparkling view beyond.

She'd decided to close the Friday session of her senior seminar on Masters of Psychological Fiction with a quotation from Henry James's *The Ambassadors.* It was a section that rarely failed to move her to tears. She offered up her passage after a lively discussion about James's complicated relationship with, and attraction to, a younger protégé, the journalist Morton Fullerton. She had ignored her inner alarm about making sentimental gestures to undergraduates, telling herself it was a fitting punctuation to one of the most satisfying classes of the semester.

Drawing her battered first edition of the novel out of her bag, the one on which she had blown a month's food money in graduate school twenty-five years before, Bettina held it aloft for a moment of reverent silence. Then, in the voice she reserved for reading aloud—her most compelling, she hoped—she began:

"'All the same don't forget that you're young—blessedly young; be glad of it on the contrary and live up to it. Live all you can; it's a mistake not to. . . . Do what you like so long as you don't make my mistake. For it was a mistake. Live!'"

Tears misting her eyes, she looked out into the class at the last "Live!" only to see two students yawn, one check his phone, another adjust her

1

backpack on her shoulder, and three others, blank faced, prepare to bolt for the door. Another young woman, in the front row, leaned forward and offered her a crumpled Kleenex, inquiring about allergies in a congested voice.

Cursing herself for an idiot and a sentimental fool, Bettina dismissed the class.

Of course, she agonized as they filed out, the subject of youth was not magical, nostalgic, pertinent, or even worth mentioning for these students, the oldest of whom was twenty-one! She really must write—preferably in blood—on each page of her schedule to remind herself never to humiliate herself in this way again. Another reason not to switch to an electronic calendar, she thought.

After slinking down the corridor and closing the door on the blessedly cluttered refuge that was her office, she dumped her class notes and books on the desk. She ignored the blinking message light on the desk phone and left with her purple backpack slung over one shoulder. If she hurried, she'd have two uninterrupted hours at the Austin University Research Center, the sole place in her life where predictability reigned supreme.

"Coming to check out the cemetery of lost souls for yourself?" A reedy voice wafted through the hushed corridor.

Bettina stiffened, but she relaxed when she saw the smirk on the library guard's face.

"Bad joke, huh?" The guard, a young woman of about twenty with limp brown hair and watery, hazel eyes, winked at Bettina. She then lifted a shoulder toward the rows of scholars seated in the special collections room, all bent intently over rare photographs and letters encased in clear plastic protectors. Bettina winced at the bent posture of one researcher, his neck craning forward at a painful angle.

"What d'you say, they all auditioning for *Night of the Living Dead* or what?" The guard giggled. "They don't have your energy, Professor Graf, most of them. Let's put it that way. I oughta know—I took your Female Moderns class." Her young and hopeful face met Bettina's with a familiar do-you-remember-me appeal.

Bettina squelched a smile as her foundering memory yielded up a name. "Judith, of course. Last spring, wasn't it?" She peered over the guard's shoulder to examine the room more closely. Judith had a point: the combined pallor of the faces in the reading room was alarming. If you narrowed your eyes, all you saw was a sea of white with scarcely a smile or a wink breaking the surface. However, to Judith she said, "Well, they're just more . . . *serious* than perhaps you realize."

"Huh. Coulda fooled me. Sorry, but I got to check your reading card."

Bettina found it interesting that Judith's speaking style varied so markedly from the meticulous essays the student had turned in the year before. "What are you doing now?" she asked Judith.

"Graduating in May. Looking for a job," Judith offered with a gloomy shrug.

This revelation held a clue to the guard's verbal syntax. A job search in this economy was bound to make seniors regress a decade or so, spurring a longing for a world where their parents paid the bills, meals appeared magically on the table, and an after-school job supplied funds for iPads and movie tickets.

"Well, good luck." Bettina watched, unnerved, as Judith scrutinized the small color photo gracing her faculty special collection identification.

"God, Dr. Graf, when was this taken? You look like a movie star."

Bettina restrained herself from snatching the card out of Judith's fingers. She kept her tone light. "That's not very flattering, Judith, to imply that I'm an aged ruin in comparison to the photo."

Judith had the grace to blush. "No . . . I just meant, you know, the perfect hair and makeup . . ."

As the student looked confused, Bettina added mentally, *And the unlined skin, the sagless chin . . .*

"I've never seen you look like that," Judith finished lamely.

"Thanks just the same." Bettina tucked the ten-year-old card away as Judith's fingertips relinquished the sliver of plastic. "I've got to run."

Bettina sucked in her stomach, pulled her shoulder blades together, and walked briskly into the reading room. The dreaded five words, mantra-like, pushed into her brain: *I am no longer young.* Her fiftieth birthday loomed in under two weeks, and everything conspired to remind her of its approach. The young student wiggled her fingers at Bettina in farewell, unaware of the consternation her casual comments had caused her former professor. Most likely, Bettina thought, Judith assumed she was being complimentary by sharing her opinion that the reading room dwellers were insipid. Bettina resolved to acquire a new ID card as soon as possible, preferably one taken on a day after an inadequate night's sleep so that her live self might sparkle compared to the photo.

Rounding the corner into Reference, Bettina noticed the dean of the Liberal Studies College, Alec Martin, seated at a terminal. She held her breath and turned her head aside, hoping to pass unseen.

Although she shielded her face with a curtain of her wavy auburn hair, on this occasion Bettina did not escape Alec's notice.

"Professor Graf!" His even front teeth gleamed in a too-white smile, Bettina noticed.

"How good to see you," she said.

He scrambled to his feet and pumped her hand. Bettina motioned for him to resume his seat and, conscious of the looks of two students at neighboring terminals, whispered, "Hi. Can't stay. Miriam needs these materials before her three o'clock class." She glanced at her watch, noting the lameness of her fib—it was already three thirty. "I guess I'm hopelessly behind schedule. Sorry, Alec."

"No, no, please wait." The dean waved her toward the empty corridor. "I must ask you something."

Bettina smothered her protest and allowed him to manipulate her elbow as a rudder to steer her out of the room. No wonder undergraduates were suspicious of libraries—they were almost certain to run into professors if they visited one.

"Professor G— . . . Bettina . . ." Alec's voice vibrated with a peculiar energy. A man noted for his caution, the dean seemed awash with excitement. "You've heard that Nyhus is going to resign?"

With a longing look down the corridor—was there a women's room she could dash into?—Bettina nodded. Only a blind and deaf newt could have missed the news that the provost, the university's chief academic officer, had announced his defection to the University of Wisconsin.

"I'm wondering if you'll serve on the search committee for the new provost," he said.

Bettina noticed the slight flush across his broad cheekbones, heightening the almost imperceptible scars from a teenage bout of acne. His eyes turned downward under her gaze. In that moment Bettina saw his raw ambition: Alec coveted the provost's office and, possibly, the presidency. She groped in her bag for a Kleenex and tamped it firmly across her lips. Alec was either barking mad or a comedian. Surely he knew the cadre of campus heavy-weights, a group that did not count him as a member, had already plotted, vetted, and ordained the next provost? Those who held the reins of power at the institution regarded Austin University as the very pulse of the great state of Texas. Alec was but a tiny hiccup in the über-flow of power that transfused the institution.

"It's very hot in here," she said simply, stuffing the tissue into a pocket after she had snuffed all reaction from her lips. She gave him a sober nod. "Alec, of course, if you need me I will serve. Or I should say, I'll agree to be nominated. There will be an election, I presume?"

Alec brushed aside her question. "And would you be willing to chair the search committee?"

Bettina cocked her head, fascinated by a thin aureole of baby-fine hair sticking up from Alec's crown. She wondered, not for the first time, how ambition positively electrified some men.

She cleared her throat. "Alec, that's very flattering of you, but I'm assuming that the chairpersonship of this committee will be determined by the president or his advisory committee." She didn't know how else to alert him to the fact that a mere dean—of liberal studies, no less, not pharmacy or law or business, entities which really mattered in the grand hierarchy of the university—was likely to have zero input into such an important appointment as the chair of the provost's search committee.

"Oh, but I've just come from a joint meeting of the provost's office, the regents, and the deans of the colleges. Your name came up, and I volun-teered to suss you out on the subject. You know, very informally."

Bettina registered that in every conversation, Alec used a British expres-sion. The poor sod probably fancied himself in one of the hallowed colleges of Oxford. Adding to her annoyance was the fact that her friend Darryl, now vice president of research, would have attended this meeting. Why hadn't he called to tell her this news? Bettina shook her head and stifled an urge to sneeze. Best to get away from this pathetic soul before he made any more misguided assumptions that he would later hold her responsible for.

5

"I consider it my duty to serve," she said hastily. "If I should be asked." *By a reputable person,* she added to herself.

Bettina made a grand show of gaping at her watch and, with a half-wave, strode down the corridor and around the corner. The elevator deposited her on the ground floor. As she exited the research center, she lamented that in a mere ten minutes the one place of refuge in her twenty years at Austin University had been snatched away. To think that she had allowed Alec, someone she avoided whenever possible at official functions and with whom she never, ever socialized, to sully this one pleasure. For the second time today, she lambasted herself as an idiot. If she really couldn't protect herself any better than this—giving students and administrators the power to send her emotions into free fall—she needed a new profession. She whispered fiercely at herself the advice she freely dispensed to friends and family at exasperating moments: *Get a life.*

And so later that day when she collected the mail at home, Bettina resisted throwing out the envelope with a return address marked "Silver City, New Mexico." It was mid-March and eighty-five degrees in Austin; the thought of cooler weather in the not too distant future and high, dry air prompted her to slide a thumbnail under the flap. She received a paper cut for her trouble. Eyeing the envelope with a wary eye, she reached for a letter opener.

Inside, written on cream paper with a deckled edge, was an invitation to participate in a literary festival. The sender was Patricia Mendoza, a former colleague from graduate school who'd left the academy in a huff a decade before. After a stint in law school—too similar to academia—she'd trained as a career counselor only to reject that too. In her view she'd just spent too much time listening to people who only wanted to talk about themselves. Recently Patricia had started a business as an events planner. One of her clients was a lodge in Silver City, New Mexico, in the southwest corner of the state. New owners had taken over the Oso Grande Lodge, a glorious property at the edge of the Gila Wilderness. "All pine trees, views, and inspiration," Patricia's invitation enthused. A handwritten note was attached saying that the lodge and the occasion—"think of a modern salon"—seemed a perfect place to arrange a reunion with her three Austin colleagues. Bettina recalled that Patricia had mentioned this festival at a reception last year, and that her good friends Miriam and Fiona had expressed doubt that the venture would actually come together. But it seemed it had.

Bettina hefted the invitation in her hand; it had a weighty feel. New people and places had changed her life before, so why not now? Turning the paper over in the afternoon sunlight, she reached for her phone to consult Miriam. The festival involved presentations of famous women in history. Perhaps the past could lend a sprinkle of glamour to the present.

Two

Miriam Held took a farewell turn along the board-walk that traced the inlet before heading to her car. As she clutched the brim of her straw hat against a brisk Gulf Coast breeze, an armada of white riding the choppy waters arrested her. She gripped her binoculars.

A squadron of white pelicans drifted in the current in front of the pier. Paired off two by two, their heads bobbed and dipped into the water, their feet trailing, their bodies curving toward one another. Each supple neck angled toward its companion bird, as if inviting the other to dance. And it was a dance, a sensuous orchestration of scooped beaks and weaving torsos as they fed, filtering the rippling water through the seine of their mouths. Necks bowing, bodies curving, they glided across the water's surface in a gastronomic minuet.

Miriam held her breath, afraid any movement at all might disrupt the birds' ritual. The pod of pelicans coursed in time to an invisible score. Their streaming was too sinuous to be a march, even a majestic one. *Brahms?* Miriam wondered. *Or Schubert?* She leaned against the railing, a tickle of desire rising in her throat at the sight of such synchrony and grace. Had she ever seen bodies more attuned? She thought not.

As the last pair of birds floated away from her, Miriam turned to go. But in front of her a ragged wing jutted up from the water. Then she noticed the bird's crooked neck drifting on the surface, its beak frozen half-open. A dead gull trailed the waltzing group, its feathers dirty and dull. Her spirits, soaring a mere moment ago, plummeted, and Miriam steadied herself on the hand-rail, imagining she saw a dark-red stain in its wake. A spattering of cold rain seeping under her jacket collar sent her hurrying for the shelter of her car.

Inside her Subaru Outback, Miriam's cell rang. "Yes?" she said as her old friend Bettina Graf's number popped up.

"Where are you?"

"Down at the coast. In Port A. Remember the whales bubble-netting in Alaska? I just saw something—"

A persistent whine emanated from her phone. ". . . can't hear very well," Bettina was saying. "Just wanted to tell you the invitation came through."

"Invitation?"

"For the festival. In Silver City."

"Oh." Miriam felt flat-footed. "But I must tell you about the pelicans."

"What? New Mexico. It's in New Mexico."

"I'm talking about pelicans. In south Texas. P-E-L-I . . ."

"Can't make it out. You're completely garbled."

Miriam held the phone away from her ear. How could Bettina hear nothing that she said when she could hear her friend perfectly?

"I'll call you when I get home. I was just going to hit the road now."

"Nome? Not sure what you mean," Bettina said, her pleasant contralto rising in laughter. "Tonight. Call me tonight."

Miriam ended the call and put the phone on the seat next to her. The dead bird unsettled her. It struck her as one sign of coming turbulence, and her phone cutting out was another. She remembered now that she'd agreed to speak at the gathering Bettina had mentioned. And on a topic—"The Locked-Room Mystery"—that now also seemed alarming. The still too-recent death of her female colleague, a woman who had been attacked and left to die in her office, still haunted her. While many people thought of the university as cushioned from reality, Miriam knew that academia was not a safe place.

The gull's broken wing and twisted neck flashed again before her eyes. Since moving to Texas, Port Aransas had always been a place she'd come to restore her sense of peace. The small town, accessible only by ferry, had an isolated charm. The dancing pelicans had taken her back to her innocence and hope—and youth—when she'd first come down to the Gulf Coast in the late 1980s. But today the dead bird appeared as an ominous symbol. She placed a hand on her own neck. It felt solid and a tad fleshy, as usual. And very alive. But as she well knew, a person bursting with health one minute could be rendered lifeless the next.

Miriam wondered at the fact that she and Bettina had found the idea of the upcoming festival appealing over coffee one morning not long ago. Perhaps they'd seen their ability to pick up their lives again as a sign they were no longer under the shadow of the suspicion, broken trust, and paranoia they'd experienced during the murder investigation. What hubris.

Miriam appreciated the calm and stability of her life more than ever before. She needed fresh air—and the canvas of woods or sea—rather than small spaces and artificial light. The idea of confinement among a small group of people, even very creative ones, in a secluded inn for almost a week felt claustrophobic.

The day had turned cloudy. Perhaps she was overreacting, she thought, as she started her car to head for home.

Three

Bettina replaced her cell on her desktop after calling Miriam. Her usually reassuring friend sounded perturbed about something, but Bettina would just have to wait to find out why. She checked her computer screen. Four o'clock. Two hours before she had to begin dinner preparations. Prime writing time, if only she could concentrate.

Bettina had left the door of her study ajar, leaving open the possibility of rescue from the usual distractions of the house or at least the comfort of a visit from Barney, her aged golden retriever. She sat stiffly for a moment, hoping to hear his toenails scuffing along the corridor's worn pine planks. A black dog brush lay on her desk amid the toppling piles of papers and correspondence. Untangling Barney's heavy coat was guaranteed to keep her from her task for an additional half hour. She waited, but the dog didn't seem forthcoming.

She shifted her pen container, put two stray paper clips into a drawer, and stared at her closed laptop. It seemed she would have to get to work. Pushing the sleeves of her green pullover above her elbows, she moved the jagged piles from around the computer. The state of the office—peach slip-covered sofa in tatters and coated with dog hair, ceiling fan cockeyed on its pole, three months' worth of filing spilling onto the floor—seemed metaphoric of the disorder of her scholarly life. Bettina leaned forward and massaged her face with both hands. Her skin felt dry, and surely there were new creases around her eyes.

She lifted the lid of her laptop and touched the track pad to wake it up. She'd promised her publisher a new outline and a first chapter from her much-delayed critical study of Virginia Woolf's fiction by May 15. She had one month to meet her deadline, and that meant accomplishing six months of work in just thirty days. Glaring at the screen, she keyed to her finder to find the latest notes for the project, only to find herself drawn to the lure of her outtakes file, entitled "VWmusings.doc."

She noted that she hadn't opened the file for three weeks. Not surprising, as she couldn't remember a single thought she might have moved into the document. In fact, the shift from the slow start of the semester to the frenzied end of term had driven critical thought in general from her mind. She simply got nothing done these days. How had this state come to pass? She had been promoted at only thirty-eight to full professor and had published three books by the age of forty. In comparison, the past nine years had been a desert of accomplishment. She winced, thinking of the affair two years before with Darryl Hansen, which had pushed her marriage to a precarious point. The episode was a sorry highlight, an indication of the distracted flight typical of her forties. While she and her husband Marvin had returned to a stable state, and her two children had both graduated from college and launched fledgling careers, her study of Virginia Woolf had languished in the accumulating debris of her office.

Bettina drew a deep breath, her chest stretching the fabric of her pullover into a second skin. It was time to put clarity to the disorder of her work life and resume a routine of concentration and discipline. With a hopeful lift of her eyebrows, she began to scan the file. To her delight she found a few pages under the intriguing title, "Move the Tree to the Middle."

She scanned the first paragraphs she'd written about a central character in Virginia Woolf's novel *To the Lighthouse*. Visiting her dear friend Mrs. Ramsey and her family, the painter Lily Briscoe despaired of escaping the voices that interrupted her life: dinner parties with outspoken men who expected her to listen to them and asked no questions about her life, the chaos of the Ramseys' children careening in and out of the house as they hunted for lost shoes and socks and earrings. Bettina smiled at the memories of her own children and husband asking for every item of clothing they possessed, how to find the ketchup, the ice cream, the hidden jar of mustard. Somehow she had managed to work in spite of, or perhaps because of, all the commotion.

Throughout the novel, Lily Briscoe searched to find the key to her own artistic vision, surely the pursuit of every artist and writer. Like everyone else in Mrs. Ramsey's orbit, she hoped to capture an undivided moment from this graceful and lovely woman, the ultimate reflector of the selves of those around her. Her own students, with their shy and anxious glances as they hoped for her approval, gave Bettina an inkling of what people expected of this beneficent being. She read on:

> The tree in her painting eluded her. It stood off to one side, as forlorn as the bloblike shape of a tree in a child's drawing. It commanded no attention. The eye graced over it, searching for more substantial signs of life. Lily felt the tree was like her, never center stage, always hugging the periphery, grateful for a look or a sigh floating in her direction. The tree, like her life, was so indirect, so insubstantial, so lacking in consequence. When would its time come?

Bettina had identified with Lily when she'd read the dinner party scenes, where a fellow guest, the tense Mr. Tansley, who showed no interest in Lily's work, constantly ranted about the difficulties of his research, the trying state of his career, his need for recognition. How many times had she been in such a position when a colleague in similar distress kept her from getting a word in edgewise? Even her simple *yes* in between the barrage of words brought a defensive, "But you can't possibly understand!" assuming that what she would say would be critical of his—or her—personhood and greatness. Bettina felt at one with poor Lily, who tried not to scream as she listened to Tansley's mantra: "Women can't write, women can't paint":

> The tree in her painting wavered in her mind, it began to dissolve. No, wait, she said silently. Don't go . . . She moved the salt and pepper shakers on the table into a new formation. That's it, I will move the tree to the middle!

Bettina's full lips turned down as she set aside this fragment. Of late, her own life needed the tree moved to the middle. Here she was, turning fifty in ten days' time, her manuscript stalled on a wayward trestle instead of speeding ahead down the main railway, her son and daughter off living their own lives very successfully (thanks, Mom, for asking, but we don't really need anything), her dear husband Marvin happy with her the way she was (though she feared she really needed a little friction to be at her best), her career not the satisfying thing it had been in the past. Her life cried out for innovation, stimulation, or at least rehabilitation! She simply couldn't go into the beginning of her fiftieth year (or would it technically be her fifty-first?) with a whimper rather than a bang.

The words "move the tree to the middle" lifted off the page and fluttered in her brain. A new project, yes, that was what she needed. Something more creative. The strained faces occupying the library earlier in the day came into her mind—God knows she didn't want to turn into an academic drone like so many of the middle-aged professors she knew. Her dear friends Miriam and Fiona were exceptions, thank God. Patricia Mendoza's invitation to the festival flickered in her mind's eye. She'd find out if performing Woolf's character—or at least these key scenes from the novel—might fit the parameters of her event. She'd minored in drama as an undergraduate. Why not try a new form of scholarship, one where the audience actually responded?

Bettina typed slowly the word "Lily." A storied name in literature. There was Lily Bart, Edith Wharton's heroine eaten by the society she alternately courted and shunned. And Lily Langtree, the Jersey girl who became a society queen and the mistress of Edward VII. Both of these women used men for advancement. Neither of them stood alone like Woolf's character, a spinster who finally moves out of the shadows and onto center stage in her own psyche.

Bettina herself had never contemplated the spinster life, having married at twenty-four. But she knew all about hovering on the margins of the page, as must any woman who had been a mother in charge of young children or worked in institutional life anywhere in America.

After Lily's name Bettina typed "postmodern heroine." Make that "hero." *Authoress, poetess, sculptress*: these diminutive versions of professional roles awarded to women artists in the days of Woolf and Wharton rankled Bettina. Most women were entirely too obedient, too nice, too quick to deny their achievements. Bettina to this day could recite whole conversations with Tansley-like administrators where she had nodded or smiled in the face of illogical assumptions instead of challenging them. She recalled being surprised by a male colleague in the mailroom one day when she had been copying an article on Carolyn Heilbrun after she had resigned from Columbia, embittered, she said, by a relentless boys' club. The senior professor in her department had watched her, saying, "Aren't you glad that couldn't happen here?" Bettina remembered just staring at him, mute with surprise. Bettina was happy to relinquish that hesitant part of youth. These days she'd have offered up the article between slices of bread and asked her colleague if he'd like to taste the experience for himself.

Bettina thumped her desk with a freckled fist. Onward to Lily Briscoe (and others like her), who, released from the pages of Woolf's novel, would finally have her day and her say squarely in the middle of her own story. It didn't matter that scarcely anyone in the attention-deficit-addled environment of the cyberage had ever heard of Lily Briscoe, or even, much more tragically, Virginia Woolf herself.

Four

Miriam parked her green Subaru in the driveway just as the car clock registered 6:00 p.m. Thank God that drive was over. The bucolic two-lane road in south Texas branched into a US highway teeming with unwashed trucks, most crawling but some screeching past or cutting in front of Miriam's car at each crest of the hill. By the time she passed Lockhart and headed into the Austin sprawl, it was all she could do to hold onto the wheel rather than cover her eyes.

She hoped her spouse, Vivian, would have martinis ready. "Vivi?" she called from the kitchen as she tossed her keys on the counter.

Instead of martinis waiting in frosted glasses, there was a note. "Be back by 6:30. Would love a drink . . . xo"

Sticky from the drive, Miriam raided the freezer for an ice cube, which she placed on the back of her neck, hoping to revive her energy. If she sat down before making the drinks, she'd still be plopped there when Vivian arrived.

The landline rang as the first cold drops oozed under the collar of her blouse.

"Miriam, have you heard the great news?" a robust voice sang into her ear. Before Miriam could manage a greeting, the voice tumbled on, seemingly without a breath. "The festival is on. In the most gorgeous spot. Southwestern New Mexico. You'll love it. Actually, we're structuring it like the revival of Chautauqua that's gotten popular again. Think of it—folks gathering in the summer in tents at the turn of the last century to hear famous people lecture around the country, bringing culture to small-town America. And now historians and literature scholars like us get to bring the past to life by presenting famous Americans to audiences, highlighting their major achievements as well as choosing aspects of each character's life that resonate with our time. We'll be putting together our own Chautauqua right here. A small audience will be invited to the performances, mostly in the evenings, and encouraged to ask questions after each presentation. First they ask questions of the character . . ."

"Patricia?" Miriam hazarded, thinking again she must deep-six the land-line. She fumbled for her glasses and her schedule. Given her earlier conversation with Bettina, she should have expected this. "Remind me when this might happen . . ."

"Of course it's me. And it's not *might* but *will* happen! Remember that fabulous idea I had? Or maybe it was your idea. The one about getting together a select group of performers and writers and exploring famous women in history?"

"Mmm, yes . . ." Miriam recalled a long arm, at the end of which was a huge prawn. Oh, of course—the cocktail party in honor of the new liberal studies building. Why had Patricia Mendoza been there? Something about public scholarship.

"Bettina called to talk about this earlier today," Miriam said. "But I don't think the keynote you and I had discussed will be appropriate," she added hastily. "Not at this. I don't perform, as you know. I can barely write my name these days."

"Ha, very funny, Professor Held. I've read at least four of your books, so you can't palm me off with your humility dodge. Plus, it's typical in these Chautauqua events that there be workshops or lectures, so your keynote will be perfect."

Miriam closed her eyes, remembering why Patricia had been such an irritating graduate student. For a moment she'd forgotten that she'd advised Patricia's dissertation twenty years before.

"And the festival is in September. Last six days. It should be just gorgeous then—"

Miriam headed off her reverie. "But I think you've forgotten mysteries, Patricia—mysteries, that's what I'd said I could talk about. You probably want something more political or historical for this event—"

"Mysteries," Patricia repeated, as if it were a foreign word. "Remind me what slant you're taking . . ."

Miriam was always patient when someone asked her the subject of the book she was writing—after all, she could barely keep a project in her sights in its early stages, so how could anyone else? "Classic women mystery writers: Dorothy Sayers, Agatha Christie, Ngaio Marsh."

"Hmm." Patricia seemed skeptical. "Seems a departure for a high-culture vulture like you . . ."

Miriam felt a surge of irritation, but before she could reply, Patricia switched gears. When she wanted something, she was endlessly flexible. "No problem. The mystery theme is perfect. For one thing, most writers have tried their hand at one. Even your beloved Gertrude Stein wrote *Blood on the Dining-Room Floor.* But I've had an idea."

Another one? Miriam braced herself.

Patricia's voice increased in intensity. Remembering another quality of her graduate student behavior, a tendency to speechify, Miriam's eyes strayed to the liquor cabinet with longing.

"What if each of the characters invited had a legacy of conflict with at least one other figure?" Patricia chuckled. "Your dean's wife, for example, Barbara Martin, has been traveling all over the country as Mabel Dodge Luhan, the great patron of the arts. A major figure in New Mexico history, of course, introducing writers like Willa Cather and D. H. Lawrence to the state."

Miriam thought Mabel Dodge Luhan an underappreciated figure in history. In addition to Luhan's literary output and her appreciation for Native American art, Luhan collected personalities in her Taos compound like a strategic magpie. The choice of the storied heiress as a subject added a new dimension to her view of Barbara Martin. Miriam had found her aloof and unreadable at their first meeting. But, back to the task at hand. "Yes, and how is the presence of Mabel Dodge Luhan a conflict?"

"With Gertrude Stein. First, she and Mabel were pals, until Mabel made a pass at her in Italy in front of Alice. They were Mabel's guests, at the Villa Curonia, which seemed doubly rude. Alice was furious. The three of them never saw each other in person again."

Miriam pushed her glasses to the top of her head, weary from Patricia's veerings from literature to gossip and back. Though, she did have to admit, what was literature but recorded gossip? It seemed to her she had written an essay on that very thing. But she must focus, or she'd be as scattered as Patricia. "But then you must have a Stein. Or an Alice B. Toklas. I told you I don't perform." Miriam's first book had parsed Stein's ideas of language.

"Never fear. Just giving you an example. Actually, there's a woman in California who's done Stein for years. She's been participating in this revival of Chautauqua for at least two decades. I'll ask her. Jane Auckler. Do you know her?"

"Yes, I know Jane. But she wasn't doing this back then—she really says that, that she *does* Stein?" Miriam wondered how that might be managed as the famous Picasso portrait showing Stein as powerful and charismatic popped into her mind.

"Ha, ha. Just actor talk."

"But I thought you said these people were scholars."

"They have to be both, don't they? The research isn't enough. They have to make it lively and interesting, to hold an audience. These presentations are not academic but are geared to a general audience who wants to learn about prominent people in history."

"Hmm. Perhaps many of my colleagues need this training to be effective in the classroom."

Patricia didn't seem to have heard. Miriam recalled that teaching evaluations hadn't been the high point of her student's career when she was getting her PhD.

A belated chuckle from Patricia indicated that she had heard Miriam's comment after all; her brain had simply sprinted to the next conversational thread. "Your book on Dorothy Sayers inspires me—I don't suppose you'd consider presenting a dialogue between Harriet Vane and Peter Wimsey?" She spoke of Sayers's two famous sleuths as if they were dear friends of hers.

"No performing," Miriam said firmly.

"No? We'll leave that then . . . for now. So, let me tell you what I'm thinking."

Miriam propped her glasses on her forehead. "Mmm."

"We'll convince Bettina to perform Virginia Woolf. She said something today about being fascinated by some character in one of the novels, but that might be too obscure. Lily something. Or Lucy? All those novels are running together for me." She laughed again. "How clever of Woolf to have all of her characters' thoughts intersecting like a giant quilt—she's showing us her theories of stream of consciousness!"

"I think Woolf expected a bit more of her readers than that. You make stream of consciousness sound like a frayed cook throwing all of her ingredients in a Cuisinart," Miriam said, frowning. Bettina's voluptuous figure and wavy auburn hair flashed before Miriam's eyes. "You know, Bettina doesn't *look* anything like Woolf . . ."

"That doesn't matter in the slightest in this form! The whole point is not to be literal. *Essence* is what we're going for."

"All right. You said something about conflict. Who is the thorn in Woolf's side?"

"Um, her husband, Leonard?"

"I thought this festival, er Chautauqua, was about women in history. And didn't they get on rather well, considering?" Miriam had always admired the Woolfs' literary partnership, in spite of what seemed to be incompatible sexual lives.

"Oh, you're being literal again. Let me think about it." Patricia switched to a more serious gear. "The 2016 election enraged me. But it energized me too. I've decided to work on Victoria Woodhull."

"The early feminist?" Miriam's estimation of Patricia rose several notches. Woodhull had been a trailblazer. She recalled that she'd been the first woman to run as a nominee of a major party for the US presidency.

"Exactly. I'm calling my piece 'The First Woman.' Woodhull was such a nonconformist—you know she spoke out for free love and called the financial bargain many women struck in marriage a form of prostitution. In the nineteenth century! She had courage. And like women from the beginning of time through Hillary Clinton and after, she was bullied by powerful men . . ."

"Torn down and torn apart," Miriam chimed in, an old anger rising at the slow turn of the wheel of progress.

". . . But she wrote a lot, particularly speeches—she toured the country as a sought-after speaker. Her writings are dense and difficult, but I'm hoping I can make the language work somehow."

"I think that's a fantastic idea. Maybe Woodhull was the original 'Nasty

Woman' who inspired others to rebel! It sounds like she would have relished the phrase. Most people don't know that a woman ran for president in, what was it, the 1890s?"

"1872. She headed the Equal Rights Party and ran against Ulysses S. Grant."

"I look forward to learning more about her," Miriam said sincerely. "And just think—it took forty-eight more years after a woman ran for president for women to get the vote in this country."

The two women were silent for a moment. Miriam added, "We all need to hear about her. By looking at that turbulent era in American history you'll dramatize the politics of our own polarized time. With similar class issues as well. I believe Woodhull rose from poverty through grit and determination."

"And a bit of luck. Which ran out right before the election—a long story I'll share with you in September. But she ended her life back on top. In England."

Even though Miriam admired Patricia's enthusiasm for her subject, her own energy began to flag. "As I said, I look forward to hearing more. Oh, I meant to ask you, what are you calling this happening?"

"'Women on the Edge.' Doesn't that have a fabulous ring?"

"Um, well, you might have something there, but—" Miriam felt a pulse of alarm. Wasn't Patricia herself always on the edge? Why did she need a special event about it?

Before Miriam could continue, Patricia interrupted her. "I do hope you'll help me with someone else . . ."

Miriam counted to five. Even though this was the most interesting conversation she'd ever had with Patricia, she was tired from her drive and impatient to get off the phone. She vowed she'd give Patricia just one more minute. "Yes?"

"Our friend Fiona. Do you think you could persuade her to perform Edith Wharton? She seemed intrigued with the idea when we all discussed it."

Miriam's younger colleague and friend, Fiona Hardison, had made a splash with a creative biography of the great American writer several years before. She doubted Fiona would leap to participate, but anything to get this woman off the phone, so she recklessly offered, "Why not? I'm seeing her for coffee tomorrow. And now I really must go."

"I'll be sending you an email . . ." Patricia carried on even as Miriam lowered the phone. For Patricia, speech was thought, her happy burble a roller derby of colliding impulses. Fiona, on the other hand, had uncommon good sense and a logical mind-set that made her shine in a crisis. Not that Miriam planned on events turning south in the near future.

Five

Fiona chose two 1930s silver pins in the gallery off the dining room of the Oso Grande Lodge. She earmarked the eagle pin, which showed a bird in profile with a fierce expression, to give Miriam, and she selected the starburst ringed in turquoise for Bettina. She'd had a meeting with her literary agent in Los Angeles, so her two friends had urged her to make a stop in Tucson on her way home to Austin, rent a car, and drive to Silver City. "We can't possibly go to Patricia's festival unless you vet the place first," Bettina had declared.

"Me? But I'm an old camping person. I'm not sure you can trust my taste."

Bettina's green eyes glittered like cut glass. "Ha! I've known you for ten years and not once have you gone camping. Face the fact that those days are over, at least when you're traveling with us. Just take a few photos, ask to see their nicest rooms, and eat at a different restaurant every meal."

At the lodge, Fiona wandered out to the porch, where bird feeders of every description hosted black-headed grosbeaks, juniper titmice, and a handful of woodpeckers. The woodpeckers squawked at Fiona's arrival. They flashed black and white as they scattered to a nearby tree, a beautiful spreading juniper with neat rows of square scales on its trunk—an alligator juniper, she discovered when she questioned the staff at the lodge.

The morning spring air was bracing but not cold; Fiona's burgundy sweater over a blouse kept her toasty.

She sat in a porch swing, waiting for her partner Darryl to join her, watching a wisp of cloud streaming toward the top of a nearby mountain. The birds alone promised to ensure Miriam's happiness, and the place's other amenities—acres of walking paths, comfortable king-size rooms, mountain views—were sure to placate Bettina. Bettina worked hard, both in her university position and as support staff to her husband and two children, and, like many ambitious and successful people, she had an equally hard-driving appetite for pleasure. Many of her colleagues envied her classic looks, wit, and seemingly effortless execution of her life. Fiona, four years younger and privy to her friend's struggles as well as her triumphs, simply appreciated her.

"There you are." The deep voice sounded relieved.

Fiona ran her fingers through her short, blonde hair and cast a wary look over her shoulder. She'd had an uneasy feeling all day that someone she didn't want to talk to from the university would be lurking in the bushes, casting a pall on a delicious stolen weekend. Then she planted a kiss on Darryl Hansen's tanned and handsome face as he slid next to her on the swing. He had flown in from Austin, and they'd driven over together. "I'm feeling very lucky," she said simply.

"Not as lucky as I am. Here we are in this beautiful place." He glanced down at their feet gently touching as they sat together. "I can't imagine being here—being anywhere—without you." He kissed her, clasped her hand, and relaxed back in the swing.

Fiona squeezed his hand in return. She had finally cast aside any worries about the attraction that had once flared between her lover and her best friend. Darryl and Bettina had a very complicated romantic history in the years before Fiona had arrived at AU. Fiona had felt doubly betrayed when the two of them had an affair right after she and Darryl had broken up a couple of years back. She and Darryl were separated, so it had been none of her business, yet at the time all she could see was that Darryl had seemingly leapt from her arms into Bettina's. The whole episode had plunged her into a queasy examination of what constituted fidelity and the bonds of friendship. The affair hadn't lasted long, but it had pained Fiona to see her ex-boyfriend and her dear friend together. Bettina's marriage to Marvin had survived, and Darryl and Fiona had gotten back together. She had finally forgiven them both.

She basked now in the easy affection between her and Darryl. "What, me? You know that old joke that academics are the kind of people no one wanted to dance with in high school? You're the exception, the boy everyone wanted to dance with in high school."

"Now there's a compliment." Darryl laughed. "I won't tell you what high school really felt like. Somehow I suspect you've been there."

"How about I pretend that I don't remember?" Fiona smiled at Darryl, who so easily deflected any mention of his charm. The fact was that he gave an impression of ease, concealing the effort he'd clearly put into his career and relationships. Even her own mother seemed dazzled by him each time the couple visited her.

Fiona hooked an arm through Darryl's. "You know, these clear skies might not last. How about a hike after we eat? I read about a trailhead only a few miles away."

Companionably, they went into breakfast. On the table was a copy of the Albuquerque newspaper. Fiona picked up the front section, Darryl dove into the business pages, and they spent a few minutes reading as they sipped an excellent brew of dark-roasted coffee beans topped with fresh cream.

"Listen to this." Darryl hastily set down his coffee cup. "'Alec Martin, dean of liberal studies at Austin University, is one of four finalists for the university's provost position. Martin, a New Mexico native, grew up in Las Cruces and went to Colorado College before getting graduate degrees at the University of Colorado.' I don't know what's weirder, reading about a colleague at a lodge near a huge wilderness area where you're feeling deliciously remote and far, far away from Texas and AU politics, or finding out that Alec has finessed a political coup that sets my teeth on edge!"

"Let me see that." Fiona read the article for herself. "Good Lord. Alec doesn't deserve any publicity. He promotes himself, and that should be enough." She rubbed her forehead. "Doesn't this job have your name on it?" She knew Darryl had stepped down as dean to take on the directorship of graduate studies, a position with the rank of vice president. The last provost had been plucked from that very position.

Darryl sat back and rolled up the sleeves of his cream-colored shirt. The lines around his eyes registered a deep strain. "That's not the problem. If you read on, you'll see I'm a finalist too. It's that Alec could be in real trouble over some missing funds. And his running for the provost's position means the scandal will just be bigger if the rumors are true."

The sinking feeling of losing what had been a lovely stolen weekend assailed Fiona. "Alec can be a fool. At one time, believe it or not, he was a fine scholar of political history. Now he's a sorry has-been kept afloat by pure cronyism."

A look of surprise passed over Darryl's face. "I didn't think your institutional memory went back that far."

"You forget I'm a pupil of Miriam's. She's a living repository of AU lore, and not just of the Department of Literature and Rhetoric."

Darryl smiled his slightly lopsided smile. "Nothing gets past her. Remember the story of Bluebeard? The young woman married to him steals the key to the closet where, she discovers, he's hidden all the grisly bodies of his former wives—the key keeps bleeding, broadcasting the fact that Bluebeard has gotten away with murder. Many times. As long as Miriam's around, the blood can't be washed away as if it were never spilled."

Fiona felt a tingling in the back of her neck. "Funny you should bring up murder. Miriam is giving a keynote about the locked-room mystery. Right here, at Oso Grande, in late September, where some of us are convening for a salon on notable women in history. Something about this Alec Martin thing makes me think he's gotten away with murder too. His career has been just too perfect."

Darryl rose and picked up their cups. Before heading to the beverage bar for a refill, he said, "He may be headed for a fall. And soon."

Six

A month later, at the end of April, Miriam and Darryl were flushed out the exit of the university union ballroom by a surging wave of departing faculty members and guests. As the press of people fled through the double doors, Miriam clutched at the slender blue scarf draped around her neck.

"Lord," she said, rearranging her clothing as people spilled out onto the sidewalk some minutes later. "I was almost throttled by the stampede."

"The smell of humiliation does that to people. Makes them bolt. Anywhere is better than the scene of the slaughter."

Darryl referred to Alec's keynote speech at the annual faculty awards' banquet. The dean—out of, what, inebriation? unconscious suicidal desires?—had laid waste to the honorees in a systematic way.

Miriam shook her head, recalling Alec's nasal voice as he gave a certificate promising supplemental publishing dollars from the university bookstore to an assistant professor of history: "You're at it again, Roger. You got this award last year. Are you going to make the university pay for every book you publish? Watch out, you might become too expensive for us to keep." The dean flashed a jaunty smile, as if expecting applause, and then moved on to the next award.

"I don't know," Miriam said. "For me the worst was when the dean presented Bridger with the lifetime achievement award and then urged the poor man's three ex-wives to stand up as well."

Darryl shook his head. "That served Bridger right. If you insist on seducing your graduate students, you can't expect your colleagues to grovel at your feet too."

Miriam reflected on how reactionary academics like both Bridger and Alec really were, seemingly deaf to the accusations of sexual harassment ricocheting around the university—and the world. But knowing Darryl was behind a zero-tolerance policy in these matters, she could afford to be playful. "Is that a sexist remark? First of all, what of the feelings of the wives? Second, are you assuming that female students collapse in awe at the knees of male professors?"

"Oh, is that what they're doing at the knees of their professors? I thought maybe something a lot more fun." Laugh lines rippled on the skin around Darryl's gray eyes. "Well, I wouldn't know, actually."

Miriam laughed out loud at the mild flush on her handsome colleague's face. "As Bettina would say, that's too hot for these hands to touch."

"Hottest were those awful introductions," Darryl said. "My God, did you hear him say that our President Price was aptly named because he always went with the highest bidder?"

"That was one of the worst. Especially in light of the public outcry over the president accepting what appear to be bribes by magnates to get their names on every new building on campus." Miriam smiled sadly, thinking of the day's headlines in the *Austin Journal Observer*, which were protesting a multimillion-dollar donation to the university by an energy CEO whose company was being investigated for tax evasion. "At least Price announced that AU was not accepting Bobby Joe Morgan's money. Or should I say blood money?"

"Well, Texas isn't the first state to have a hangover from corrupt corporations and politicians. And it won't be the—" he broke off. "Hang on!"

They had reached the street, and the door of Miriam's Subaru, when a woman with long, blonde hair tripped over the curb and fell against Darryl's arm. "Ohhhh, I'm sorry," she gasped. She clutched her ankle with a grimace.

"Mrs. Bridger?" In a quick reflex, Darryl bolstered the woman's flagging right side with one arm. "Are you all right?"

After a moment of rummaging about in her memory, Miriam recognized her as the second of the award-winning Bridger's wives who had been paraded before the audience by Alec.

The woman nodded, impatiently extracting a wisp of hair that clung to her mouth. Miriam noticed that her nose looked pinched and whitish, as if the air were frigid. Even though it was still April, the evening air couldn't have been below seventy degrees.

"God, yes, I'm fine. If you can say that after enduring an eternity of that bastard's drivel."

"I don't suppose you could just chalk up Alec's behavior as macabre humor?" Darryl said.

Miriam put a hand on her friend's elbow and exerted a subtle pressure. Darryl was usually so tactful. The blonde woman burst into a rough laugh. "Oh, it was funny all right, if you like your humor of the killer variety, sort of like shooting fish in a barrel with a deer rifle." She put a hand on Darryl's shoulder and smiled slightly. "I forgot that he's made you his target too."

"More like a pin cushion, of late," Darryl said.

"And this is about . . . ?" Miriam was puzzled.

As Mrs. Bridger smiled knowingly, Darryl explained. "Oh, just one of Alec's sleazy moves. When I took over as VP for graduate studies, there was an irregularity in funding for graduate student grants. A gaping hole to the tune of four hundred thousand dollars. I made a fuss about it." Darryl disentangled himself from his tie and stuffed the scrap of red silk in his jacket pocket.

It confounded Miriam that she, chair of her department twice in the last six years, hadn't known about what sounded like embezzlement in her own college. "Maybe that's why he's drinking so much," was all she said.

Mrs. Bridger's disparaging laugh rumbled in her throat with a smoker's rasp. Taking in the woman's swollen lips—chafed and red more likely from nervy biting than makeup—and flushed face, Miriam was reminded of Lana Turner in her sultry turn in *Peyton Place*, a favorite of her mother's in the rota of late-night reruns they'd watched together.

Miriam clicked the remote on her car, feeling if she stayed any longer she'd feel singed from the woman's simmering anger that threatened to boil over at any moment. "I'm sorry. It's getting late," she said to Darryl. "I promised Vivian I'd proof one of her projects. Why don't I call you tomorrow?" She improvised: "We'll finish discussing the summer grant budget then."

"Forgive me for interrupting." Mrs. Bridger's serene tone held not a hint of regret. She turned a dazzling smile on Darryl. "I'm afraid the friend who came with me tonight had to leave early. I live fairly close by. Could you possibly drop me at my house?"

"Sure," Darryl said after a pause. "Be glad to." He gestured toward his car, a cranberry Lexus sedan three car-lengths up from Miriam's. "After you," he said. He turned for a moment before he followed her to flash Miriam a grin that was part SOS and part resignation. She felt a wave of affection for him as he gently guided Mrs. Bridger down the street.

Miriam thought her dapper friend had his hands full this evening. His divorce two years ago had put Darryl into the supremely eligible bachelor category for those at AU on the prowl. Miriam knew Darryl wasn't available, his heart once attached to Bettina and now firmly to Fiona. However, even during the turbulence of his divorce, Darryl had managed to keep his affairs intimate in name as well as deed, so much so that even seasoned gossipmongers like the one they'd just encountered were kept in the dark.

Miriam's spirits were lifted a moment later by thoughts of her wife, Vivian. Give her a stable marriage over intrigue every time. What had Bettina once said of the two of them? "You two are so far from the fast lane you're in the parking lot." Her remark was gratifying in light of the mad couplings she witnessed in her department. Exciting they may be, but the predictable fallout of tears, career wipeouts, and mental meltdowns had never appealed to Miriam. At least, she amended, not since she'd met Vivian. She firmly pushed away memories of early experiments that had led to more loneliness and frustration, not less.

At home, Miriam found Vivian in her upstairs study, packing up her laptop. "Early meeting tomorrow," Vivian said. The couple's glossy tortoiseshell cat, Phoebe, opened her amber eyes from her perch on the corner of the desk and yawned at Miriam.

Miriam's lips skimmed her wife's wavy hair as Vivian leaned forward to slide the laptop case on a nearby chair. "You don't want me to edit tonight?"

"Oh God no." Vivian flashed an impish smile. "I just told you that in case you needed an excuse to get home early."

"Ha. I couldn't get away any earlier. But, actually, the evening had some

30

entertainment value. Alec positively laid waste to every scrap of goodwill he's managed to scrape together in thirty years at AU. The man was raving like a lunatic."

Vivian shuddered. "I don't know how you academics stand each other. Sniping and drooling at every opportunity, and who knows which it'll be each time a so-called *colleague* stands up to speak!"

"Well, someone has to keep our institutions going," Miriam grumbled, having thought the same thing herself earlier that evening.

The two women looked at each other, Vivian's eyes in an oval of surprise and Miriam's eyebrows raised crookedly. They burst into laughter.

"You mean someone's got to do it?" Vivian hooted. "Someone's got to endure the boredom and the bad clothes and the bad food—"

"I draw the line at the food. The faculty club has really improved—"

"Are you sure?" Tears stood out in Vivian's eyes at this revelation. She doubled over, her shoulders quivering.

"Stop!" Miriam gasped and then hiccupped to stifle a giggle. "This is unfair. Truth will get you nowhere with me. Come, let's pretend we're civilized and have a drink together while you tell me about *your* day."

Vivian, her long legs clearing two steps at a time, preceded Miriam down the stairs and into the living room. Phoebe raced past both of them and vanished in a twinkling of gray and gold fur down the hall. "You sit and relax, and I'll get us a drink," Vivian said.

Miriam sank into the worn leather sofa and closed her eyes. When she opened them, Vivian had reappeared with a tray, two small crystal glasses, a bottle of Glenmorangie—Miriam's favorite—and a small bowl of ice cubes. She then poured two inches of malt whiskey into one glass, added one ice cube, and passed it to Miriam.

"Perfect!" Miriam purred. She stared at the tray. "So formal. I feel like a guest."

Vivian sat down next to her, tossed off her shoes, and folded her legs underneath her. "I want to talk to you about something." She absently picked up her empty glass and then put it down.

Miriam felt a moment's unease. Vivian's usually mobile face looked blank.

Vivian did not pour herself a drink. Miriam took a tentative sip of hers, her tongue meeting with the brine of peat and a deep aftertaste of malt.

No wonder the Scots thought of their whiskey as food. It did nourish the tired soul.

"Sweetie, what is it?" Miriam prompted.

"Barbara Martin came to see me today."

"Alec's wife? Here? Why?" Miriam had only met the woman once, at a reception six months ago that the dean had thrown to commemorate his recent marriage, his third. She remembered her as attractive, with cropped dark hair and wearing an outfit of shimmery blue fabric. She tried to remember if Vivian had been with her at the event.

"I don't think I mentioned it, but she and I were at Brown together." Vivian's smile was uncharacteristically tight. "In the way back."

"Mmm." That the association was so long ago seemed like positive news to Miriam.

"She's spent most of her life in the northeast. She says she's at sea in Texas."

"Well, yes," Miriam nodded. "She'll get the hang of it. All of us imports do."

Vivian made a sound more like a half growl than an assent. "I'm not sure she will."

"Good grief, Vivian. Come out with it." Miriam's glass felt sweaty, and she set it back on the tray. "She's hardly your responsibility."

"No. But she wants friends. Her new husband's under some kind of political cloud, and she's finding the university unfriendly."

Austin University was claustrophobic and certainly rife with cliques, but unfriendly? Miriam had always found the Texas style more of a come hither than a rebuff. "Oh. What can her secret be? Just try and keep most of these people away, I've always found!"

Vivian looked profoundly unhappy. "Miriam. Barbara was my first lover."

Miriam hadn't known this, but then the only detail she knew about Barbara Martin was Patricia's remark that the woman was touring a performance of Mabel Dodge Luhan. Luhan had been a notorious troublemaker, especially in matters romantic. Hopefully this trait did not apply to Barbara. "Well, remember, I was once involved with Isabel, long before I met you. I can't really fault your taste."

The murdered former chair, once Miriam's lover, had been a woman of great brilliance and larger ambition. Miriam had actually been a suspect in her death, and her chest tightened in familiar dread at the memory. She took Vivian's hand and waited.

"Oh God, poor Isabel." Vivian bowed her head. "I'm surprised Barbara didn't pump me for information about that." Vivian poured herself a drink. "I haven't seen Barbara for, oh, thirty-some years. Lord, we were eighteen! Things didn't end well. I guess most first relationships don't, do they? I didn't expect to ever see her again once we graduated."

Miriam's voice was soft. "Well, these people sometimes turn up. When we least expect them. Is it really so important now?"

"Not to me!" Vivian's face paled and her voice was hoarse. "But I don't trust her. All the time she was here I wondered what she wanted. And how she might hurt you."

"Me?" Miriam sat up straight. "The police investigated me for killing Isabel. Not many things are worse than being accused of murder. Don't worry about me." Nightmares still plagued her about Isabel, her handsome face and elegant figure, destroyed in an instant by an unstable person's rage. If Isabel could be felled so suddenly, no one was safe.

"Oh, Miriam. Barbara can be dangerous when she wants something."

Miriam gave Vivian's hand a squeeze. "And what does she want?"

Vivian's face looked hot and almost allergic. "I'm afraid she wants me."

Seven

Alec hesitated on the doorstep of the small, square house on West Lynn. A small, silver nameplate to the right of the doorbell announced:

DAPHNE ARBOR, THERAPEUTIC AND PSYCHIC CONSULTATIONS

His wife, Barbara, had insisted that he come to Arbor for counseling, but as he stood in the small courtyard of the house overgrown with twisting wisteria vines, his misgivings surfaced. The tangled vines reminded him of his life. Some of the vines seemed dead, the gnarled bark denuded of foliage in the same way he would soon be stripped of his professional standing if he didn't find a way out of the boondoggle he'd created.

He reminded himself he was only keeping this appointment to please his wife. She was convinced that Arbor's reputation for insightful solutions was just what he needed for behavior that she had labeled "agitation." He knew his problems went much deeper than an unstable mood. Barbara's parting words that morning echoed in his head: "For God's sake, Alec, stop brooding. Forget the past. Eyes on the prize!"

What Barbara, a woman of action, didn't seem to realize was that the past was his playground. His field was history, after all. But, anxious to appear open and flexible to his wife, he submitted to her advice. Alec raised his hand, the skin scored by wear and weather, to ring the bell. But before the first peal of sound, the door opened, and an extraordinary figure stood before him.

Daphne, a towering woman with the ample proportions of an Artemis, had a mane of silver curls that grazed her shoulders. Her weathered face was marked by a strong nose, a generous mouth, and a gaze made disconcerting by her mismatched eyes, one piercingly blue, one a tawny cat's eye.

"Dean Alec Martin?" She inquired in a warm, husky tenor. As he nodded, she bowed slightly from the waist, her curls flowing forward like a gleaming wave, and swept a hand toward the interior.

Alec obliged, wishing he'd worn a hat or gloves so that he could occupy himself with removing one or the other. Not since his graduate school days, sitting alone on one side of a table facing the cerebral firing squad that was his dissertation committee, had he felt so exposed. The woman's stillness commanded his attention. He sucked in a breath, reassured by Daphne's imposing demeanor that perhaps she could shed light on his predicament.

Feeling every bit like the timid sixth grader he had long ago banished from his memory, he walked through a small waiting room dominated by a carved-oak grandfather clock, which chimed the quarter hour in a minor key. He checked his watch. "Um, perhaps this isn't a convenient time?" He fought a moment's panic. Barbara had gone too far this time, making an appointment with a psychic of all things. He half-turned to go back out the door.

But Daphne's voice urged him forward: "This way." Wearing a long, indigo dress, she suddenly brushed by him and entered a large, open space lit by soft light from a sleek chrome table lamp. Cushions lined the walls, and two leather sofas anchored both sides of a black and red rug that fairly pulsated in a lightning bolt pattern.

Alec blinked, finding the carpet, with its energetic angles and intersecting lines, mesmerizing.

"Navajo," she said, following the downward cast of his eyes.

Daphne sat in the center of one sofa and indicated that he should sit across the low table from her in the other. A variety of wooden boxes rested on the table surrounding a pliant sack of dark purple that contained something square; an oversize block of index cards perhaps?

With a sigh he sank into the camel-colored leather, his rear wallowing comfortably into the cushions. Daphne sat across from him, leaning forward, her broad shoulders square. "May I have one of your hands?" she asked imperiously.

Dazzled by her tone, he offered her his right hand. Daphne grazed his

35

rough knuckles with her fingers, then she laid the back of his hand in the palm of one of her own. Her touch, feather light, contrasted with the fierce fixedness of her face. She traced the lines across his palm with soft, pliant fingertips. Alec felt a strange prickling sensation across his palm that traveled up his arm. He resisted the impulse to jerk his hand away, but after a moment he felt some of the tension in his shoulder melting away.

She gently relinquished his hand. "You must reduce stress in your life at once," she said. "I recommend a course of meditation and will give you a list of able teachers on your way out. But that's not why you're here. Neurophysiological stress is of course a symptom you've lived with your whole life—you don't really notice it anymore—but your concerns are more immediate. More demanding." She smiled, the skin creasing on the sides of her broad mouth. "So much so that you are here. When you so clearly would rather be almost anywhere else."

"Well, no. I . . . uh, it's just . . ." Alec gulped air for a few seconds. *Steady on*, he counseled himself. "There is something . . . er, important . . . that is bothering me," he said, his clear baritone voice wobbling a bit.

"Yes," Daphne said softly. "You stand at the intersection of a great divide. Will you go forward, and change your life dramatically, or will you hesitate, and continue on the path that may lead to greater status and reward but which, I assure you, is dangerous. And the fruits of this path are by no means assured. You take a risk either way, and that is what torments you." She nodded. "Tell me about it."

Sweat broke out lightly across Alec's chest. "I am taking a gamble." He laughed shakily. "No risk, no reward."

Daphne gazed at him shrewdly. Her blue eye, he noticed, was slightly hooded, while he found her tawny cat's eye unnerving in its wide intensity. "You must not assume all risks are equal."

"What?" What was the woman talking about? He saw her turn away, as if disappointed. "Wait," he said, his voice more urgent. "I'm not here to waste your time." The moisture on his chest congealed into a drip. He shifted uncomfortably. This was incredible. Here he was, dean of the oldest and largest college at Austin University, afraid this dragon of a woman would get bored with him. It was ludicrous, and yet . . .

He licked his lips. He couldn't just blurt out that he had shifted funds in his administrative accounts. Instead he said, "Perhaps I've been impetuous.

36

Well, let me explain. I've allocated resources to fund a new center that will be revolutionary in its impact. It will put Austin University on an even larger map. Yes, it's a gamble. And the provost was against me. But he is resigning. I . . . well . . . my aim is to take his place."

Daphne's gaze softened sadly. "Ambition is a consuming thing, is it not? It makes us stretch the bounds of . . . many things. Responsible and allowable financial maneuvers, for example." She picked up the purple pouch and slid out a large deck of brightly colored cards. "Do you wish me to tell you if the time is favorable, the odds for you or against you, or—?"

He gripped his hands together between his spread knees. "I've invested a good deal of my own money as well as my reputation in this. I've bought land at the eastern edge of the campus, across the freeway. It's the logical location for the new building." He hastily added, "I bought the land not to profit, of course, but so it will be available for the university when the time comes. I don't have to tell you about how quickly Austin real estate is scooped up when advantageously placed." He attempted a smile; he really must be more careful about what he told this strangely appealing woman.

Unexpectedly, Alec felt overwhelmed by the magnitude of what he was attempting.

His eyes filmed over with tears; his voice took on a moody note. "But it's the administration that really stands in my way . . . I fear the force of reactionary thinking."

As Daphne's striking eyes focused on him, for a moment Alec feared Daphne might realize how irregular his situation really was—he knew how rare it was for any dean to go so far out on a limb for a center not even in the proposal stages yet, and especially to commit his own funds. It didn't occur to him that he was revealing his obvious financial greed and his fear of others' "reactionary thinking" in the same breath.

Daphne simply asked, "Your new center. It's called?"

"The Center for Psychology, Politics, and Religion. Someday, the Alec R. Martin Center." He looked up, his pale-hazel eyes eager. "Think of it: it will be a place where great debates about fundamentalism versus humanism can take place, a crucible where a new way can be found, a way to distill tribal foment into rational thought, if you will. A gathering of scholars who can show the world a new way to deal with the destructive forces of hysteria and reactionary thought sweeping the globe. I imagine a convergence of myth, archetype, and cultural exchange." Alec paused for breath, his narrow chest inflating.

"But you don't have the support you need."

Alec's chest deflated, his shoulders slumping forward. "No. Not yet. But, as provost, I will have the platform. And at AU that's the same thing. My investment so far, my reordering of the college's financial priorities, might seem unorthodox to some. But the money I've committed—while substantial to most people—is a mere fragment of the endowment of AU. I admit I've extended myself, and the College, a bit. But the outcome will be worth it hundreds of times over."

"I was under the impression that a center for religious thought already existed at Austin University." Daphne touched her necklace of sterling-silver beads like a talisman.

"Not at the level I envision," he said.

At this Daphne sat back and studied the floor for some time. Alec stared at her, willing her to have an answer for him, buoyed up by her prolonged silence. His fingers strayed to the buttons of his heather-gray sport coat. He began twisting them until he noticed that the middle button was hanging by a thread. He folded his arms across his chest.

"You say you've extended yourself a 'bit'—this clearly concerns you."

Alec took out a white handkerchief from his pocket and dabbed at a fleck of saliva on his bottom lip. "When you take a risk like I'm taking, well, you'd have to be delusional or possibly megalomaniacal not to be worried." He smiled awkwardly, and then he said with sudden intensity, "I've been careful all of my life. I'm sixty years old. I've got, what? Five years, seven before I'm put out to pasture? I have no children. But I'd like to leave a legacy." He felt the pressure of tears once again, and he cleared his throat. The woman's calm was excruciating.

"Are you a scholar of religion?" she asked neutrally.

He leaned forward. "History. But I see East and West locked in a fatal battle. Humanity will have no further history without détente."

"I am well aware of the shocking state of world events, Dr. Martin." Daphne held up a hand as if to restrain Alec's torso from angling into her personal space. "Please shuffle these cards. Meditate on what you wish your psyche to reveal. I will tell you ahead of time that unless you can remove the glare of your own ego in this project, you will be just another blind man stumbling toward the cliff of his own destruction. Remember your training as a scholar. Think. Analyze. Reflect."

"Um, tarot? I didn't anticipate . . ." He drew himself up. "I don't think such a method very relevant here. You must understand, I have only limited time before my investment must be realized."

Daphne pushed the cards closer to him. "We'll just select one card as a focus for our deliberations. Not to worry. It's simply a place to begin."

Alec shuffled the cards and then cut them impatiently and sloppily into three piles when told to do so. Daphne's hand hesitated above each stack as if the cards emanated a subtle vibration. She picked up the smallest, most disheveled cluster. Her tanned fingers turned over the first card: the Tower. Two figures tumbled headfirst from the top of a castle parapet, their plight heightened by the lurid flames consuming the monolithic structure. A king's gold crown hurtled through space after them, surrounded by bolts of lightning.

"The Tower." Daphne pronounced the name with a particular reverence.

Alec felt light-headed, and he giggled uneasily. "Well, how appropriate I suppose. AU has a rather famous tower, as you must know."

Daphne pursed her plump lips. "Oh, yes, I am very familiar with it. Do you have an office there?"

"Used to. Third floor. Our college moved to—"

"Death to the old order," Daphne said dreamily. "Some interpreters of the cards say death to the patriarchy. In ancient times the card referenced the death of the king, and the resulting chaos and shift in hierarchy, you see. Nothing short of revolution, if you will. But of course we always look at the cards on a rather more personal level."

"I see you're something of a historian yourself," Alec said nervously.

Daphne's eyes drifted upward, giving her face a rapt expression. "How fascinating that the AU tower is best known for the sniper attacks over fifty years ago, and for suicides. In the tarot, the Tower signifies an imperative to purify—one's motives and actions for example. Yet the two towers are similar. In all mythologies, death is the ultimate purification. The gods sent mortals to Hades to experience transformation . . ."

Daphne hesitated a moment and then resumed with a firm tone. "You see the plummeting figures? The ground under them has crumbled, and they must adapt. It is essential that you choose to let go of ingrained patterns and thoughts that no longer serve you. If you do not change voluntarily, the universe will see to it for you."

"If one could believe in such things," Alec protested, his face registering distaste for both the card and Daphne's pronouncement. He hastily removed his hands from the table as if to prevent contamination by the Tower's symbols, but not before Daphne noticed how his cuticles were inflamed and torn.

Daphne tapped the card. "Dean Martin, you came to see me. Surely a researcher of your caliber has found out that my practice contains a strong spiritual dimension. And yet you really don't want to hear anything I have to say. Tell me, why did you come here? For reassurance?"

"I've heard that you have unique insight. And an unusual perspective."

"Both are true," Daphne said flatly. "But insight offered to those with closed minds and hearts is a poor thing indeed."

Alec's fingers fumbled to release the top button of his blue oxford-cloth shirt; his tie was positively choking him. What was the temperature in this infernal room? His forehead gleamed dully. "I just need to know. Can I do this? Is my . . . my investment . . . safe? Are my ambitions reasonable?"

Daphne scooped up the cards from the table and smiled. "You mean, dear Dean, will you be caught? I'm afraid you've come to the wrong place for that information. Perhaps a priest would be more appropriate if absolution is what you seek."

Eight

Barbara lounged on her back patio, enjoying the steady murmur of water spilling from the cupid fountain in the center of a planting of peach and cream roses. Over the two years they'd known each other, Alec had attempted to interest her in his attachment to Victorian tea roses. Although Barbara enjoyed her husband's various gardens, she wasn't attuned to plants herself. She considered herself more of a social animal. Or perhaps a political one.

She sipped her morning latte, mulling Alec's reaction to his session yesterday with Daphne, the psychic. Barbara preferred to think of her as more of a therapist, and indeed among Daphne's many accomplishments was a license as a professional counselor. She knew that Alec had gone to see the counselor against his better judgment, but his level of upset over developments at the university had left him sleep deprived and edgy, and she'd persuaded him he needed to see someone. He'd balked at making an appointment with a psychiatrist or a clinical psychologist. Over the past six months, she'd seen how rigid Alec's thinking was. She now doubted her judgment in getting married so soon after her divorce from her ex, Thomas. For the first time in her life, she'd panicked, about money, about being alone.

When Alec returned from the appointment late in the day, his face flushed, he'd thrown his briefcase under the hall table so that it skidded against the wall.

The thud of the briefcase was both irritating and a warning. "How'd it go, dear?" She'd asked carefully, giving him a peck on the lips.

His lips barely brushed her cheek. "The woman is preposterous!"

"Oh, I thought you might find her insightful."

"Insightful? Jesus Christ!"

Barbara regarded the strands of silver hair streaking across his forehead. Once she'd have soothed him by smoothing them back from his brow. But now his petulant face stopped her. She managed to say, "Look, it's a beautiful afternoon. Let's just go sit outside for a bit. I've made us Manhattans. Come on, honey."

Alec pivoted into the living room then yanked off his tie and tossed it on the arm of a sofa. He covered the tie with his sport coat. "A drink. Good."

She took him by the hand and led him outside. She kicked off her shoes inside the patio door. Barefoot, she was an inch shorter than her husband. Alec's lean body and hawkish nose gave him a patrician air she'd once admired. Until recently she hadn't thought he'd looked a decade older than she, but the past months had worn him down. She led him to a wrought-iron rocker. "Just relax, and I'll get the drinks."

In a few moments she handed him a chilled glass, dropping into a chair opposite him. "So tell me about it."

Alec leaned back in his chair, slipped on a pair of aviator glasses, and sipped his drink. "Ah, that's better." His forehead relaxed.

Alec reminded Barbara, not for the first time, of that actor decades ago from *Mission Impossible*. She smiled. *Impossible* was how her friends had seen this fairly recent marriage. They'd only seen the buttoned-up professor. But Alec had been playful and sexy when they'd first met. That side of him had faded steadily over the past year, however.

She prodded, "Well?"

"Well, yes." Alec smiled. "Your Daphne is unique. I'll say that for her. Those mismatched eyes! I felt she was watching me from every corner of the room."

"I know what you mean." The bourbon slid smoothly across her tongue. "She does appear to see everything." Barbara thought back to when she'd consulted Daphne about marrying Alec over a year ago. That big, handsome face had regarded her, impossible to read, impassive yet entirely focused. Her words haunted Barbara now. "An opportunity," Daphne had told her. "A big monetary advantage. But the future is cloudy."

"Cloudy how?" Barbara had pressed her.

The psychic had dropped her eyes. "Just be careful. Keep your head. And don't open your heart too much." Barbara had been perplexed, thinking those odd words to tell a woman on the verge of marriage. But perhaps Daphne, for all her gifts, hadn't seen that Barbara never did open her heart very much. She'd always thought that hearts had ribcages for good reasons: containment, protection. *Keep your boundaries, and don't give too much away* had always been Barbara's motto. Thinking back to this meeting, Barbara almost missed what Alec was saying.

". . . the wrong person to come to for absolution, she said. That was kind of offensive. I wasn't asking for that."

"What were you asking her for?" She put her drink down on a round table of blue and red tile.

Alec rustled in his chair, unbuttoned his cuffs, and rolled up his sleeves. "Good question," he said hoarsely. "Stupid of me to ask for advice anyway." He looked up at Barbara, his hazel eyes naked, pleading.

Pierced by his wanting expression, Barbara placed her hand around her cold glass and kept her face composed. A part of her wanted to put her arms around him, suggest that they go to bed. But a larger part of her pulled away. *It's too late for that.*

"Barbara, I've made a bit of a mess. The college funds . . . I can get a loan, of course, but it's a stretch. I've been foolish."

She didn't reply right away. "How much?"

"Close to half a million. Less than chicken feed in the Austin University scheme of things. A year's worth of light bulbs for the campus probably costs less than that. It's just that—"

"Yes?"

"—that my money is tied up right now. Real-estate investment trusts, that sort of thing. Not liquid."

Barbara recoiled from his insinuation that she should bail him out. Thomas had left her a small trust. She and Alec had signed a prenup agreement. "I'm afraid I'm tied up too."

Alec's laugh sounded like a half bark. "You or your money? I can untie you, if you'll let me."

Only the week before, on the night of the annual faculty awards dinner,

Barbara had half-carried her husband into their house. She fumed that she had wasted hours of her precious life at such a ridiculous function. By the end of the evening, Alec had been dead drunk. His behavior had been disgusting. And stupid. More than stupid. He hadn't absorbed the lesson that when circumstances are the most precarious the good strategist knows that his behavior must be the most proper, the most impeccable. Good Lord, had the man never played chess?

On the ride home, Barbara drove Alec's sedan, certain that given the way his drinking was escalating, she'd never ride in a car with him behind the wheel again.

"Don't worry about it," he repeated. "No big deal. A bunch of stuffed shirts anyway." His head rolled on the headrest and flopped toward the window.

"But that crack about Bridger? Insulting his wives, for God's sake!"

"Not his wives . . . No, no, meant to show him for the grandstanding bastard that he is." His voice faded in and out.

"Alec, get a grip. Don't you see that there was only one grandstanding bastard on that podium tonight, and it was you?" Barbara made a hard right into their driveway, waited for the garage door to open, and then slid the car inside. As the door lowered behind her, she drew a shaky breath. Safe from prying eyes at last.

Alec stiffened, then covered his face with his hands. "Oh, Barbara, not you too?" Tears leaked down his face. His breath broke in ragged sobs.

Barbara marshaled patience. "I'm here, honey. Don't worry. Let's just get you to bed. Things will look better in the morning." She sincerely doubted that platitude, but she was at her wit's end.

Haltingly, they made their way from the garage into the kitchen and down the hall to their bedroom. Grateful that the house had only a single story, she slid him onto the edge of the bed.

"I'll just take these things off." Alec yanked at his tie and fumbled with his shirt buttons. Finally he kicked off his shoes and just crawled between the covers. Barbara stared at the pile of clothes strewn by his side of the bed. A teenager would have made a neater job of it. She shoved the shoes under the bed with her foot. He could pick up after himself in the morning.

As snores vibrated through the room, she made her way down the hall to her office. The space boasted a spectacular watercolor of a Norwegian fjord in summer, a mountain peak cresting the blue sky with its doppelgänger reflected in the water below. She closed the door, arranged herself in a reclining chair, and picked up her cell.

"Jane?"

"Hi, sweetheart. I've been hoping you'd call."

Tension drained out of Barbara's throat at hearing her lover's voice. She'd met Jane Auckler at a conference in San Diego three months ago. Their first conversation, at dinner after a panel, had awakened Barbara's yearning for an intelligent, witty companion. She'd felt like a woman in a fairy tale, awakened from a long, numbing slumber.

"I wish you were here. The drinking. It's horrible. I can't tell you how depressing my life with Alec is right now. He's paranoid too. He's even accused me of having an affair."

Jane's low voice grew warm. "Well, at least he still has some sense of reality."

"His instincts are right, but of course he assumes it's a man. He suspects the dishy Darryl Hansen, but I've heard he's hitched to Fiona Hardison."

"Maybe Hansen is the generous type?"

Barbara snickered. "As you know, sex with men is not on my mind these days."

"So . . ." Barbara heard ice cubes collide as Jane took a sip of something. "Your marriage has sprouted gray hair, and Alec's suddenly grokked to the fact. When can you come out to see me?"

Barbara sighed. "How many conferences in California can I pretend to attend before Alec finds out? But he's so preoccupied with his own problems. They're mounting by the day! He used to seem so smart, so organized. But now . . . maybe early signs of dementia? His executive functions winding down? Who the hell knows?"

"Or cares, no? Why don't I come to Austin?"

"Soon. Why don't I come to you this weekend?" The thought made Barbara shiver. The first time she and Jane had gone to bed, she'd asked, "Do you care that I'm married?" And Jane had said, "No, because I don't think you will be for very long." Barbara had asked her what she meant by that, but Jane had only whispered, "Let's not talk," her body, long and fit, curving around Barbara's.

45

Barbara ran her hand over Jane's hip and thigh. "You have the most beautiful hips." *Imperial hips*, an old friend had called them, whenever he'd see a slender but well-built young man. The thought flew away as Jane began kissing her, from her throat all the way down to her thighs.

In her office, Barbara held her phone tighter and breathed into the phone, "Oh, Jane . . ."

Nine

Bettina turned her left profile to the full-length mirror in her bedroom and considered the period costume she'd assembled for the performance salon in New Mexico. Her mid-calf dress, in cream silk variegated with gold threads, hugged her shoulders and breasts and then fell freely past her waist to fit snuggly around her hips. Her brown Mary Janes had a two-inch block heel. Buttons secured the straps and gave the shoes an early twentieth-century look. Completing her costume with a bronze cloche hat, she cocked one hip. Deciding it was both feminine and comfortable, she hoped it might evoke both Virginia Woolf and her era.

For two months she'd been locked in a war with Patricia Mendoza. Patricia wanted a Virginia Woolf for her festival, while Bettina forged ahead with plans to present Lily Briscoe as a neglected everywoman, an artist who lacked connections or fame. Woolf herself was bolstered by the cultural frisson of the Bloomsbury group, a dazzling group that included painters, critics, and writers. The daughter of Leslie Stephen, a prominent thinker of the day, Woolf had opportunity to hone her critical skills throughout her life.

Bettina sensed the partial surrender of compromise coming. "Give us Woolf and read choice passages from *To the Lighthouse*. You'll be smashing!" Patricia's breezy pronouncement ignored the months of preparations—"Indeed months! A lifetime!" Miriam pronounced—that Bettina would have to endure before she'd dare show her face as such a momentous icon as Virginia Woolf.

On second thought she didn't think she could pass herself off as Virginia Woolf, even if being *smashing* meant falling on her face. Bettina visualized hiding behind a series of masks. She tore off the hat and released her shoulder-length hair from its knot behind her head. How had she let herself be talked into this! Besides, her figure tended to the robust—not to put too fine a point on it. Not to mention that her broad face couldn't be less like the fragile and ascetic beauty of Woolf. The title of one of Bettina's favorite essays, "Feeling Like a Fraud," flared behind her eyes.

At that moment her husband, Marvin, taking a break from his greenhouse, popped into the doorway. "Hi, doll. Cool threads," he said, face flushed from the hothouse May day.

Marvin, with the heavy build of a Marine Corps Sergeant, which he once was, anchored Bettina to the present. In the great scheme of things, this Chautauqua was minor. And yet the challenge of bringing Woolf into the current conversation appealed to her.

"If only I could waltz into the dean's graduate reception in this *just for fun*. Instead, I'm supposed to be credible in this outfit for the women's history festival."

As usual, Marvin ignored his wife's self-doubt. "Honey, you're always credible." His graying-blond buzz cut glinted in the light from the recessed lights in the ceiling. "I'd say *in*credible too."

Bettina groaned. "That's what scares me." She accepted a kiss on the ear from Marvin and watched him disappear out into the hallway, most likely in search of food.

To evoke Woolf, Bettina decided she'd wear a broad-brimmed hat instead of the cloche. Clothing was the least of her worries. A script would be nice—and soon.

The following Monday, the beginning of May, Bettina arrived at the Corner Café at 8:00 a.m. In spite of the drizzly morning, she wore large tortoiseshell sunglasses. She and Marvin had celebrated their twenty-fifth wedding anniversary the night before. The stress of the previous week had melted along with the ice in her third vodka on the rocks. This morning Bettina had noticed a new puffiness around her eyes that she put down to the rapidly dwindling minutes of her forties. Forty had once seemed impossibly mature; now seen from the waning end of forty-nine, the decade seemed positively a holding tank for youth's last stand. When announcing her distress at breakfast, Marvin had shrugged shoulders made even broader by intense work at his landscaping business and simply grinned. "Vintage Bettina. Every man should be so lucky."

"Stop being so kind," Bettina had retorted crossly. "It makes me feel even worse."

The first Monday of every month, Bettina met Miriam and Fiona at the Corner Café, a bright yet cozy local bakery near the university.

Bettina, the last to arrive at the café, noticed that Fiona's skin appeared smooth and rested on this Monday morning. Reflexively, she touched the bruised-looking skin under her own eyes.

Fiona's ash-blonde hair was short and spiky, reducing her forty-six years by a decade. Her clear, gray eyes turned to Bettina in welcome. "I hear congratulations are in order."

"Oh, you know about the anniversary?" Bettina took off her sunglasses and smoothed her forehead. "Today it just makes me feel older. Not wiser, not grateful. Just getting closer to that inevitable something I don't want to think about."

Fiona angled toward Bettina sympathetically. "Maybe this will take your mind off all that," she said, her alto voice rising a note. "The word is that there's a financial scandal brewing in the dean's office. One that our dean is going to have trouble wriggling out of. It's big. I was told more a tsunami than the perfect surfing wave he's managed to ride in times past."

Bettina looked surprised. "Fiona, 'tsunami'? 'surfing wave'? This doesn't sound like you. Who have you been talking to?"

A flush spread across Fiona's fair face. "Daphne, actually. She dropped by to ask what I knew about Alec, and when I said nothing, she ended up telling me that. In confidence of course."

Miriam cleared her throat. "Ladies, you've scooped me once again. I was out with Darryl the other night and thought I'd heard some hot news to tell you." The skin around her pecan-colored eyes creased. "I should have known that once a rumor makes its way to me it's too cold to need refrigeration for days."

Fiona poured her mentor another cup of tea. "If it's any consolation, Miriam, that makes two of us."

Bettina reached toward the plate of raspberry Danish that had appeared on their table. She took one and delicately touched her tongue to one corner where the filling threatened to burst through the pastry. "Delicious," she pronounced, reaching for another and nodding as their waiter inquired about a refill on her coffee.

Miriam thoughtfully raised her cup and then put it back down. "There's something deeply disturbing about Alec. When someone abuses power, and people begin to spread rumors, meanwhile keeping their heads down, it reminds me of the anger and paranoia surrounding Isabel's death. Alec seems desperate. I hope he doesn't harm himself." *Or someone else*, she thought.

No one spoke for a moment. Bettina sighed. "Miriam, it's not good for you to get distressed about this. Last year was so painful when the police investigated our department—for you particularly. I think it's best to stay clear of Alec, and that goes for all of us."

"I hear he's drinking heavily," Fiona said.

"Drinking?" Bettina retorted. "Then he takes his cocktails garnished. A sprinkle of Ambien here and a dash of Valium there. Maybe yummy to him, but destabilizing to most of us mortals."

Fiona raised her eyebrows and helped herself to a Danish while there still was one to be had, as Bettina had made serious inroads on the four that had been deposited only minutes before.

Miriam addressed Bettina. "It might be more serious than you think, my droll friend." She cleared her throat. "But let's talk about the festival, the Chautauqua Patricia has put together. September is closer than we think. Fiona, you said the location is stunning."

Fiona was pleased to see that Bettina was wearing her new turquoise pin she'd brought back from southwestern New Mexico for her. "Luxury and nature—it's quite perfect."

Bettina turned to Miriam. "Is it true that Vivian has agreed to present Alice B. Toklas? And does this mean that you're going to give us a Stein after all, to complete the original lesbian power couple?"

Miriam's eyes drifted skyward as she dabbed at a smear of cappuccino froth from the corner of her mouth. "Vivi has said yes to this madness. And a woman I've seen for years at conferences, Jane Auckler, is coming from LA to anchor the festival as Stein. I couldn't possibly do it. You know, Vivi has never been onstage in her life."

"Courage," Fiona muttered. "Speaking of, do you think it's too late for me to back out?"

Bettina shook her head. "You can't. We're in this craziness together. It seemed like such a lark when it was in the outback of my calendar. But of course as the time gets closer . . ." She stared at the now-empty plate of Danish with a look of longing. "But this is wonderful. I hope this means we'll get to see some glimpses of the Edith Wharton research you've been talking about forever."

"You'll see it almost as soon as I do." Fiona suddenly looked impish. "But wait! Patricia's always telling us not to be literal, so maybe I should work on Woolf and you conjure up an Edith Wharton!"

Bettina said, "One idea might be for you to work on both of them." When Fiona's shoulders slumped, she added, "I'm in too much trouble with someone I know something about. Besides, I just don't think I can cultivate the air of old money, not in just five months."

"Now I'm really terrified. That's a detail I hadn't even thought of." Fiona massaged her forehead as if the skin felt too tight. "In fact, I haven't given any thought to credibility with a real live audience. I think I'm doomed."

Miriam said, "I'm afraid we all are. Except for Patricia. She told me that Victoria Woodhull, whom she's portraying, was a famous medical clairvoyant. Knowing Patricia, she's probably confident that the spirits are on her side."

"I'd take anything that would have my back at this point. The only thing that's comforting me is that Patricia said on this first experimental go-round of Chautauqua in Silver City, she's invited a select audience, so I'm hoping they'll be open-minded. And forgiving." Fiona looked at her watch and gathered her briefcase. "Well, I have class in fifteen minutes. At least I can still teach. I think." She waved at Bettina and Miriam as she headed for the door, her toned legs and arms swinging. "See you at Alec's garden party Friday afternoon, if not before."

Miriam and Bettina sat in silence for a moment as if becalmed in the wake of the younger woman's energy as she briskly left the café. Bettina murmured, "She's like an advertisement for going to the gym." She smoothed her peach top over her stomach. "I suppose I should just suit up and join one."

Miriam laughed. "Let's see, you say this every three months. I wouldn't worry. You look wonderful."

"Flatterer," Bettina said flatly and then put out a hand, palm up. "More please." She straightened in her chair. "Hang on. Don't look now but Barbara Martin is sitting across the room by the window. Too bad I can't ask her for advice about shaping my performance for a contemporary audience. Her Mabel Dodge Luhan presentation is supposed to be very witty."

"Oh my God," Miriam said. Fortunately Barbara was to her left so she could take a look without craning her neck. The woman had high cheekbones and a rather lush, downturned mouth. She hoped that Vivi had misjudged her motives the other day. "Do you think she and Alec are happy together?"

"Who knows?" Bettina shrugged. "Other people's marriages are one of the last great mysteries. I'm sure the geniuses at Apple are working on an app this very moment to make that not be the case. However . . ."

Barbara opened her purse, deposited some money, and stood. She looked formidable, a good five feet nine inches tall with a generous, well-proportioned figure. To Miriam's surprise, she headed straight to their table.

"Bettina, so nice to see you again." Barbara pursed her lips, which looked no less lush up close. "Professor Held, we met once very briefly."

"Call me Miriam, please." Miriam regarded the woman's shiny, well-cut hair and wide-set brown eyes. There was something imperious and impervious about Barbara. "Um, would you like to join us?" she asked, a touch too late.

"Can't, must run. I suspect we'll get to know each other well," Barbara said, taking a step back and repositioning her lizard-skin shoulder bag more firmly. "I'll see you in Silver City in not too long."

"Oh," Bettina said. "For a moment I'd managed to put that out of my mind. But yes."

"Alec is so looking forward to it," Barbara said in a perfunctory way. She appeared to be about to add something, but then she was silent.

"He's performing?" Miriam's face froze in a smile.

"Oh no. God no! That's a very funny thought." But Barbara didn't laugh, and Bettina thought the woman spoke with a curious lack of enthusiasm as she added, "He comes with me whenever I have a big event. I couldn't possibly do it without his support."

Miriam and Bettina exchanged a glance. "Didn't you get married recently?" Bettina asked with a smile.

"Almost a year ago," Barbara said, raising her chin. "But we've been together longer."

"And did he make a promise to accompany you?"

"Well, yes."

Bettina cocked her head to one side, her green eyes merry. "Ah. Husbands are so accommodating that first year. Well, let's hope he has the fortitude to keep it up."

Miriam hurried to say, "I'm sure Bettina means in light of all of the obligations Alec has as dean."

Barbara's voice was airy. "I consider it his duty. After all, this is my *work* we're talking about."

"Er, yes," Miriam agreed, not meeting Bettina's eyes.

Barbara inclined her head. "I'll perhaps see you both at the reception this week." She raised a hand as she headed for the door.

Bettina waited until Barbara left the building before a strangled giggle erupted from her throat. "Is it our *duty* to go?"

"You are a disgrace! Yes, in your case, it is definitely your obligation. Or should I say your penance?" Miriam took a Kleenex out of her pocket and dabbed at her eyes. "I don't know what to think of that woman."

"I do. She's perfect for Alec. I'm sure the roof of their house fairly levitates with their self-regard."

"Why so hard on her?" Miriam asked, relieved that Bettina shared her own instincts. Yet she also knew that when Bettina had one of these manic attacks of hilarity, it was usually because she was uncomfortable about something.

"I know it takes one to know one, but believe me, that woman is trouble." Bettina folded her arms across her chest as if the room were cold. "Ask Darryl about her. Her consulting firm was hired by a certain dean to beef up the fundraising in Liberal Studies."

"She's a development professional?"

"Well, she is now. She has connections with oil interests in Houston. And she's already raised over a million for his cause. They seem a perfect pair. Even though my instinct is that Alec's third marriage is already on oxygen, and that the canister is empty."

"It didn't sound that way to me at all," Miriam protested.

Bettina did not appear to have heard her. "Of course Barbara would have Houston connections. Oil and the great state of Texas have always been in bed together." She thought a moment. "I believe her training is in public relations."

Miriam tossed her napkin on the table. "You know, you really are a snob. A lot of perfectly intelligent people go into public relations. Just because your Ivy League graduate school didn't have a major in such a practical field. Or should I say a program not part of the traditional humanities or sciences as decided in the early 1800s or whenever Henry Adams was a renaissance scholar . . ."

"You mean a degree in Communication? Where former Business School students go to sulk when they don't make the grade?" Bettina tapped her finger on her plate to capture the lone crumbs of pastry left there. Then she brushed them off, having thought better of adding even one more empty calorie to the day.

"Now you're putting me on."

"Of course I am. You forget that my son majored in Communication Studies. And went on to do very well on the LSAT. Of course, he didn't go to law school. Too traditional for Carl." Bettina sighed. "I would've liked an attorney in the family."

"Anticipating legal problems?"

"No. Just a path not taken for me. My dad was a lawyer. I must have been madder than mad. Choosing English literature over a profession in which there's a hope of making money."

Miriam nodded. "Worried about Marvin's business again?" Bettina's husband had left the safety of a tenured professor position in the Botany Department to start his own company, a nursery: Marvin Gardens.

"Always. You know how Marvin and both my children are entrepreneurs. Compared to them I feel like a staid workhorse slogging on the wheel. Or maybe I'm in the grip of the loneliness of the long-distance runner. Or something. I know I'm lucky to have a decent job. Maybe I'm just feeling stuck in my own research, and worrying about money seems more concrete. Disregard everything I say today." She worried one corner of her lower lip with her teeth. "Except the warning about Barbara. I don't think I'm paranoid about that."

Miriam picked up her discarded napkin and twisted it around one hand. "I just found out that Vivi used to know her rather well."

Bettina listened as Miriam recounted Vivian's fears. "Maybe Barbara should be the one who's worried. My mother used to have a saying, 'There's nothing deader than an old love affair.' Or was it an old lover?"

Miriam's scalp prickled. Had her own mother told her something similar? She seemed to remember a certain grim intent in such pronouncements. "But that could refer to Vivian as well."

Bettina's face tensed as she looked over at the door Barbara had recently exited. "I wish Daphne were here. The woman has an aura. But what does it portend?" She leaned closer to Miriam and spoke quietly. "Perhaps it's time for us to pay attention. And watch our backs too."

Ten

Barbara watched her husband brooding at the breakfast table, thrashing the newspaper pages about, and muttering to himself. The garden party was scheduled for the next afternoon. Her voice brimmed with impatience. "Alec! If you're this upset, just cancel the damn faculty reception. On this of all years, it's a ridiculous affair and not worth your mental health!"

"That would make everyone think me guilty. They'd believe all the hideous rumors." Alec's pale face had a sickly sheen.

"But they're true, aren't they?" Barbara scrutinized his face. "Your eyes are bloodshot. Have you been up all night?"

Alec nodded. "Who can sleep with all this going on? Maybe you're right. I should cancel the party. But it's too late."

He looked at Barbara with a doglike hopefulness. "How about I leave town, you say I'm terribly ill and at the Mayo Clinic or Cedars-Sinai or some other great hospital, and you stay here to get rid of the guests?"

Barbara, surprised, laughed uncomfortably. "Remember the 'Get the Guests' part of *Who's Afraid of Virginia Woolf*? I think this is the worst idea you've ever had."

"God," he groaned. Alec lowered his head onto the surface of the table and whispered, "I don't think I can move. I'm totally paralyzed."

Barbara put aside some notes she was reading for a development meeting at the university later that day. "Honey, what if you really are ill? Maybe the idea of the Mayo isn't a bad idea. Or MD Anderson but of course we can't assume it's cancer."

Alec took several deep breaths and, as he attempted to sit straighter in his chair, shuddered. Barbara thought she'd never seen anyone actually move like that before—his skin quivered like a dog shaking himself.

"Barbara, we have to talk."

"We are, dear, we are. What is it?"

"I can't go on. Not knowing what I know."

She removed her reading glasses. "Uh-huh. Um, you mean because you feel so ill?"

"No. The political and financial mess I'm in. And then . . . there's you."

Proceed carefully, she coached herself, taking a moment. "What about me? I'm really fine. Dreadfully worried about you, of course, but—"

"I think you've betrayed me," Alec said, his voice as limp as a dead fish.

"Alec! That's simply not true. I know I've had to travel some, especially back to Houston and occasionally New York and California, but . . ."

"Who is he? Dear God, please don't tell me it's someone I work with."

A moment's panic struck Barbara. She wasn't ready for this kind of confrontation. Not yet. "It's no one. You know I'm devoted to you." Guilt stabbed at her.

"You've been so distant. You treat me like I'm a pariah."

At this, impatience overran remorse. "Oh, for fuck's sake. You're treating yourself that way, can't you see that? Look at you, you can barely hold yourself together. You're acting like you're finished."

"I might be just that. Finished. It's a wonderful word, so final."

Barbara attempted humor. "Only you can act like you're at death's door on the one hand and on the other parse your vocabulary!" But when Alec's face only collapsed further, she tried another tack in an attempt to put some steel in his spine. "Dear, you've got to buck up. Otherwise, turn yourself in. But in any case, do something! Sitting and stewing will just make you bonkers."

"I can't. I can't." He covered his face and began to sob.

Barbara went to him then, rubbing his back and murmuring soothing sounds, but nothing seemed to reach him.

The next morning as Alec backed his silver Maxima out of the garage, he nicked his side mirror on the driver's side so that he had to get out of the car and snap the mirror back into position. He shook a fist in the air as he ripped out a series of curses. One of his neighbors, picking up her newspaper from the lawn, watched curiously.

Resuming his seat, he cranked the car, grazed a hedge of pampas grass flanking the driveway, and drove away in a flurry of pea gravel. He picked up speed when he reached 38th Street and ran a light at the access lane of I-35. Outraged honking around him didn't shift his stiff posture behind the wheel. Jaw and neck locked forward, he resolutely made his way onto Cherrywood Avenue, and from there to the Safeway store.

He careened into the grocery store lot, screeched to a stop, and parked crookedly so that his car took up two spaces near the door. He ran into the store, mumbling under his breath. Five minutes later he ran out of the store with a small bag in his hand. A woman entering the store later reported that he was wearing sweatpants and some kind of slippers on his feet.

Again settled at the wheel, Alec reversed the car, narrowly missing a shopping cart that had been abandoned near his car. Heedless to other traffic entering from the street, he raced out of the lot, accelerating so that he barely cleared a right-hand turn onto the street.

His cell phone rang, and he removed one hand from the wheel to answer it. "What?" he shouted. "What?" he repeated, this time very loudly as if attempting to be heard over an airplane engine. A man on the sidewalk jumped out of the car's way as the Maxima's right rear tire bumped over the curb. Alec then yelled in a high register, "WHAT ARE YOU SAYING?" The same man later described Alec's voice as "a frantic, bleating sound."

A moment later Alec's car slammed into a metal post. The front end of the vehicle crumpled as the engine ground to a halt. For a very short time, the street was silent. Then, scurrying feet, shouting, and approaching sirens filled the air. Alec did not stir.

Eleven

The first Friday in May, Miriam woke to the sound of a manic oriole singing to welcome the sun. She didn't think the oriole was supposed to be here; it had its flyways confused. She turned over in bed to find Vivian's round, blue eyes on her, already alert. "Ugh."

Vivian blinked. "Excuse me?"

"Not you, honey. Ugh that I have to go to Alec's garden party this afternoon. Won't you come with me? Please?"

"I don't think I'm up to being a faculty wife today. And Barbara will be there." Vivian's eyes closed, and a deep furrow appeared on her forehead. "Now that's truly ugh."

"Hmm. I saw her at the coffee shop the other day. She's kind of attractive if you like animal spirits."

Vivian punched at her pillow. "Animal spirits? I don't think so. Reptile, maybe."

"How can you say that when you loved her once?"

"I did not love her. We had sex. I knew nothing about sex then and was grateful to find out something about it with *someone*. I don't think we ever pretended to be in love. It was the '80s for heaven's sake."

"Oh. Well, that's something. That you didn't love her."

"Darling Miriam. Do not feel competitive with Barbara. I don't think I even like her anymore!"

Miriam felt a foolish smile begin on her face. Before Vivian, no one in her life had ever called her "darling" aside from her dear mother, who had died much too young, at sixty. The endearment made her feel precious. "Say that again."

"I don't think I like her."

"Not that, you goof." Miriam leaned over and kissed Vivian on the lips. "I must get up. The sooner I begin this day, the sooner it will end."

It was only 7:00 a.m., but over tea and the newspaper Miriam launched into strategizing her wardrobe for the 3:00 p.m. party, visualizing which colleagues she'd like to talk with and how to avoid those she hoped not to see at all. Vivian, up late the night before finishing a project, had gone back to sleep.

The *New York Times* was proving difficult. Images of her shoe bin in the closet upstairs (boots or sandals or clogs?), an imagined scenario of Darryl sidestepping the woman they'd run into after the awards ceremony, and Bettina's pronouncement about Barbara—"that woman is trouble"—garbled the words on the page. Their cat, Phoebe, materialized for her morning infusion of warm milk as Miriam brewed another pot of tea.

At 8:30 a.m. the doorbell rang. Miriam opened the door to find her two friends huddled like conspirators in the overgrown oleander hedge that ran along the front side of the house. Fiona advanced toward her wearing navy-blue shorts, a turquoise T-shirt, and tennis shoes followed by Bettina wearing one of Marvin's white shirts and jeans. Pink trainers were on her feet.

"What are you two doing out walking this early?" Miriam asked as they stepped inside. Fiona glanced over her shoulder with a quick furtive motion and then closed the door.

Bettina grasped Miriam's hand and led her to the living room. "Sit down."

Miriam took her customary seat in her scuffed recliner and herded the magazines and books into a more manageable pile on the coffee table. Sunlight streamed in from a bank of windows at one end of the large room.

Fiona, already on her way to the kitchen, said, "I'll bring a glass of water. Actually, I'll bring three. We just heard some bad news."

Miriam began to feel seriously alarmed when Fiona brought glasses from the kitchen on a tray and the two of them then sat opposite her on the sofa. She knew Vivian was safely upstairs. Both of her parents had already died and she was an only child. If something had happened to Marvin, surely Bettina wouldn't be on her doorstep. "What is it?"

Fiona stalled, not sure herself what to think of the news she was bringing. "You haven't heard from anyone at the university, have you? Or the police?"

"No. Why do you ask?" Miriam gripped the handle of her empty teacup, which she'd been carrying when she answered the door. She put it carefully down on the coffee table.

Miriam looked at one friend and then the other. Bettina's eyes looked murky and unreadable.

Miriam removed her glasses and put them on again. Her own eyes were having trouble focusing. "Someone has to start at the beginning," she said.

"It's Alec," Bettina said. "He's had a fatal crash."

Miriam's anxiety prompted her to say, "Hasn't he been having one all year?"

"For real," Bettina said. "A collision. The car was totaled. And so was he."

Fiona leaned back into the sofa and expelled a breath. "Bettina and I were about to go for a walk when Darryl called."

"But where did this happen?" Miriam had the urge to go back to the kitchen and get the local newspaper as if it might tell her something more.

"Near the parking lot of his neighborhood market."

"Alec at a grocery store?" Miriam wondered. "He doesn't strike me as someone who does anything as pragmatic as shopping. I know there's the garden party later today, but the college is catering it."

"I have no idea." Bettina untied her pink trainers and slipped them off. She crossed her legs under her and folded up the sleeves of Marvin's shirt. "His wife needed aspirin? He stopped in before work for a bagel?"

Miriam leaned forward and grasped her thighs, grateful for their solidity. "Don't you think it's too convenient?"

"What do you mean?" Fiona asked. Stunned by the news of the car accident, she'd only half-listened to Bettina's theories about a fatal assault on Alec. Now it appeared that Miriam shared Bettina's certainty as well.

"He was in such trouble," Bettina offered. "And his problems would have infected the whole university. Darryl thinks there might be a possibility of containing the financial leaks now that he's gone."

"I doubt that," Miriam said. "Nothing can stay a secret now. Not when the perpetrator of the scandal has just died. Someone will ask questions."

"Someone has already been asking questions," Bettina said.

Miriam nodded. "Yes, that's what Alec's 'accident' implies. And now everyone connected with him will be scrutinized as well." Miriam brought her hand out from the pocket of her robe, revealing a smashed yellow Post-it Note. "All communications will be sifted through." She gestured at the paper. "Down to the most casual scrap." She dropped the Post-it on the coffee table. "Nothing will be private."

The square of yellow paper appeared to shock Fiona out of her trance. "Neither of you think it's an accident, do you?" she blurted. "I don't get it. The man had poor judgment, yes, but he was hardly the scourge of the campus."

Bettina cocked her head at Fiona, raised one plump hand, and ticked off three fingers in rapid succession. "One, the man seems to have embezzled a large quantity of funds from Liberal Studies. Two, he wanted to be provost and obsessed about it constantly to people who didn't want to listen. Three, he insulted some very big guns at a major AU function. There will be a scandal. The media will want to know why money—public funds no less—was entrusted to such a nitwit so clearly past his prime. And that is just the beginning."

Miriam saw Fiona's agitation in the way she twisted a single strand of hair through her fingers over and over. But like the high school debater Fiona once was, she kept her voice earnest and level, as if employing the voice of reason to drive home her argument to the judge. "I don't think we should jump to conclusions. Even if all that is true, there are ways of farming faculty out to pasture. Both of you are implying that his car accident wasn't what it seems. Aren't you being extreme? I know you're both thinking of the horrible way Isabel died. But that was completely different—she was brutally attacked and left to die. It was nothing as pedestrian as a car accident. That could happen to anyone. Why assume the worst?"

Bettina's green eyes regarded Fiona speculatively. It was all Fiona could do not to flinch. Her friend, whose understanding gaze in normal conversation often wrapped Fiona in a gauze of calm, now swept over her with all the comfort of an acid bath. "Because it's beginning to look like Alec might have made fools of some very prominent people. Someone has to pay the price for that."

Fiona's voice cracked, poised between a statement and a question. "You don't mean murder . . ."

The word *murder* made Miriam freeze. She felt a tremor in her hand and wrapped it around her glass to make it stop.

Bettina fiddled with the bottom buttons of her white shirt, which had come open, revealing a fold of pale flesh. Her face was grim. "You said it first."

Twelve

Lt. Susan Crane watched the erect, well-dressed woman come through her office door accompanied by her sergeant, Joe Mason, a slender man in his early thirties. Barbara Martin, wearing flats, stood at least two inches taller than Joe, who barely topped five feet seven in thick-soled boots. While Joe shut the door and then retreated to the back of the room, Crane rose from her desk and held out her hand, which Barbara touched with only the tips of her fingers. Barbara looked ragged, tense, and tired.

"Thank you for coming, Ms. Martin." Crane straightened her wire-rimmed glasses, her blue eyes gently regarding the recent widow. "I'm very sorry about your loss." Crane indicated a small, square table with two chairs off to the side of her desk. "Please take a seat. I understand that this is a difficult time, and I appreciate your willingness to meet with me. I know you spoke to Sergeant Mason yesterday, but I'd like to hear again your impressions of yesterday morning. Any details you can think of. Would you like a glass of water?"

Barbara shook her head and lowered herself carefully into the seat farthest from the desk as if she were unsure of her balance. She placed her bag on the floor as Crane took the other chair and placed several pages of notes in front of her. "I tried to be detailed yesterday afternoon when I talked with your sergeant. I know I wasn't in good shape then. I'm afraid I'm not feeling very well now either. This has all been so . . . so painful."

"Of course. And if at any time you'd like us to stop, please say so, and we'll continue this at a later time."

Taking off her dark glasses, Barbara wore a shocked expression as she

64

wearily took in the institutional metal desk, the single window, the beige paint, the plain shelves on the back wall, and the nondescript armchair. She closed her eyes briefly. "I'm wondering if I should call my lawyer after all."

"That is, of course, your decision." Crane indicated the telephone at the edge of her desk, picked up a sharp pencil, and tapped the eraser end on the table. She waited.

"Well," Barbara said in a low voice, "I'm happy to tell you what I know, but it isn't much. I guess I'm afraid of wasting your time."

Crane smiled and looked at Joe, who sat quietly in a corner of the room behind Barbara taking notes. "Believe me, nothing you can tell me is inappropriate or unwelcome. In a case like this, we simply have to gather the facts." She spoke sympathetically. "Tell me about the morning of yesterday, May 5, as closely as you remember it. Where were you?"

Barbara fidgeted with the knot on the rose scarf flowing down the front of her cream-colored blouse. "At home, of course. Well, not of course, I actually was supposed to be doing a performance at one time that day, but then there was the garden party. Alec needed me." She stopped abruptly as if she'd said too much.

After a few calming breaths, she continued. "We—Alec and I—were hosting the annual dean's reception at our house in the afternoon. Catered by the college, of course. I'd actually tried to get Alec to hold it at Old Main on campus instead. He seemed nervous and out of sorts, and I didn't think he needed the extra stress of a garden party. Plus, early May weather is atrocious, a complete steam bath." She flashed an irritable smile at Crane. "If you've lived very long in Austin, you know what I'm talking about."

"Yes, I couldn't agree more. So Dr. Martin was at home. And you were with him."

"I said I was." Barbara's voice was sharp.

Crane continued as if the other woman hadn't spoken. "The party was just hours away. And yet he left the house before such an important occasion."

"It seems unbelievable now. He was eating breakfast, and we were out of apricot-peach preserves, and he threw a fit. He said he couldn't possibly continue eating without them." She fidgeted in her chair, crossed her legs. Her slacks draped softly around her ankles.

"And so did you offer to go and get some for him?"

"I didn't even have time to think of that before he leaped up, grabbed his keys, and stormed outside."

"I see." Crane consulted the notes in front of her. "And he took the silver Maxima sedan rather than the black Mercedes sports car. Was that the car he typically drove?"

"Yes, that was his car, though once in a while he borrowed my Mercedes. We sometimes argued about it. Well, I must admit he bought it for me, and I rarely let him drive it. It was a gift to me, after all. If he'd wanted the Mercedes he should have bought it for himself. Christ," Barbara swore softly.

"I'm sorry?" Crane looked up and again caught Joe's eye.

"Oh, nothing. It just irritated me, that's all. Alec could be so fussy about cars and clothes and—" She bit her lip and reached down to draw a tissue from her purse. "Of course it's those little things we miss the most when we lose someone, isn't it?" She pressed her fingers to the bridge of her nose.

Lt. Crane nodded. "The everyday things, yes, they are the hardest. You were saying he took the Maxima. What happened then?"

"He was backing out of the garage, and I called after him. I said, 'Alec, you really don't have time to get worked up over the preserves! The caterers will be arriving in less than six hours.' I don't think he heard me. The store is just across the freeway. It can't be more than ten minutes away even if you don't drive like a bat out of hell. Which he always did." She turned around and smiled at Joe with a touch of flirtation. "You know . . . male drivers."

"And that's the last time you saw him?" Crane spoke quietly.

For a moment Barbara looked stunned. "Well, yes, it is." She fumbled with her tissue and brushed it under her eyes.

Crane placed the pencil to one side of the table. "You have no idea if he stopped anywhere on his way?"

"No. But he left here around seven o'clock, and the crash occurred something like twenty minutes later I think, just enough to get to the store, nab that one item, get back into his car, and . . ." She started to cough.

"Joe," Crane asked, "would you hand Ms. Martin a bottle of water from the fridge?"

"Of course." Joe walked to the corner of the office behind Crane's desk and selected a bottle of water from the small fridge. He crouched down to a shelf and unwrapped a stack of cups. On his way back to his chair, he placed the bottle and the cup on the table in front of Barbara. He ran a hand through his short, red hair and resumed his seat.

"Ms. Martin, would you say that your husband was depressed?"

Barbara's mouth turned down in a pained way. "He was under a lot of stress. Work, faculty grievances, the cross fire of campus politics . . ." she gestured vaguely. "You know."

"You weren't married very long." Crane cocked her head to one side. "Would you say the marriage was a happy one?"

"I certainly felt hopeful about this marriage." Barbara bowed her head, silent, and then said flatly, "I'm afraid my husband had a serious drinking problem, Lieutenant. I didn't realize how serious when I married him."

"I see. Was he getting help for this problem? Were the two of you seeking help?"

"I'm not prepared to discuss that right now." Barbara tucked her glossy hair behind her ears with an abstracted air.

Crane looked out at the cedar elm trees outside her window, the narrow leaves trembling in a slight breeze. "Ms. Martin, please tell me about the cell phone call."

Barbara uncrossed her legs. "What?"

"The dean's phone registered a call approximately . . ." She consulted her notes. ". . . approximately two minutes before he crashed. The number was your own cell."

Barbara frowned. "I'd almost forgotten that."

"Really? That would have been the very last time you heard your husband's voice." Crane pursed her lips, opened her mouth, but remained silent. The detective's light hair reflected the platinum glare of the fluorescent lights overhead.

"That's correct." Barbara adjusted her scarf again. "The very last time," she echoed.

In a patient voice, Crane said, "Please tell me about the call. Did you call him?"

"It's so utterly trivial." Barbara put her head in her hands.

"Let me be the judge of that."

Barbara unscrewed the cap from the water bottle and with steady hands poured a thin stream into the cup. She took a sip of water. "He called me, actually. I asked him if he'd already gone into the store."

"Yes?"

Barbara's voice was dogged. "He said yes, that he was just exiting the parking lot."

"And is that all?"

"Not quite. I heard the engine of his car kind of rev up. And then I heard him say, 'What? Oh my God! Wait!'"

Crane's voice was thoughtful. "Do you have any idea what he was referring to?"

"No. Well, I assumed he saw someone he knew. Or that someone ran out in front of him. That would explain how he lost control of the car and crashed into that utility pole." She looked up, a hopeful expression lighting up her face. "Wouldn't it?"

Lt. Crane rose from her chair and walked around to the front of her desk. She perched there about two feet in front of Barbara. "Ms. Martin, I'd like you to think very carefully back to that phone call. You talked to him right before the moment of impact. We've now examined the phone. He didn't call you—you called him." She was silent for a long while, examining Barbara's face. "Did you suggest to him that you were going to leave him?"

Unexpectedly, Barbara laughed. "What? Oh, that is one of the most outrageous things I've ever heard. Do you think if I were going to leave my husband I'd choose the morning of an important university function to tell him, and bring it up on the phone when he's driving in the car?"

"I'm simply asking the question." Lt. Crane smiled slightly.

Still laughing, Barbara shook her head. "Absurd. Of course not. I have to leave now."

Crane gave her a disappointed look. "Let me ask this another way: Were you involved with someone else?"

"Are we speaking different languages?" Barbara stood up. "We are finished here. Please address any further questions to my attorney."

"Of course," Crane said. "I'm sure we'll be speaking again soon. Good day, Ms. Martin. Joe, will you show Ms. Martin out?"

"I'll show myself out, thank you." Barbara picked up her bag, squared her shoulders, and walked stiffly out the door.

Joe hastened to shut the door behind the departing figure. He turned to face his superior and shook his head.

Crane reflectively brushed her short, fine hair away from her forehead.

"There are several things troublesome here. Tell me what you observed, Joe, from the moment Ms. Martin arrived."

Joe nodded and leaned against the door. "She's very controlled. And careful. I don't see real grief or even shock in the way she behaved here today."

"Hang on a minute. Was she much different when you interviewed her yesterday after she'd been informed of the accident?"

Considering, Joe crossed his arms across his chest and stared at the ceiling. "Not really. She appeared surprised, but at bottom she was still and watchful. Assessing me as if to gauge if she was appearing appropriately shocked. There were no tears. Her face was flushed, not pale. I remember thinking there didn't seem to be any risk of her fainting. She seemed flustered, as she did today, when I brought up the cell phone. When I told her that her husband's cell phone had been flung onto the floor during the impact, she closed her eyes. She did not volunteer that she'd been talking to him."

"And of course at that time, the phone hadn't been examined fully yet," Crane interjected. "It's clear that the call was incoming."

"Right, the deceased did not initiate the call. She's defensive, boss. She's protecting herself. And maybe someone else."

After a brief silence, Joe added, "It doesn't add up. The idea that her husband would dash out for something as trivial as jam on the morning of a key event, and then just happen to be on his phone, losing control of his car. I don't like it."

"I agree. There's much that doesn't add up. Alec Martin's death is suspicious. And his wife is a person of interest." Crane pushed herself away from the edge of the desk, her compact figure poised to move. "Let's get a coffee. To begin with, we know she's a performer, Joe. A very seasoned one it appears."

Thirteen

Barbara returned from her interview with Lt. Susan Crane and slid into a corner of the living-room sofa. She noticed how closely its wine color resembled that of blood. The sight made her queasy. She spoke out loud: "Alec is dead." *Dead is a clunker of a word,* she thought, heavy, final, a word that drops like a rock. But only the silence of the house answered her.

Every atom of her body felt stilled. She watched her hand lift her cell and punch Jane's name in her speed dial, seemingly on its own.

"Barbara, love . . ." Jane answered. Barbara didn't speak. The calm tone of her lover's voice acted as a compress on her aching head.

"I just had a horrid interview with the police." Barbara felt strangely disembodied from her voice. "I didn't say anything about you, of course. I—"

"Shhh." Jane's voice was soothing. "Try to be calm. It wasn't your fault."

Barbara squeezed her eyes tightly shut. "But before he died Alec asked me again about whether or not I was having an affair, and this time I . . . well, I choked. I bungled my answer. I denied it. 'I'm devoted to you,' I finally spat out, but it was too late. He's convinced it's someone at AU. And a man, of course. He has such a limited imagination."

"He's gone, Barbara. Alec has no imagination now."

"Oh, God, you think I'm callous, that I don't care."

"I know you care, but not like you once did. Look, who knows about us?"

"No one. I have said not one word one to anyone."

Jane breathed softly into the phone. Then, resolutely, she said, "The only reason I ask is because his death is being investigated as suspicious, yes?"

"It seems to be. I guess any one-car crash has to be. Maybe it was suicide. He was in a terrible place. Frankly, that's my guess. He couldn't hold his head up anymore."

Jane murmured something. Barbara couldn't quite hear her, but her own words rushed on. "His integrity was soiled, his reputation—these are things a man like Alec lives for. He loved the university. He couldn't ever see a life beyond it. I mentioned retirement once to him. He looked at me like I was speaking Urdu. I guess he liked being a cog in a wheel, as long as it was a bright cog, one that caught the light. But now . . . he thought he'd lost me, which, well, was, is, true . . . his career on the rocks, his image tarnished. What did he have left?"

"What all of us have: ourselves. If we're drowning, we have to swim."

Barbara cringed, imagining her late mother responding to Jane's remark in approval: *The woman has spine, I'll say that for her.* Barbara pushed the image away. She could only see Alec sobbing, his shoulders drooping over the breakfast table, finished.

"And if you don't have a self?" she whispered to Jane. Barbara bowed her head. Jane didn't know what it was like to be lost.

"Oh, you have a self, don't worry about that," Jane said. "But be careful. They always suspect the spouse. That's what worries me."

For several days after receiving the news about Alec, Miriam found herself paralyzed, unable to research or write. The news that the police were treating his death as suspicious rather than as an accident electrified the whole campus community. She prepared for the semester's last week of classes in a numb haze. Among the many projects torturing her was the keynote for the women's festival in Silver City. She'd promised to get it to Patricia Mendoza by mid-May, only a week away.

Finally, exasperated by her spouse's pacing and early awakenings, Vivian said, "Can't you make use of all of this turmoil for your speech?"

Miriam allowed that she'd try it. After a string of false starts, she found it was a relief to write about murder rather than discuss it in the hallways with colleagues or to make vain attempts to avoid obsessing about it with Bettina or Fiona. After managing a few paragraphs, she decided to read them out loud to see if they made sense. She faced the mirror in the bathroom upstairs, scanned her imaginary audience, and recited:

And now for a meditation on murder. Human beings may be blundering and offensive, but they are also very hard to kill. We are large mammals, very resourceful, dedicated to survival. A careless footfall can pulverize an ant or even a toad. But strength, resolution, and cunning are required to bring down the roughly one hundred and eighty pounds of stubborn flesh that was Alec Martin. Oh, I know what you're thinking—what about the unfortunate soul who trips in her garden, smashes her head, and dies instantly of a cerebral hemorrhage? That act requires neither strength nor cunning. It's true that sometimes death simply happens. But one can never count on such a tidy end, not if one were depending on it. Here the role of luck plays its part. In fact, the turn of the wheel of fortune may be the single most essential component in life, so much so that I say, forget planning! Give me plain vanilla serendipity every time.

But I'm not talking about naïve souls such as ourselves who lack cunning or malice. There are those whose goal in life is to beat the odds, without relying on them in the least. The foolproof murder is a goal sought as fervently today as in Arthur Conan Doyle's nineteenth century.

She paused. "The foolproof murder." Miriam pronounced again. It just might do. Then it hit her that her example wasn't just hypothetical, that she was talking about a real human being, a man she'd known and had worked with for years. She'd been so worried about her failure to make progress on her lecture, "The Locked-Room Mystery," that she'd decided to use Alec's accident to try and motivate her thinking. But it felt like tempting fate to mention him so soon after his death. His mysterious death. A car accident, a fatal head injury. And what killer was she talking about? She still held out hope that there wasn't one. She'd best delete Alec's name or use a notorious case from the past as an example. And she still needed to weave Dorothy Sayers into the talk. At the moment, it all seemed beyond her.

Her phone vibrated in her pocket. Daphne's number came up, and she accepted the call. Her friend's husky voice filled her ear. "I'm in your neighborhood. Do you have time for a cup of tea?"

"Yes, come over. I need to be distracted. And, of course, I'd love to see you," Miriam added. She and Daphne had met in the late 1980s, when both of them had lost their fathers and participated in a grief support group. They'd begun getting together for the occasional coffee soon after. Within a year of meeting, they'd become good friends, indulging their passion for jazz and Tex-Mex food in small clubs and eateries downtown and on Congress Avenue south of the Capitol.

In five minutes Daphne swept into the house wearing a deep-purple cotton dress. She gave Miriam a ferocious hug. "You poor woman. I hope you're not afraid for your safety."

"My safety?" Miriam was still preoccupied by foolproof crimes. "I haven't thought about it."

Daphne took her hand and gently led her to Miriam's favorite chair. "You are, as always, so worried about others, I know."

Miriam, feeling empowered by having voiced the beginning of her lecture, resisted sitting down, indicating that Daphne should sit in the worn leather recliner herself. "Thank you, dear. But I'm really fine. Let me get you some tea. Ginger all right?"

"Perfect." Daphne kicked off her shoes and followed Miriam into the kitchen. Miriam and Vivian's house had originally been a schoolhouse in a small Texas town at the turn of the last century. The prior owner had moved it in the 1920s from Liberty to Austin into the Hemphill Park neighborhood, a bit north and east of Austin University. They'd built a new kitchen ten years before, salvaging the longleaf pine from the school's former gymnasium—an adjacent building—for the flooring.

"This wood is so creamy and soft on my feet," Daphne said, not for the first time.

Phoebe appeared and brushed against Daphne's skirt. Miriam had never noticed before how perfectly Daphne's one tawny eye matched those of her cat.

Daphne opened the refrigerator and removed a block of cheese. "May I? I need a snack." At Miriam's nod Daphne rummaged in the cupboards and proceeded to fill a plate with crackers, cheese, and slices of apple. They sat down at the table in a small nook next to the kitchen that faced the backyard. A blue jay, prowling the branches of a live oak tree outside the window, snared a white moth from a glossy leaf as Daphne bit into a slice of apple.

"So," Daphne said, never one for small talk. "Alec Martin came to see me two weeks before he died—to consult me, no, to *tell* me about his project for a center for religious studies. I do not exaggerate when I say the man had a manic gleam about him."

"Hmm. You know then about his financial difficulties?"

"The rumors reached me before he did. But I wouldn't have needed to know. You should have heard the man—the easy way he conflated his private funds with the public ones of the university. He must have thought me very slow or very uninformed."

"You're saying he underestimated you?" Miriam knew that anyone who dismissed Daphne as a mere psychic or a crank was a fool.

"So annoying." Daphne reached for a slice of cheese and munched for a moment.

"But I know a red flag when I see one—this one was huge enough to blaze from planet earth into the stratosphere. I knew I couldn't dissuade him from self-destructing, but this . . ."

"Surely you don't think it was suicide?" Surprised, Miriam sloshed tea onto her saucer as she removed the tea bag.

Daphne raised both palms in the air as if to halt traffic. "Oh, no. I don't think him capable. He had a mission. I didn't see depression. Fear maybe. Panic. But not despair."

"Do you know his wife?"

"Barbara? Yes, she came to see me once. Why?"

Miriam heard caution in Daphne's neutral tone. "I'm not sure. Bettina and I ran into her not too long ago. There's something about her . . ."

"She's very sure of herself. I'd say she knows what she wants," Daphne said. "But that's usually a quality you admire." She slid another piece of cheese on a cracker.

"She seems ferocious," Miriam said, her face reddening. "I think she frightens me. You know, she was once involved with Vivi when they were young?"

"That can't be why she frightens you. Vivian adores you."

Miriam absently picked up the last piece of cheese on the plate and bit into it. The familiar, sharp texture of the white cheddar reassured her. Barbara's statuesque figure and handsome face filled her brain. "I don't know."

"That's the problem. None of us does. There's something very strange about all of this." Daphne stood up and pushed back her chair. "I want to show you something. Come. Don't think about it. We'll take my car."

"But the tea will get cold," Miriam protested.

"There's always another cup of tea," Daphne said, taking Miriam's arm and propelling her through the kitchen, into the hall, and out the door.

Daphne drove a red Mini Cooper coupe. The tires protested as they pulled away from the curb. Miriam had forgotten how much her friend's erratic driving terrified her. Daphne tailgated a white pickup on 38th Street then screeched ahead of it as a red light turned to green, passing in the bike lane and displacing a woman on a Schwinn Cruiser who leaped from her bike into the bushes.

"Silly woman," Daphne said, "as if I wouldn't have stopped for her."

"You *didn't* stop for her!" Miriam protested.

"Do you want to drive?" Daphne said, taking a sharp turn into a 7-Eleven and hitting the brake so hard that Miriam hung from the shoulder strap for a moment before settling back against the seat.

"No. I'll take my chances," Miriam said, breathless. "Go ahead. Plus, I have no idea where we're going."

"To the scene of the crash, of course," Daphne replied.

They crossed Interstate 35—the lights were, as usual, not timed properly even though Daphne sped up to make it through both points where cars speeding across 38th Street had to yield to the interstate access road traffic. Daphne headed north on Cherrywood Street, took a sharp right on 45th, then accelerated even though she had to make another right into the Safeway parking lot. "Thirty-five miles per hour—it can be done!" She sprang out of the low-slung car with dexterity in spite of her height and long skirt. She walked from the lot in a diagonal about a half block to the grassy berm that separated the sidewalk from the street. "Alec Martin hit this metal post at a speed of thirty-five miles an hour."

"That doesn't seem that fast. Didn't his airbag deploy?"

"No it did not. And he didn't have his seatbelt on. He'd bought something at the store and didn't bother—you recall he lives only about a mile from here. It doesn't take much of an impact to get a closed-head injury."

"You're saying he went out of the lot, jammed on the accelerator, and hit that post?'

"Exactly. That's why I clocked my speed coming in here. It's very easy within a half block, even from a dead stop, to get up to thirty-five."

Miriam nodded, thinking of Vivian's propensity to gun the engine after the light turned green. She had easily reached forty miles per hour in less time. Miriam had noticed because their street had a speed limit of only thirty.

"And," Daphne extended her arm toward the parking area, "do you see the long drive he could have taken from the lot into this soft turn? If it was early and there were no pedestrians, he could have raced out of this lot at a good clip."

Miriam swept her eyes from the exit of the supermarket farthest from the street and tried to gauge distance. "If he was really in a hurry. And not paying attention."

"Most people are not paying attention when they have single-car accidents," Daphne said patiently.

"How do you know all of this?" Miriam took in the cracked parking lot, which baked in the early May heat. A few crepe myrtle bushes had grown large enough to block a clear view of where the street intersected the lot entrance.

"Common sense," Daphne snapped. "And a friend of mine is with the police."

"Susan Crane?" Miriam asked, pronouncing the name of the only person she knew on the Austin Police Force.

"A colleague of hers." Daphne crouched near the ground and studied the post.

Miriam looked closely as well—it did seem to have a fresh dent in it. Although who could tell? The thing was riddled with pockmarks from thirty years' worth of scrapes from bumpers and doors.

"What could have occurred after he left the store to either upset him, terrify him, or distract him?" Daphne asked.

"Are you sure you're not with the police?" Miriam said facetiously, but Daphne did not laugh.

"All will be revealed," Daphne retorted.

Later that afternoon Miriam resumed work on her lecture. Daphne had almost convinced her on the way back to her house that Alec had been ambushed. But how? She wrote steadily for an hour, crossing out sentences, adding others, and scribbling thought balloons on the page before copying the result into her computer. She'd make Alec anonymous later; for now his suspicious accident spurred her on.

Once again she read the paragraphs aloud, this time not in front of a mirror but sitting before her laptop in her downstairs office. She reread the last sentence of what she'd written earlier and then kept going.

The foolproof murder. A seemingly impossible feat. But not for the person who laid waste to Alec, God rest his unlucky soul. Our perpetrator tweaked the chosen method of destruction perfectly, making Alec's downfall appear not a matter of misfortune but of fate. So ingenious was the killer's plan that for days after the murder, Alec's end was thought to be caused by a simple accident, a date with destiny. A sad occurrence, but surely a haphazard one.

I ask you to contemplate a mind facile and arrogant enough to predict that an act of premeditated violence would appear, one hundred times out of one hundred, as just a bad break. Casual, unfortunate, just one of life's little surprises. Like a slip on a slick staircase, or a skid in the shower, or a burst vessel in the brain, it was something that could happen to anyone. At any time. But Alec's death would not have happened at any time. Just at one: on a Friday morning, at rush hour, in the one-mile drive from the victim's home to his neighborhood grocery. Call it designer's delight. Call it devil's play. Call it the perfect crime.

Fourteen

Three days later, Lt. Susan Crane rubbed the corner of her right eye, dislodging her round wire-rim glasses, and shot a cautious glance at her wrist: 1:45, five minutes until class adjourned. She sat in the last row of seats in a classroom in Helmsley Hall, observing Miriam Held teaching a senior seminar on archetypes of gender. Professor Held, her squat form erect in the room's center, trained her round face on a young man in the front row.

The student, muscular and rangy, wore a vintage T-shirt emblazoned with the slogan, "Silence = Death." "Dr. Held, are you saying that difficult women like Circe, who turns Ulysses's men into pigs in *The Odyssey*, are actually agents of enlightenment rather than harm?"

Miriam took a step toward him and nodded in approval. "Absolutely. Circe was considered a witch, as were many powerful women throughout time. By persecuting these women, our society walls off inconvenient and not always rational emotions. Men have strong emotions like passion and jealousy. Sometimes they're capricious or disloyal. They just don't always admit to these feelings."

"The shadow," a student in the second row with a platinum streak at the crown of her brown hair said. She made an annoyed sound, half cough, half laugh. "But I'm a little tired of women always appearing like evil incarnate in these stories. Circe had to defend herself from warriors breaching her shores. Why do women have to instruct society at their own expense?"

"Our society regards the price of wisdom as too costly, perhaps." Miriam shrugged, and raised a cautionary finger. "It started with the story of

Eve being tempted by the Serpent, no? Women are traditionally receptive, as Eve was. The Serpent brought knowledge to the Garden. Adam, like many men—like many people—would have preferred to live in ignorance." Miriam paused and scanned the class. She liked these curious and alert honors students. "Being perceived as evil is the price we women pay for being so emotionally intelligent."

The class laughed. Miriam continued, pointing to the first student's T-shirt. "Silence equals death. That's very emotionally intelligent. Yet would we call this young man feminine for wearing it? Not necessarily, but we might think him someone on the margins. Activists created the phrase during the AIDS crisis, often accompanied by the image of an upright pink triangle. Recall that the Nazis ordered homosexuals to wear an inverted pink triangle in the concentration camps.

"These oppressed outsiders occupy the same position as women in culture: from the margins come society's truths. When the majority doesn't want to hear these truths, the outsiders are ignored or given second-class citizenship or, in some cases, imprisoned or killed. The urge to repress the shadow is powerful."

Miriam frowned at her watch. "We're overtime. We'll continue on Friday." She looked startled. "Our last class day. And, don't forget, your final essays are due then."

As the students broke for the door, Crane made her way to the front where Miriam was packing two books and a folder into a canvas bag.

"Sergeant Crane!" Miriam's voice was friendly but wary. "Are you thinking of returning to school?"

Crane smiled. "Pretty interesting place to be. Actually, thanks partly to our work on your colleague Isabel's case, I've made lieutenant."

"Congratulations."

Crane stuffed her hands into her jacket pockets. "Thank you. And please call me Susan. But no, I don't think I'm ready to come back to class. Not just yet."

"Ah. Well, I don't suppose you came then just for the pleasure of watching me teach?"

"No." Crane's light-blue eyes darted around the room as if making sure it was empty. "May I accompany you back to your office?"

Miriam picked up her bag, noting how heavy it felt. She trudged through the doorway. "It's on the seventh floor, but the elevator is just down the hall."

"So," Crane began in a neutral voice, "all this talk about the shadow. Are you a student of Jungian psychology?"

Miriam raised her eyebrows, remembering how the detective had a habit of surprising her. "No, but I suspect you might be."

"A very amateur one. I have a sister in Denver studying at the Jungian Institute. I peek at a book or two of hers when she visits."

"This is no doubt about Alec?"

"It concerns his death, yes." Crane held open the door, a slab of nondescript gray metal. They stepped into the corridor, the walls a medium gray but with occasional lighter spots where posters had been removed.

"This building desperately needs a renovation, don't you think? It's a modernist box, but there's nothing modern about it." Miriam spoke conversationally, her mind flailing about for a reason for Crane's visit. "I can't believe I've taught in it for over twenty-five years."

"You probably don't notice it unless you're with someone who doesn't work here," Crane said calmly, her steps slowing as they reached the elevator. She punched the button, and the two of them listened to the motor whine as the mechanism creaked to meet them at the third floor.

"Obsolete, wretched machine," Miriam muttered, placing her body against the sliding door so that it wouldn't snap shut behind her. "Best to leap on—this beast would as soon snap off your arm as take you somewhere."

Crane jumped aboard lightly. "Isn't Austin University one of the most well endowed universities in the country? Strange that such a clunky thing hasn't been updated."

Miriam laughed. "One would think. But this is the Department of Literature and Rhetoric, Lieutenant. We take pride in our eccentricities. Or that's what I'm told."

Crane's lean face broke out into a shrewd smile. "Eccentricity is all that the liberal arts can afford, is that what you mean?"

"Well put." Miriam's voice crackled in appreciation.

"I was an American Studies major here, once upon a time," Crane said. "I remember AU's pecking order."

"Yes, the Business School has functional elevators. But, of course, the building is newer." Miriam paused and fumbled for her keys. "Here we are."

The office had a small table with three chairs off to one side of the desk. Miriam extended a hand to one of them. "Please don't look at the desk. I'm behind on a deadline." She looked at the desk, littered with folders and books, and wished she could throw a tarp over the whole mess and start over.

"So, you've once again given up the chairmanship of the department?" Crane asked as she took a seat, unbuttoning her heather-gray wool jacket to reveal a simple ivory blouse. The buttons, shiny with a pearl finish, winked in the fluorescent lighting of the office.

Miriam waved a hand and lowered herself into her desk chair. "Good riddance. I've done it twice now. It was the least I could do after poor Isabel's death, but . . ." Miriam sat up straighter. "But, tell me why you're here. I'm sure you didn't come to hear me complain about the lack of funding in the humanities."

Crane shifted in her seat, one hand fumbling in her jacket pocket. Miriam recognized the signs of an ex-smoker. "Coffee?" she asked.

"No, thanks. Look, Professor Held . . ."

"Miriam, remember?" Miriam felt her mouth go dry in a sudden flash of nerves. Why did Crane want to talk to her?

"Miriam. You know that Dean Martin died seven days ago." Crane's blonde eyebrows, almost nonexistent, rose slightly.

Miriam nodded.

"We're still treating his death as suspicious, I can tell you that much. However, I wanted to ask you what you know about Barbara Martin."

The name caused Miriam's insides to lurch. "Almost nothing. I mean, I've met her twice."

Crane pulled a small notepad out of her jacket pocket. She paged through it. "One of your colleagues thought you went way back."

"No, it wasn't me. But at least one person here knew her when she lived back East," Miriam stammered, thinking of Vivian. Then she frowned. "You know, I haven't heard a word about her since Alec's accident. There's a memorial service planned on Sunday."

"Yes, I know. The thing is, Professor Held, Miriam . . . Barbara Martin was originally scheduled to perform in Dallas last Friday. The day Dean

Martin died," she added automatically. "And yet she was seen going for a walk in her neighborhood early that morning."

"And when you called Dallas, you found out the event was canceled and that Barbara Martin had never appeared there?"

Crane smiled. "Elementary, my dear Doctor. Yes."

"So she could have been in Austin that morning. Pardon me, you probably can't say."

"I can tell you that she freely admits to being with her husband that morning." The detective fumbled with her pocket again, and this time she brought out a pack of chewing gum that she offered to Miriam before removing a piece. "She did mention the canceled performance—she wanted to support her husband at his reception."

"Oh, the loyal wife, and all that," Miriam said.

"Right." Crane stripped the wrapping off the gum, rolled it up, and seemed to think better of putting it in her mouth. She wrapped it in its wrapper and tossed it into the trash can near Miriam's desk. "Addictive stuff," she said. "I'm trying to cut back. The thing is, the Martins were married only a short time. Most recent brides—" here Crane smiled— "would be prostrate with grief."

"But not this one?" Miriam wanted to keep the detective talking. Her comments fascinated her, and their conversation was wonderful fieldwork for her lecture too. "Pardon me, ah, Susan, but I think Barbara Martin is not your typical bride. And I don't just mean because of her age, which is probably around fifty, fifty-five." Miriam paused. Vivian had just turned fifty-two, and Barbara had been an undergraduate at the same time, so they must be roughly the same age.

Crane shifted in her chair and adjusted her glasses. "'Typical bride.' A quaint expression these days. But please, say more."

Miriam folded her hands in her lap. "Well, I don't know the woman well as I said. And please know that I don't usually speak so frankly." Miriam cautioned herself to be quiet—why was she babbling like this? Something about Susan Crane's open, fresh face made her want to confide in her, so she disregarded her inner warning and continued. "I have to say that I find her very ambitious, possibly opportunistic." Inside, Miriam cringed. Her attitude had everything to do with Vivian. She'd turned into a possessive spouse.

"Really?" Crane sat very still. "Interesting. It won't come as a surprise to you then that one of your colleagues said something to that effect. Another said, and I quote, 'She fucked her way to the top.'"

It was Miriam's turn to be silent. A panel discussion at an arts symposium when she was an undergraduate popped into her mind. Two famous writers were hurling slurs at each other in the student union ballroom, escalating their insults and their volume, until one said, "What do you know about struggling to make a career? You've always fucked your way to the top." The phrase had been a conversation stopper back then. Now it just seemed sad. And sadder still that all these decades later, powerful people continued to use and abuse others for sex. If Barbara had married Alec as a business arrangement, it seemed like she'd made a bad investment. "Oh," Miriam replied to Crane.

"Would you say that marrying Alec Martin might have been a good professional move for her?" Crane paged through her notebook.

"I used to think Alec had family money," Miriam said. "And perhaps he did. But his recent actions seem to indicate that this surplus was gone, or insufficient. He wanted to become provost and then president of the university. In our little academic world, that means huge power. But, you know, Barbara struck me as someone who didn't care for small worlds. I'd say she had larger aims. Of course, if Alec had become one of the chief executives at AU, that would have opened doors for Barbara—onto nonprofit boards and that sort of thing."

"But even that sounds like only a first step for a woman of grander aims, if your assessment is correct," Crane said.

Miriam scanned the wall opposite her desk. Both of the framed posters were cockeyed. "Good grief. I can't believe I'm talking like this. I don't know anything about this poor woman's life."

Susan Crane tucked her notebook into her jacket pocket. "That 'poor woman' is about to collect on a three-million-dollar life-insurance policy. Perhaps that amount of cash will jump-start her career as well."

Fifteen

The investigation into Alec Martin's death ground through the summer, its lack of a conclusion increasing Miriam's sense of foreboding as the season wore on. Even so, the summer passed with unbelievable speed—travel to Oregon for the Shakespeare festival, a visit to Vivian's mother in Maine, too many books unread in spite of great intentions—dropping Miriam once more into a new fall semester.

The term had barely geared up to speed when Miriam found herself traveling to Silver City for the Chautauqua, "Women on the Edge." Patricia had arranged for a car to take her from the airport in El Paso. Exiting the car, Miriam slipped on a pair of oversize maroon sunglasses. The glasses were old, two prescriptions ago, but she liked them. They made her feel disguised and yet a bit glamorous too. Given that her physique was short and portly (this last according to her somewhat elderly doctor), glamour was not a part of her self-concept. But if her calculus included ideas, that altered the story. She'd had one or two of those in her life that she was proud of.

A breeze stirred her skin. She sniffed: clean, dry air. In late September. Astonishing. Miriam had been living in the shallow, humid bowl called central Texas for decades. The word "crisp" did not apply.

The twin doors of the lodge—heavy, scarred wood with tarnished-brass door latches—greeted her after she walked up the path towing her rolling bag, which kept getting hung up on the gravel.

She raised her hand to use the gargoyle knocker, which was in the shape of some kind of creature. A bear's head? That would be the obvious choice, given the name of the place: Oso Grande. But it didn't look quite right . . . Maybe it was a wild boar? Were there wild boar in New Mexico? Fiona had said something about javelinas running wild. Before she had a chance to rap the iron gargoyle, the doors swung wide.

"Ah, it must be Dr. Held. Come in, come in," said a woman in a full skirt who grasped Miriam's hand. "I'm Brenda Perez, the manager—"

She was interrupted by a hearty shout of "Miriam! Thank goodness."

Miriam did not even have to glimpse the round, bright eyes or the high forehead framed by dark, curly hair to know who it was—her old student Patricia Mendoza.

"Pleased to meet you, Brenda," Miriam said before she withstood a squeeze from the robust Patricia, one of those people who were not aware of how imposing their physical selves might be to a short person. Miriam's, "It's been a long—" was muffled as her face was crushed into Patricia's mid-chest.

"She walks, and talks, and she's here!" Patricia said in a folksy way, thrusting Miriam at arm's length. "You never change. Or I should say you never age. How do you do it?"

"Here, let me take this." Brenda grasped Miriam's gray rolling bag, sparing any need for Miriam to reply. Each of the woman's broad wrists displayed a wide silver bracelet burnished to a high polish. "I'll take this to your room. It's in a cottage in the back with a private little patio. I hope you'll like it."

Miriam hurried after Brenda, giving Patricia a little wave. She really needed to unpack and settle down before she could face her former student. Her energy was like a high wind rolling toward the unwary. A gale. Something a little scary. *A lot scary*, Miriam thought, her compact legs carrying her toward the other end of the building and out on a gravel path to the cottage where she was staying. The building had four large rooms surrounding a common living room in the center.

At the door to Miriam's room, Brenda told her the guests would assemble for dinner at seven.

"Have you been here long?" Miriam asked.

"Oh yes, since the place opened, ten years ago." The manager's voice was low and musical. "Many people come here to let the beauty soothe them. I've lived in the area many years."

Without thinking Miriam said, "Ah, so you know where all the bodies are buried then. We must talk."

Brenda suddenly stood very straight. A fearful shadow crossed her face.

"A figure of speech," Miriam said. "You know, as in the saying, 'Where there are dead bodies, the vultures will gather'? I did see a few vultures when I arrived."

"I don't like to talk of such things," Brenda said in a quiet voice. Her fingers tightened on Miriam's luggage as if for ballast. In a moment, resuming her position as host, Brenda smiled slightly. "I'll see you at seven o'clock, then. Let me know if you have questions." The woman touched her throat and hurried down the corridor.

Strange, Miriam thought. She hadn't noticed that Brenda had worn a cross or a necklace. Perhaps the throat gesture was some kind of Catholic shorthand? Miriam couldn't help but think that growing up Jewish in the Midwest had its disadvantages. There were so many references that she didn't recognize.

Safely in her room, Miriam arranged her few possessions in the pine armoire, tried out the two chairs—the one by the window was the most comfortable—tested the queen bed for firmness, and then slipped out onto her patio with a book. The tensions of the day retreated as she looked out onto native grasses with their golden seed plumes waving in the breeze, bird feeders abuzz throughout the grounds, and the glorious mountains beyond. The air was dry and, in the September twilight, cool. She sniffed. Not pine scented, she noted with disappointment. Maybe the scent was too subtle for her—her sense of smell had been muted since she had tripped over the clothes she'd left outside of the shower, fallen, and hit her head last year. She checked her watch: it was only six o'clock.

She resisted the impulse to call Vivian, Bettina, or Fiona. All three would arrive tomorrow. She'd already called Vivian during the drive from the airport to let her know her flight had landed safely. She didn't want any of them to think she was feeling desperate. In truth the coming gathering troubled her. The event had loomed up in her calendar for months now. Patricia's idea of inviting six scholar-performers to perform historical figures at Oso Grande seemed benign. Yet her student's idea of including Gertrude Stein, Alice B. Toklas, and Mabel Dodge Luhan, three women who not only knew each other in history but in some cases had grudges against one another in the past, did not seem prudent to Miriam. Patricia, though, liked action; she was fond of phrases like "Friction makes change" and "Change is the spice of life."

Since Alec's death in May, Miriam's dread had only grown. His death had been labeled as suspicious, but so far no one had been arrested as a suspect. Alec had created ill will with enough people that as time went on, the fumes of paranoia poisoned the campus more than ever. Daphne, of course, had no doubts that his death was planned and not an accident at all. What would make a very entitled, very busy man who was hosting a reception that was going to be fully catered burst out of his house early in the morning to do an errand at a grocery store he never went to? Alec was unlucky, true, but also willfully ignorant. Of his own limitations, of the amount you could stretch incredulity even with gray hair and a PhD after your name, of other people's perceptual abilities—in other words, people were twice as smart as Alec thought they were, even as he himself was four hundred percent less gifted than he thought he was.

Daphne had reported to Miriam that the police still observed Barbara. And they probably continued to monitor half the faculty as well. Miriam's mind drifted back to the dreadful awards dinner. Alec hadn't cemented any loyalty there.

Miriam braced herself for more surprises during the festival. Perhaps Susan Crane might appear unofficially, disguised as an early twentieth-century figure, the better to observe Barbara. If so, Miriam hoped for one of her favorite mystery writers, Dorothy L. Sayers or Agatha Christie, even though Crane seemed more like a contemporary type. Sue Grafton? Elizabeth George? More theatrics. A field day for Patricia.

She made her way back into her room, pulled her bottle of single malt from the closet, and poured two fingers into a glass, then she retreated back to the patio. What was she doing here? Unfortunately, besides her research, the only book she'd brought with her was Edith Wharton's *Tales of Men and Ghosts*. She opened it to a story called "The Eyes," where a woman is visited by the malevolent spirit of a seducer. She put the book aside.

Oso Grande Lodge seemed full of ghosts. Chief among them was the woman called Brenda, a full-figured woman with hair worn in a thick twist at the back of her neck. She seemed like a Mother Superior figure to

Miriam, pleasant and orderly, discreet. There was something deliberately opaque about her, as if she had much to hide and was determined to keep it hidden. Miriam had noticed a thick scar on the back of her right ankle when she preceded her to the back of the property. A dog bite? A knife wound? Brenda's calf-length black skirt failed to hide the mark.

Jane, a colleague from California who had agreed to reprise her performance of Gertrude Stein for the Chautauqua, joined Miriam at dinner. Miriam noticed that Jane's short, wavy hair was even more blonde than she'd remembered.

Jane's full face lit up when she saw Miriam. "Thank goodness you're here at least. My luggage has been lost. Serves me right for arriving a day early." She glanced down at her cream-colored vest and brown chino slacks. "I know Stein was known not to give a fig about clothes, at least in her early years, but let's hope I won't be wearing this for five days."

"Don't worry, we'll think of something." Miriam had no ideas at the moment. At least five inches shorter than Jane, she knew she had no wardrobe help to offer. Vivian was tall but slender, and Alice B. Toklas had a completely different style—part gypsy, part enchantress—so they'd have no help there.

They selected a few hors d'oeuvres from a small table off to one side before joining Patricia—who had decided to appear in her Woodhull costume for some reason, perhaps to inspire them?—at the dining table. Miriam noted that all of the items were very healthy, of the cucumber and fruit variety as opposed to the heavier meatball and rich-canapé style Miriam favored. "I hope they won't expect us to speak without proper food." She patted her ample stomach. "I suppose it will do us all good to fast a bit."

At that moment a platter of prime rib was making its way out of the kitchen. "Well, I don't think we're at the fasting stage yet," Jane said, snagging a piece of cheese with a toothpick.

Once seated, Miriam tipped her head toward Patricia at the other end of the table and whispered to Jane, "She looks better than I've ever seen her look. Have you seen the Victoria Woodhull she's promised us?"

"She's organizing all this and performing, and not just as anyone. As one of the most notorious suffragists of her day, famous not only for advancing the cause of women but an advocate of free love as well. She and her sister were the first women to found a brokerage firm on Wall Street! Gutsy. I do like her hair cut short this way, as Woodhull wore it at the peak of her fame. With her beautifully tailored black brocade ensemble, complete with a cape the Victorians wore so well, she does look stunning—I think she's lost twenty pounds since I saw her last! Do you think she's responsible for my lost luggage?"

"Ha," Miriam said. "That's it. Maybe everyone arriving tomorrow will have that problem, guaranteeing that we'll all look shabby next to her while she wears one stunning outfit after another!"

Cutting a slice of roast, Jane said to Patricia, "Remind me to tell you about a colleague who's begun work on the celebrated African American journalist Ida B. Wells, who fought against lynching in the Jim Crow era. Another activist woman born in the nineteenth century. You might want to include her next time. What led you to Woodhull?"

The mere mention of her subject's name animated Patricia; her words tumbled out. "The election, of course, followed by the groundswell of the women's march in January. The bravery of women coming together and coming forward . . ."

Jane interjected, "The walls of silence are tumbling down at last."

"Yes, and I felt I had to contribute in some way. Woodhull faced so much discrimination for her radical views on suffrage and marriage. I think she's been forgotten, and I aim to change that."

Miriam raised her glass to Patricia. "Your timing is perfect! Woodhull was intelligent and stunning, a very good orator, and very successful in finance as well. Truly a Renaissance woman."

Patricia, looking pleased, turned her attention to one of the servers.

After a few minutes of concentrating on her food, Jane scooted her chair even closer to Miriam. "So, tell me about Barbara Martin. Half of Patricia's emails have been devoted to Alec Martin's accident . . . which she thinks was actually murder."

"Lord. Patricia thinks it's a murder, and she doesn't even live in Austin. Why doesn't she just publish an essay in the *Chronicle of Higher Education* and lay out her theories? But Alec's death really does appear to be a mystery to be solved . . ."

Patricia at that moment placed a hand on the ornate pearl brooch at her throat. "What are you two talking about?"

"You," said Miriam. "Look at you. We're admiring your dressmaker."

"Oh! Thank you." Patricia's face flushed. "But we shouldn't talk about clothes. I'm so sorry, Jane, about your lost bags."

"Tell us the plan for the first evening." Jane waved a hand as if her costume was a slight matter.

"Well, I wanted Miriam to give her keynote then, but she suggested that you perform first since Gertrude Stein was famous for her Saturday nights in Paris. You can set a cultural stage for our get-together."

Jane nodded. "I like the idea of making the event like a private salon as Stein did in her atelier, a gathering of friends." She looked around the dining area adjoining a huge living room. "And that wonderful room is perfect as a stage for our little community, even though the art on the walls is southwestern rather than European." She gestured at a series of photographs depicting the extensive adobe tiers of the Taos Pueblo, one of the oldest pueblos in the southwest. Opposite it was a large painting of a dramatic chasm, the Rio Grande Gorge, where the cliffs appeared to plunge precipitously from the sky to the bottom of the world.

Miriam had read that the Gorge was a rift valley where the earth's plates had separated almost thirty million years ago. She and Vivian hoped to drive up to Taos to see it after the festival. She admired the room along with Jane. "The plaster walls and the wood ceiling are very authentic, aren't they?"

"Yes, and the round wood beams, called vigas, came from pine forests in the area," Patricia offered. She turned toward Miriam. "Um, Miriam," Patricia said. "You know, in the current revival of Chautauqua, the scholar-performer, after giving a monologue in character, first takes questions from the audience as the character and then removes a small item of her costume—a hat, a scarf, or a tie—and takes questions from the audience as herself, the person who has brought the historic figure alive in the context of the present time. So we need a moderator. I hope you don't feel like I'm springing this on you, but I'm hoping you'll moderate the event. I know Gertrude here will keep the conversation flowing—" she extended a hand toward Jane—"but we want to keep on schedule and make sure the discussion is focused."

Unsure whether she felt put out or flattered by Patricia's suggestion, Miriam quickly said, "But wouldn't Gertrude, the ultimate salon hostess, be the logical choice?" Miriam hoped Jane might find this suggestion appropriate and even enticing.

Which she did. "I'd be happy to," Jane smiled.

Her cheeks were flushed, and Miriam couldn't help but notice that she looked uncommonly well. She'd forgotten what lovely cheekbones Jane had, and surely she'd shed a few pounds too . . . Miriam thought back to Patricia telling her that she never changed. Seeing her colleagues looking so trim made her resolve to work on her waistline and fitness. *As soon as I get back home and settled*, she temporized, reaching for her wineglass.

Jane took another bite of salad. "How big an audience are you expecting for the public events?"

Patricia said, "We think about forty to fifty for each presentation. There are six performances plus Miriam's keynote, so that makes for a full schedule for our time together. I'm hoping we'll be able to publish the scripts from our proceedings. I confess I've handpicked the audience as I'm floating this event as an experiment—several book clubs and people in the visual and literary arts here. If it works we'll expand it next time, or maybe take this one on the road! Most Chautauqua program planners choose a theme and hold auditions. For this first one, I selfishly wanted to bring this group of women together, so thank you for agreeing to come."

Miriam resisted the urge to check her calendar for a means of escape—surely she could find an excuse to just go home? "Women on the Edge" was scheduled for six days. She already felt restless, and it was a day before anything began. She began to wish she could live in the locked room instead of making it the subject of her lecture.

The mere idea of such a room was so reassuring that Miriam excused herself, confirmed with Jane that she'd meet her for breakfast, and made her way to the back of the building, past the coffee and tea caddy and out the double French doors to the cottage and into her own room. After locking the door, which she'd been happy to discover had two sets of latches, she sought the only control she had, which was her pen. She settled into the small desk under the window to the back portal and opened her notebook. She cracked the spine as she opened to a new page and selected a red pen.

Alec Martin = a Janus figure. Two-faced. But rather than see both the past and the future as in the myth, he changed his mask to feed his desires. He didn't look back, only forward, to his imagined triumphs. Barbara seems much more skilled. Inheriting three million dollars so conveniently. A pile of cash. What does it mean to her? What can she do when she has the money that she couldn't do before?

Miriam paused, then she crossed out the rest of the sentence after the words "has the money." "What can she do when she has the money?" she said aloud, underlining the words. She resumed writing.

Things to consider:
1. Barbara goes around the country as Mabel Dodge Luhan, one of the country's most moneyed benefactors of the arts in her time. Her attraction to the character of Dodge Luhan shows that Barbara finds wealth fascinating in a huge way.

Miriam circled the words "wealth" and "huge."

Not only wealth, but power. Mabel had sexual power, financial power, cultural prestige.
2. Mabel was a troublemaker. Vivian says Barbara was—and is—as well. Does she want something from Vivi?

Miriam's pen left a nasty glob of red ink by the word "want." She swiped the ballpoint on the paper calendar blotter on one side of the desk.

3. Why attend this event? Who is here who can get her closer to what she wants?

Miriam closed her journal. Barbara would reveal her motives. Everyone always did. The woman had married Alec, hadn't she? A narcissist of the first order. Barbara valued self-importance. Had to if she linked herself with Alec. She'd seen him as a stepping stone. But maybe his adoration of her was so blind—uncharacteristic of a narcissist unless it reflected on him (Miriam decided that it had)—that he buoyed her up on a daily basis.

Reflected back her dazzling self. Miriam poured herself another single malt. Just a tiny one to wash her own harsh judgment out of her mouth. Yet she couldn't help but think how the Martins were so obvious, such preening paragons of self-regard. She felt another stab of guilt. One of them was dead. *Sorry, Alec,* she thought as she tipped the glass and swallowed the smoky liquid. *Rest in peace.* She shuddered. She hadn't poured just one finger of Scotch but two. Oh well. Or, as a former colleague had always said, "C'est la guerre." At that, she changed into her pj's and went to bed.

Sixteen

Barbara arrived the next morning in one of those mountain rains that flash-dump a half an inch of rain and then charge on to the next destination before you've moved from your bed to your back door. Barbara stayed in the car and flashed her lights and waited until someone came with an umbrella to help her into the lodge. Oso Grande operated with a minimal staff, and since the gardener was in the woods looking for mushrooms for the evening's meal and the waitstaff were serving breakfast, that left only Brenda, the manager, to trudge into the rain and liberate Barbara from the car.

Miriam watched all of this from the windows in the lodge's living room, where she'd gone early to check for a newspaper and had stayed to watch the storm. She checked another box off in her mental assessment of Barbara Martin: drama queen. Anyone else would have enjoyed the fairly rare sight of rain in New Mexico—splashed in a puddle maybe, opened her mouth up to catch drops, or just made a dash for it.

But Barbara's arrival was an event, and she might as well enjoy it. As she hadn't found a newspaper and the internet seemed to be down, she decided she'd check to see if breakfast was ready.

On the way into the dining room, Miriam encountered Jane, still wearing her chinos from the evening before. "Any sign of the lost luggage?" Miriam asked.

"Yes. A phone call from the airport in Tucson. The word is that the bags will arrive this afternoon by four."

"In time for your performance. That's good." Miriam drew her own phone out of her pocket. "You must have Verizon. I'm getting no bars at all. Blasted AT&T."

Jane's level gray eyes did not blink. "They have a landline here, actually. My phone was in my luggage."

"Oh." The two friends looked at each other, Miriam suppressing the impulse—the bane of a life spent teaching—to say something about the wisdom of packing your cell phone and checking it anywhere as unreliable as an airport.

Jane's laugh was musical. "I understand the Eagle has landed." They walked together into the dining room.

"Have you been working on your laugh?" Miriam asked. "I read somewhere, and it's always stuck in my mind, that Mabel Dodge described Stein's laugh like a 'juicy beefsteak.'"

"It sounds easier than it is to duplicate that. Think about it: What does a steak sound like?"

Miriam was about to reply with some variation on the word *sizzle* when Barbara looked up from the counter that held the coffeepot and assorted fruit juices, teas, and condiments. "Miriam, you're already here!"

Miriam stepped forward. "Barbara, I don't know if you've met Jane Auckler from Los Angeles."

The two women regarded each other for a long moment. Barbara and Jane were both tall women with impressive physiques, and Miriam felt like a referee in a prizefight standing between them.

Barbara grasped Jane's hand and held it a moment too long. "Patricia has spoken very highly of your performance."

"Thank you." As Jane extricated herself from the handshake, she said, "I'm very sorry to hear about your husband's death."

Barbara's brown eyes looked glazed for a moment. "Yes, it was very sudden. Did you know him?"

Jane appealed to Miriam. "I think I met the dean when you invited me in for that lecture—what, three years ago?"

Miriam nodded as Jane murmured, "Such an energetic man."

As Barbara did not reply to this comment, Jane and Miriam busied themselves pouring tea, measuring milk, and choosing a selection of fruit. As they picked up their cups and bowls, Miriam saw Barbara's gaze sweep over

Jane's short hair and broad shoulders as she said, "I see you look even better in earth tones than Gertrude did."

"You're too kind. You'll notice when I'm in costume that I'll be wearing brown and beige and more brown!" Jane attempted an easy laugh that signaled to Miriam that she was relieved to have the conversation back on a neutral ground. "Gertrude wasn't exactly the peacock in the clothes category that your Mabel is."

Strange how these scholars referred to the characters they'd performed or interacted with by their first names, as if they were dear friends, Miriam observed. Fiona had lately begun referring to Edith Wharton as "our Edith."

Miriam chose a table by the window, and as the two women joined her, she reflected that there was much to learn in this place. Oso Grande was indeed an alternate cosmos, one marked not only by craggy mountains and strange cacti but unfamiliar ways of being as well.

After breakfast, Barbara walked outside with Jane and Miriam.

"I think I'll go work on my keynote," Miriam announced.

"How about a walk?" Barbara said to Jane. "It's such a fine day. We don't get these cool mornings in September in Austin."

"I need to go upstairs for just a minute, and then I'll join you," Jane said, waving to Miriam who had headed back to the cottage.

Once Miriam moved out of view, Barbara went back inside the lodge and up the stairs to the second floor. Jane materialized by the stairwell, took her by the hand, and led Barbara into her room. As soon as she'd closed the door, Jane took Barbara in her arms and kissed her, all the while guiding them to the bed.

"That was a close call!" Barbara gasped between kisses. "You don't think Miriam has any clue that we know each other?"

"You mean really know each other?" Jane said, falling onto the bed with Barbara. "No, she seemed preoccupied. Oh, darling, it's been two whole weeks!"

Barbara held Jane tightly. Ever since meeting Jane at a program in Los

Angeles on Americans Abroad in the 1920s, they'd managed to see each other at least every other week. "I've been so lonely for you. We can't let our schedules get in the way like that ever again."

"Remember when we met and I told you that you were fabulous looking?" Jane said, slowly unbuttoning Barbara's blouse. She slid her hands over her lover's stomach and around to her back to unhook her bra.

"I think I told you that," Barbara murmured.

After that, they were occupied for some time.

"Are we rewriting history, do you think?" Jane asked later.

"Letting it play out. I really do think that, left to their own devices, this would have happened for Gertrude and Mabel. Alice was right to worry. Had she not been there, at the Villa Curonia to keep Gertrude on a leash, who knows what might have happened between the two lions?"

"Well, not this," Jane said, showing even, white teeth. Her lips were chafed from kissing.

"Ha. You're right. Who knows what either of them was really like."

"We have Stein's poems in *Lifting Belly* and the portrait 'As a Wife Has a Cow: A Love Story.' Very sensual. Their sex life might have been very, very good."

"Show me," Barbara said.

A couple of hours later, as they lay together, the sun shining brightly into the room, Barbara traced her finger along Jane's collarbones. "You have such a nice body, strong but soft too."

Jane sighed and pulled Barbara closer. "You're the best thing that's ever happened to me."

"Mmm," Barbara said and then giggled. "Do you remember when I told you in Los Angeles when we met that your Stein performance was the best I'd ever seen?"

"Yes?"

"Then I had to fess up, remember? 'Full disclosure,' I told you after we'd spent the night together. 'It's the only one I've ever seen!' I think I blushed for the first time in twenty years!"

"It was that blush that did it," Jane said. She threaded her fingers through Barbara's hair and played with the strands. "I feel we're in a secret world. For now. But maybe not for much longer."

"As soon as Lt. Crane closes out the investigation into Alec's death, we can be as open as we want to be. I just want to make sure I'm free of suspicion. I'm very ready for all that to be over."

Jane nodded. "That brings me back to Miriam. She's so worried about her keynote I can't imagine she noticed anything today. And she seems a bit worried about Vivian for some reason."

"Well . . . I know you've known her longer than I have, but I have the feeling not much gets past her. I hope you're right. As for Vivian, what I've noticed back home is that she's acting more like Toklas every day. So possessive of her darling Miriam. But let's not talk."

"Agree. *Don't speak.*" Jane tried to imitate Dianne Wiest in *Bullets Over Broadway*. She failed. They dissolved into a fit of helpless laughter.

Seventeen

Bettina rapped on the door of Miriam and Vivian's room in the back of the cottage. A flat airplane tire in Austin had delayed her arrival, and she'd missed lunch. The lodge had arranged a shuttle for her from El Paso, and it was now after 4:00 p.m.

From the quiet hall she heard laughter, and Vivian elaborately enunciate a single word: "concinnity." Bettina wondered if she'd wandered into a foreign language lesson. Latin perhaps?

Vivian opened the door, waved Bettina in with a slight bow, and said over her shoulder, "Stumped you there!"

"I have no idea what it means," Miriam agreed.

Both of them looked very pleased as Bettina stepped into the room. "Does whatever it is have something to do with me?"

"Sit down, sit down." Miriam rose and bustled to get Bettina a chair. "I don't think so. We're just playing a word game. It was my turn to define an unusual word. Vivi, tell us what 'concinnity' means."

"The word means a harmony of design, particularly in terms of literary style. I thought it fit rather nicely in terms of the weekend. And you know how hard it is to dig up something about language that Miriam doesn't know."

Bettina slumped into a patio chair. "It's after five in Austin. Do you think we might have a drink? What a time I've had. The high point of my day was Clare asking for an emergency loan."

Miriam gestured to the small terrace attached to their room. "That's what daughters are for. Pick up your chair, and let's go outside. We have Scotch of course. And vodka for you and Fiona."

The three settled themselves on the red brick surface. Beyond the wood pillars that supported the roof of the patio, fat piñon trees were layered with bird feeders in bright colors—like ornaments, Bettina thought. Clumps of native grasses in hues of brown and gold spread out into the foothills. Gravel paths wound through the trees and grasses, dotted here and there by benches fashioned from tree stumps.

Vivian brought out a tray of ice and glasses and distributed drinks. "This wonderful porch is called a portal." She pronounced the word por-*tall*. "The Spanish built them for shade on traditional territorial houses like this one."

"Very pleasant," Bettina agreed, accepting a vodka on the rocks. "Cheers. Where is Fiona by the way?"

"She's having an attack of nerves in her room." Vivian sat on a bench next to Miriam.

"But Jane is the only person who has to do anything this evening, isn't she?" Bettina scooped up a handful of peanuts from a glazed blue bowl Vivian had set in front of her and popped a few into her mouth.

Miriam nodded. "Fiona said she'll be with us in a few minutes. I don't think she quite realized what she was getting herself into."

Bettina exchanged a glance with Vivian. "That makes three of us I think. My mistake was to agree to capture one of my heroes. Woolf was so articulate and sophisticated about literature. Not to mention life. And how can I match her style? I wish now I'd said I'd take on Georgia O'Keeffe, who didn't think too much of words, or at least that's what she said. Then I could have just waved around some paint brushes or something."

"Ha!" Miriam waved as Fiona came up the walk toward their patio. "O'Keeffe was actually quite eloquent, you know. 'Words are like the wind,' she said. And I can't imagine it would be easy meeting the expectations of a New Mexico audience about one of their most famous artists."

"You have a point, I suppose." Bettina wanted nothing more than a good sulk. Too bad this lodge didn't have a bar with a dark corner and down-and-dirty blues music. "I'd just like to do something else—anything else—but what I'm supposed to do."

Miriam gave her a sympathetic look. "Just so you know," she said, "Patricia told me last night that this event is more of an experiment, a salon with a handpicked audience—readers and artists, probably history buffs too. Maybe knowing that will help relieve some of the pressure you're feeling."

"Oh, good." Bettina rolled her shoulders, which remained stubbornly tight. "Let's hope that's true." She sipped her drink. "Are you all right, Fiona?" Bettina asked as Fiona arrived and plopped down on a stool Vivian fetched from their room.

"I'm not sure. Patricia told me I could use a script." Fiona's face cleared. "You know, Wharton wasn't a big public speaker. Her friends found her entertaining and witty, but she was reserved in public. So maybe I'll just pretend that she's writing in her diary the whole time."

"Ah, a private context." Miriam nodded approval. "The audience will be the fourth wall, listening in."

"Impressive, Professor Held." Bettina raised her glass. "I didn't know you knew so much about the stage."

"Well," Miriam said, pretending to brush a crumb from her light-brown cardigan, "just between us, I did actually start college as a drama major. Don't look so horrified. Of course I washed out after the first year. Didn't have a feel for the audience."

"But you're such a good teacher, sweetie," Vivian said. "That requires a strong sense of your audience."

"That's different," Miriam insisted. "I like to teach my subject, and I can just be myself. It was all the worrying about projecting a character that I found daunting."

"Hmm." Bettina sat up straighter. "You have something there. You just reminded me of Barbara—of another thing that makes me think she's a suspicious person."

"I'm curious to know what you're getting at." Fiona's blue eyes looked perplexed. "You mean that she's skilled at reading her audience?"

"She probably can do that too. But she is a master of projecting character, I think." Bettina sucked on an ice cube from her empty drink. "Think about it. Every single one of us had a different impression of her. Vivian knew her as a seductive young woman, Miriam and I met her as a development officer who supported her husband's career, Patricia first heard of her as an actress. And Fiona—"

"I know nothing about her," Fiona responded. "She was on the arm of Alec Martin at a reception. That's all."

"Proves my point," Bettina said. "To you, she blended in as Alec's prop. She's a chameleon."

"But, Bettina, that's what we're all here to be, chameleons," Fiona spoke reasonably. "Playing at being people other than ourselves."

"For better or worse," Vivian chimed in.

"You'll see I'm right, all of you." Bettina's tone was uncharacteristically severe. "All actors may be chameleons on the stage. But we hope they have some essential core offstage. I shall be paying attention, that's all. Barbara is definitely someone to watch."

"I hope so," Miriam said. "If I have to watch her as Mabel Dodge Luhan, I'd like to enjoy myself."

Bettina threw up her hands. "Some of us have to get in costume for this opening event, and then let's go in to dinner. We have Jane's Stein monologue to look forward to. At least Jane knows what she's doing. Maybe we'll learn something from a real pro."

About forty people were arranged at long narrow tables in the great room when their group arrived. As the guests were served, Bettina noticed Brenda watching the diners and keeping the narrow hallway that led to the kitchen free of congestion. Her hair was plaited in dark waves down her back. Short and compact, with unlined skin and high, polished cheekbones, Brenda was a striking figure. The courses came and went like clockwork, and each time Bettina heard someone ask for something, she'd see Brenda glide from the room and down the hallway. Moments later one of the waiters would deposit the requested item on the appropriate table.

Had she been observing the social matrix of the festival, Bettina supposed she would have called the table where she was seated, one of four and the closest to the small staging area in front of a huge kiva fireplace, the "A" table. Patricia Mendoza presided at its head, Barbara at its foot. Along one side were Miriam and Jane, the latter in a simple dark-brown dress that fell from her shoulders to the floor. She looked quite elegant in spite of Stein's reputation for functional clothing. Bettina recalled Vivian telling her that Gertrude Stein of all people, once she became famous, favored Balenciaga couture when photographed by Cecil Beaton.

On the other side of the table were Vivian, Fiona, and Bettina, all in their characters' costumes. When asked before the dinner which character she was portraying, Bettina stated, "Lily Briscoe, as created by Virginia Woolf," to the mystification of her questioner. Try as she might, Bettina could not find the brazen confidence to claim that she was in any way a stand-in for her revered VW.

After dinner Patricia introduced Jane by asking the audience to imagine that it was 1935 and that they were part of the audience for one of the lectures Gertrude Stein gave on her 1934–1935 tour of America after her book, *The Autobiography of Alice B. Toklas*, became a best seller. "After she speaks, you may ask Miss Stein questions."

Jane stepped onto a small platform in front of the fireplace in full view of the tables. She planted herself stolidly, put her arms behind her back, and, after a long silence, began. "I always said I would not come back to America until I was a real lion. A real celebrity. And of course at the time I never thought I was going to be one. But then I wrote *The Autobiography of Alice B. Toklas*. And there was this lecture tour. And here I am . . .

"When Alice and I arrived in New York harbor, it was quite astonishing. Reporters and cameras were everywhere. The revolving sign above Times Square proclaimed, 'Gertrude Stein has returned to New York.' The front pages of the newspapers, apparently trying to imitate my style, had headlines like 'Gerty Gerty Stein is Back Back Back' and 'Gertrude Stein is Back and it's still all Black Black Black.' One reporter who interviewed me apparently expected me to be difficult to understand; he said to me, 'Miss Stein, why don't you write the way you talk?' I replied, 'Why don't you read the way I write?'"

Bettina noticed Barbara taking rapid notes on a sheet of paper as Jane talked. Barbara looked glossy and glamorous in her costume, which entailed elaborate jewelry in silver and turquoise, including a squash-blossom necklace, dazzling against a black gown.

Jane, as Stein, spent a lot of time detailing the acquisition of modernist art along with the founding of her and her brother Leo's salon, which allowed others to view the remarkable paintings. She took the audience on a tour of her and Alice's activities when they drove a van with medical supplies during the First World War. As soon as she concluded with, "I have seen the twentieth century, and I've shown you a part of it today," Barbara's arm shot up.

"Miss Stein, can you tell us about your friendship with Mabel Dodge?"

Jane's carriage got a little stiffer. "We were quite good friends. In fact, Mabel introduced my work to the world in an article that came out around the time of the Armory Show in 1913. She was a great appreciator of modern art and my writing in particular."

"Yes, but I understand that in spite of spending time at her villa in Italy as her guests, you and Miss Toklas did not visit her in Taos during your American tour."

"Well." Jane smiled, but Bettina could see she intended to cut this line of inquiry short. "My tour of America is just beginning. In fact, my exact itinerary isn't yet set. We'll be here for several more months." Jane turned to a woman in the front row with her hand up. "Another question?"

Barbara stood up. "I happen to know that there were romantic tensions between you and Mabel Dodge."

"Madam," Jane ad-libbed in character, "this is a public lecture. I don't discuss private matters in such a venue. Now, if you care to ask me about my work . . ."

Patricia Mendoza glared down the length of the table at Barbara. As if out of the mist after a mountain shower, Brenda appeared at Patricia's side. Brenda nodded as Patricia whispered something to her then marched down to the other end of the table, where she tapped Barbara lightly on the arm and spoke to her. Bettina watched this exchange, surprised that Barbara then folded her napkin on the table and followed the manager out of the room. Bettina excused herself to Fiona and Vivian and left the table herself, hoping to discover where Barbara had gone.

She found Barbara smoking a cigarette in the front hall of the lodge by an open window.

"Come with me outside," Barbara said. She opened the door so that Bettina could precede her.

Curious, Bettina complied. "I could use some fresh air."

They stepped into a courtyard filled with flowering plants in waist-high ceramic pots. The pots were beautifully glazed in blue and green and ochre colors. Drooping spires of yellow columbines lined the two gravel paths leading to separate gates. As she had on several occasions since she'd arrived, Bettina found herself drawn to the sensuous textures underpinning Oso Grande, from its adobe walls to its diamond-plastered rooms to its artworks.

Barbara dropped onto a wooden bench nestled between two metal abstract sculptures, each capped by inlaid cobalt-blue tile.

With the setting of the sun over an hour ago, the air temperature had dropped as well. Bettina, grateful she'd worn a silk jacket over her costume, buttoned the collar around her throat. She sat down on the bench and pointed to Barbara's cigarette. "You don't have another one of those, do you?"

Barbara supplied one from her purse and touched Bettina's hand as she held out a match. Very seductive, Bettina thought, as the slim fingers grazed her skin. "Why so hard on Jane as Stein? You were putting her on the spot."

"Just putting her through her paces," Barbara said. "Then the audience can see that when she becomes herself after the monologue, she can address the tension between Dodge and Stein and Toklas. She can handle it."

They smoked in silence for a bit.

"Auckler makes a prickly Gertrude Stein," Barbara said hoarsely as she exhaled a stream of smoke.

There was something almost too emphatic about this pronouncement. Bettina inched a little further down the bench, away from her companion. "I don't know her really. Miriam knows her professionally. Was Stein difficult? Certainly her work was. But I thought she let Alice do all her hatchet work for her so she could appear jolly and charming."

"How handy that must be." The other woman took a last drag and stamped her cigarette onto the ground, then she picked it up and deposited it in her bag.

Bettina heard a bitter undertone. "Yes, I suppose. My husband is the jolly one in our family, so if there's any unpleasantness to be done, it falls to me. No one would guess that he was in the Marine Corps early on. He's strong as a bull, but not in the least bull-headed." She stopped. She'd completely forgotten about Barbara's marital state. "I'm so sorry about Alec. Here I am going on about Marvin when you've just lost your husband."

"Thank you. I'm still in shock about his death. He was so vigorous."

Bettina nodded, wondering how someone with the pronounced physicality of the woman next to her could have possibly been married to a man as locked into his cerebral cortex as the deceased Alec. Telling herself that other people's marriages were generally inscrutable to those on the outside (and often to the two people involved) did not make her any less judgmental. She drew in a deep breath of dry mountain air, determined to enjoy the magnificent evening. A fountain murmured near one of the gates. In the nearby trees, a few feathers rustled as a bird settled into its roost for the night.

The silence fell away as her companion's voice pierced the air. "Alec would still be alive if it weren't for AU. That institution is barbaric. He gave it everything he had, worked like a fiend to get more resources for Liberal Arts, and all he got back was ridicule."

Bettina finished her cigarette, stepped on the butt, and slid it into her jacket pocket. She folded her arms tightly across her chest and shrank back against the bench. There was so little to be said to counter this bald statement. "I'm so sorry. Universities aren't the altruistic places people imagine. Far from it. I've found people are tribal in their exclusions of anyone unlike themselves and blatant about their desires for power and prestige. There's precious little of either to go around, I assure you. Sometimes I'm utterly ashamed of my colleagues' behavior. I—"

"It's not your fault. Alec always spoke highly of you, considered you a supporter of his." Face flushed, Barbara fidgeted with the clasp on her bag as if considering another cigarette. "Look, Bettina, I like you. I think we can be friends. Or at least be frank with one another."

"Of course." Bettina spoke automatically, but her mind was racing. She remembered that last encounter with Alec in the library, when he'd wanted her on the provost's search committee. Her cheeks burned to recall the way she'd backpedaled away from his request and the thought of serving. And how could Barbara think she knew her well enough to like her from their brief meetings? She decided against pointing that out because of the woman's bereavement.

Perhaps that was a mistake, however, for Barbara tore into another subject. She laughed with a peculiar breathiness. "I'm not sure I like Jane Auckler. Those heady academics bore me. Always trying to impress everyone with their erudition."

Surely she had to know she had been married to an academic of that description? There was now no doubt that Barbara had known a different Alec than everyone else. "But she is playing a very erudite woman," Bettina objected. "Stein was very well educated and appeared to be sure of herself. How many women of her time went to Radcliffe and then on to study medicine at Johns Hopkins? And in spite of her earthy body, she could be plenty 'heady.' All those word games. You know, 'rose is a rose is a rose' is just the tip of the iceberg." She laughed. "I've known Miriam so long, and she's such a Stein fan I feel like I know Gertrude myself."

As Bettina defended Jane, Barbara gave her a bare smile, her eyes not wavering. Her focus reminded Bettina of a large cat, a beautiful sleek one, a snow leopard perhaps.

Barbara stayed silent for some time, then she yawned. "I suppose you have a point. Several points. And since we're all stuck together for five more days, I should try and be more positive. Although you may have guessed that's not exactly my strong suit. When I say I don't like someone, I mean I don't trust someone. And that's a problem in a place like this."

Bettina was tempted to agree, as her mistrust of Barbara grew with every word that came out of her mouth, but instead she just said, "You've met Jane before?"

Barbara opened her purse and took out a cigarette. She lit it before answering, head down, fiddling with putting the lighter back in her bag. "Actually, no. She did know my husband, however—a fact she pretended to have forgotten when I met her earlier. Both she and Alec taught together in Fresno quite a long time ago. Of course I wasn't with him then," she added quickly. "But he told me that she was very political. And a beast to deal with on committees."

The way she said "beast" sounded so much like Alec himself—heated and irritable—that Bettina was caught flat-footed. "Committees do not bring out the best in humans. My colleagues might say the same about me."

"I doubt that's the first thing they're thinking." Barbara tipped her head back and studied the almost-full moon, which had just risen in a showy way over Bear Mountain, its flat orb radiating silver as it cleared the dark peak.

"What do you mean?" Bettina felt a flush creeping up her neck. Having a cigarette with this woman was like crossing a freeway on foot in rush hour. All lanes teemed with implements of destruction.

"Just that you're very attractive. And articulate. You seem to me like someone who knows her way around university politics. All in a day's work, I imagine."

"I'm not sure that's a compliment. But I have to get back inside. I want to watch Jane handle her audience when she changes from Stein back into her scholar self. I'd forgotten for a few minutes that I'm going to have to manage one of these events myself in two nights, and I thank you for reminding me of that." For a few moments, in these beautiful surroundings, she'd almost felt like she was on vacation. But Barbara's flippant comment about "a day's work" jarred Bettina into remembering that she had duties here more onerous than trying to decipher Barbara's point of view.

She rose and made her way toward the door, happy to grasp its solid metal handle. Barbara did not follow her. "See you tomorrow," she called as Bettina slipped inside the lodge.

As Bettina made her way back to her table, Jane was addressing a question from a woman in the middle of the room. "In the 1930s Gertrude Stein would never have discussed her sexuality in a lecture hall. The newspapers always referred to Alice B. Toklas as her companion or her secretary, never as her lover and certainly not as her wife. They lived together thirty-eight years, but, with the exception of friends and those in their large circle of writers and artists, they were private about that aspect of their lives."

Bettina had just retaken her seat when Miriam raised her hand and asked, "Jane, can you tell us about Stein's only attempt at a mystery, *Blood on the Dining-Room Floor*? What inspired her to undertake such a project, given that plot was not exactly her strong suit?"

Jane sipped from the glass of water on a table near the reading stand she was using for her lecture. "This is an interesting story. Stein was a great mystery fan and apparently fascinated by the murders of Lizzie Borden's parents in Fall River, Massachusetts, which were never solved. In fact, 'Lizzie' is often addressed in this short novel as if to stitch her into the fabric of the story.

"Stein and Toklas had a country house in Bilignin, near the Swiss border, where they went in the summers. The summer after the *Autobiography* came out and was such a success, Stein had writer's block for really the only time in her life. Some odd events happened in and around the house in the country—cars not starting, phones not working, a woman fell. Stein's writer's block went away when she started writing about them. In her story there isn't blood on the dining-room floor, or at least not her floor, but there is a death in the small community—a woman dies five days after falling into a cement courtyard and breaking her back. Someone suggests she was walking in her sleep before the fall, but no one knows." Jane gestured at the bank of windows and the trees beyond. "She says that the belief that more things happened in the city than the country is an illusion, that actually much more happens in the country—'the city just tells what happened in the country,' she said in *Blood on the Dining-Room Floor.*"

Jane looked placidly about the room. She took another drink of water and then directed her attention to the table where her colleagues sat. "I think Stein has a point," she said. "There is something intriguing about being away in the country with a group of people; it lends one's thoughts to odd occurrences and even unfortunate accidents, don't you agree?"

Eighteen

Fiona's script was in front of her, and as Patricia was talking, she read the first page over and over.

". . . and simply a wonderful beginning," Patricia said. "Jane, I think you'll actually have half that audience reading Gertrude Stein's work before the week is out."

"A triumph," Miriam agreed.

"Thank you," Jane smiled, her handsome face relaxed. Fiona thought she looked uncommonly attractive this morning. Of course, the pressure of performance was over for her, yet Fiona saw clearly the night before that Jane drew energy from the audience's reactions. She was clearly satisfied with how well the opening night had gone.

"You know what's tremendously exciting is that all of these women we're discussing and presenting were the architects of their own lives," Patricia said. "No one anointed them as artists or pioneers, they had to make their own way, and with much effort they did." She looked at each woman in turn and beamed. "It's an inspiration. And so are all of you."

"Thank you," said Miriam. "You're right that it's one of the reasons we all study women from history. Their lives are a blueprint for what is possible."

"How much leeway do we have with this event?" Bettina asked, a cup of coffee in front of her. The five of them had just finished their breakfast. She rucked up the sleeves of her green cardigan to her elbows. "I was wondering if we could somehow build on each event, depending upon what themes emerged. You know, make connections with each lecture or performance."

Fiona knew that Bettina was calling her Woolf evening a lecture, and she herself was calling her program on Edith Wharton a lecture-performance.

"Tell me more about what you're thinking," Patricia said, repositioning a metal hair comb in an effort to keep the unruly curls of brunette hair out of her face. "Of course, this is our Chautauqua, and while Jane and I are doing a more traditional performance and Q&A with the audience, we can fashion the event the way we want. And the people coming in the evening just expect to learn about the historical figures in the program. I don't think they care too much about the exact format. In fact, they might like to be surprised!" At this, Patricia looked pleased and surprised herself.

"Well, I was intrigued when Jane explained the *Blood on the Dining-Room Floor* episode, the idea that a series of disassociated events could be 'investigated' by a writer, in this case Stein, as if they comprised a detective story. And that the country is not the bucolic place of people's imaginings where nothing happens, but instead a place where anything can and does happen . . ."

"Bettina, let me just interrupt for a moment," Miriam broke in. "I want to thank you for that insight, Jane. You brought crime and the creepiness of the bucolic life into the forefront and paved the way for my keynote on the locked-room mystery." Miriam polished her glasses, repositioned them on her face, and squinted. "This prescription is either really out of date or these glasses belong to Vivi."

"Mmm," Patricia said, her attention still on Bettina. "And so how would you build on that, for instance in what you're doing with Virginia Woolf and *To the Lighthouse?*" Patricia asked.

"I guess Jane's remarks made me see that whatever our approach, we are making a case that the person we're exploring is a certain kind of human being. We're creating a persona that emphasizes some things and excludes others. So, for instance, when Jane presents Stein as if she is lecturing in 1935, what aspects of the person is she showing versus what is she leaving out? What is public? What is private? Which Stein is it that we get to see?"

"I agree, that's what the kind of performance I do is all about," Jane said. "Someone like Stein, like any person, has many facets, some ascendant at different times depending upon the people she is with. And then there's the problem of sketching in enough history and information about the person that those in the audience who know nothing about the figure don't feel confused."

"Exactly. So really we're all dealing with mystery. The mystery of identity." Bettina leaned forward and pressed on. "Who was Virginia Woolf when she wrote *To The Lighthouse*? Lily Briscoe then can be seen as the mask of the female artist that Woolf wears in the novel, criticizing great men, for example, who can only talk about themselves, and admiring women like Mrs. Ramsey, who make others feel worthwhile and loved."

Bettina had a dreamy smile on her face, and Fiona wondered if she identified with the character of Mrs. Ramsey. "How will that change what you share with the audience tomorrow evening?" Fiona asked of her friend.

"It leaves me free to do what I do best." Bettina's voice was firm. "Educate the audience about the way the artist disguises herself in her fictions. Remember that wonderful book *The Performing Self*? I have to say it lets me off the hook of thinking I have to perform Virginia Woolf. Which I simply cannot do anyway. But I can talk about how she as an author performs on the page: who and what emerges because of the specific interactions she lets us, the readers, see. And the excerpts I've picked out to read from the novel reinforce this idea. I hope you're not disappointed, Patricia."

"Not at all! I love it. Most of the people coming here to participate are great readers. You're offering them insights into how someone like Woolf disguises herself in her characters, revealing not just her attitudes and nature but that of the world she knew. They'll find it fascinating. And most readers never tire of hearing about the conjuring act that a great writer does when he or she writes a story. Look at Dickens, a master illusionist whether in front of an audience or reading his own work aloud as he wrote it! He became a marquee name on the lecture circuit. He may have lectured for money, but, just as with Gertrude Stein, the adulation of the crowds was irresistible."

Miriam piped up. "For Gertrude, *gloire* was almost everything. And perhaps for Mabel Dodge Luhan as well. I must say I'm very much looking forward to Barbara's slant on her. And no doubt she'll get the largest audience as a New Mexico legend."

"I'm sure you're right. But," Fiona couldn't help but blurt, "it's such a relief, Patricia, that we have wiggle room in our format here. Some of us, er, I mean you, really are performers—you Patricia, and Jane, and of course Barbara is too. But I consider myself an educator and a scholar . . ."

At the mention of Barbara, Miriam fairly levitated out of her seat. "Excuse me, Fiona, but where *is* Barbara? And Vivian? They should certainly be part of this discussion." She swiveled to take in the outdoor patio outside the dining room, empty except for two guests in wooden reclining chairs reading books. She then turned to check the great room that led to the art gallery around the corner. One person sat by the far fireplace fidgeting with a pair of binoculars. "Perhaps they've gone off somewhere together."

Jane murmured, "Oh, I don't think so—"

But no one heard her because Fiona jumped up and took hold of her friend's arm. Miriam's degree of upset seemed very out of character. "I'll help you find them."

On the way back to the cottage and Miriam and Vivian's room, Miriam said, "The odd thing is that when I left for breakfast, Vivi was getting dressed and told me she'd meet me in ten minutes. I suppose you've heard the story that many years ago Barbara and Vivi were once together."

Fiona nodded. "Vivian told me and said she wished she'd never brought it up to you at all."

A flush rising on her round face, Miriam slowed her pace. "I am really not a possessive person. Funny, I suppose, for an only child. But I'm not. But something Vivi told me made me feel that Barbara is not to be trusted, and so I worry. I suppose it's ridiculous."

The memory of Bettina's brief affair with Darryl assailed Fiona, her keen sense of betrayal a parcel she wished she could discard, wrapped as it was in a shroud of self-pity and misery. At the time she hadn't been able to accept that the two of them might have needs that didn't include her. She'd just felt wretched and excluded. "It's not at all ridiculous. Most of us don't like sharing our intimate relationships. We want our people to be just ours. And Barbara does seem under a lot of pressure. I'm surprised she didn't cancel out of this, given what happened to her husband."

They reached the cottage and walked through the empty living room and on to Miriam's room in the back on the right.

"She probably couldn't wait to get out of town and away from the scrutiny of Susan Crane." Miriam fitted a huge iron key into the lock. "Vivi, are you here?"

They stood in the open doorway and contemplated the very neatly made bed, the closet doors closed, the Saltillo tile floor warming the room with its tawny tones. Behind them, in the parking lot, a motor shut off. The room felt quiet and peaceful.

Fiona heard feet scrambling down the short steps to the cottage. Vivian sang out, "Hey, did I miss the whole meeting?" In a moment Vivian appeared beside them, her face faintly pink as if she'd been bustling about.

"We can fill you in. But where were you?" Miriam passed the mug of coffee she'd carried from the dining room to Vivian, who finished it in one swallow.

"I was on my way to meet you—God, I hope there's still food in there, I'm starving—when Barbara came out of her room and asked me if I'd mind dropping her off at some park that's about three miles away. She said she needed a walk to clear her head for tonight."

"The Continental Divide trails," Fiona said. "I was planning to go for a hike there myself in a bit. The park is right on the edge of the Gila Wilderness, and if you want to, you can go a long way in or up to Gomez Peak, the highest one around here."

"Well, Barbara didn't have a car—she had the rental company pick it up—plus she said she has no sense of direction, so I dropped her off." Vivian hooked her arm through Miriam's. "I hope you weren't really worried about me."

But Fiona was worried about Barbara. The Gila, over three million acres and heavily forested, was the nation's oldest designated wilderness area. The area around Silver City was picturesque and not as rugged as the alpine areas at higher elevations in many areas of Colorado. The mountains in the Gila appeared more rounded, almost gentle, and yet the altitudes could easily affect someone like Barbara, who lived barely above sea level in Austin. Silver City was fifty-nine hundred feet, and Gomez Peak reached seventy-two hundred feet.

Here, temperatures soared and plummeted with the movement of the sun. One pine-covered mountain dissolved into another, and the top of one saddle could appear tantalizingly close, only to fade out of reach the closer—and the more steeply—a hiker's trail straggled up its slope. Fiona wondered what kind of physical condition Barbara was in. "It's a little odd for someone with no sense of direction to go off hiking alone in a strange place. I wonder how she even knew about those trails. Did she have enough water with her at least and proper footwear?"

"Um, I think she had on some kind of modish yellow running shoes. But no daypack or anything." Vivian looked up at the flawless blue New Mexico sky. It was ten thirty, and already the sun had warmed the day about twenty degrees from the chill of early morning. "I don't remember seeing a bottle of water, no."

"Barbara doesn't strike me as the girl scout type," Miriam said. "Bettina said she was in a strange mood last night when she spoke with her. And I never saw her after she left in the middle of Jane's performance."

Fiona threw up her hands at the thought of Barbara wandering around unprepared. "Can I take the car? I'll just get my things and go over there and see if I can't catch up to her. Some of the trails over there are short, but they crisscross others, and it's easy to get stuck in a loop if you don't know where you're going. It's confusing, and the grades are sometimes intense. And the sun here is nothing to mess with. Not to mention the altitude—the dry air sucks the moisture right out of you."

Fiona squinted up at the sky, noting a wisp of contrail slicing across the clear blue. The flawless weather lulled many amateur walkers to imagine they were living in a glossy postcard of the Land of Enchantment rather than the demanding New Mexico she knew of rugged terrain and changing weather. She remembered hearing a lecture the last time she was here about the privations of the Spanish settlers as they struggled through the arid stretch they called the *Jornada del Muerto*, the journey of death. Opting to save time, they found themselves cut off from the Rio Grande and at the mercy of the blazing sun without water. "The manager, Brenda, said it's a little warm for September. I'll pack extra water."

Miriam and Vivian turned back, taking the gravel path to the main house in search of food. "I'll check in later," Fiona called as she went to her room, which was in a forward suite in the same building. It was still early in the day, and not too warm, but she hoped she'd find Barbara soon. The trails were rocky and slippery. Without hiking boots, the terrain provided training for the unwary in tripping, falling, or turning an ankle.

Fiona mulled over Stein's comments about the country as an environ full of opportunities for the unexpected to happen or ordinary things to malfunction. City people like Barbara were used to structure, and wilderness areas didn't always have convenient signposts. And certainly not extra supplies like water and proper footwear to purchase at the bottom of the nearest tree. She pictured Barbara wandering in dizzy circles on some mountain path, careening from one ponderosa pine to the next, slipping on treacherous rock falls, and wilting in the heat.

Fiona laced up her hiking boots and filled three water bottles to go into her pack with Powerbars and a light lunch. But maybe she was obsessing for no reason. Perhaps Barbara was meeting someone or just taking a stroll. Vivian hadn't said she'd made arrangements to get back to the lodge, though. Fiona couldn't help but think that either Barbara's expedition was a well-planned escape or a foolhardy whim. Neither option seemed particularly reassuring at the moment.

Nineteen

After Vivian dropped her off, Barbara contemplated the various trails leading from the parking lot. A large and confusing map posted near the road was of no help. She wandered a bit until she saw a metal gate appear on her left. As the path she had found herself on continued from there, she slipped the loop from the post and entered, carefully closing the gate and securing it. She began to stride uphill, her brain working at a furious pace.

Not for the first time in the months since his crash, she found herself arguing with her late husband: *Damn it, Alec, I'm boxed in. Why did you do it? Dying on me like this and leaving me this incriminating insurance policy. Now everyone thinks I am perfectly happy about your death. Christ. I feel Lt. Crane's eyes on me every time I go to the bank, pay the gardener, or go shopping. Even now, when I know she's in Austin and I'm hundreds of miles away, I feel watched here in Silver City. I know you wanted me to be cared for, but leaving the earth the way you did . . . Let's just say I'm inspiring the wrong kind of interest. My skin is crawling. You know what you used to say—the hills are alive with predators. And they're crawling through the grass in my backyard.*

Barbara stopped under a group of pines. The only thing keeping her in Silver City was Jane. If only they were just here on one of their heavenly weekend rendezvous. She never tired of telling Jane that Gertrude Stein and Mabel Dodge were together at last. "We're revising the historical record and setting it straight," she teased her as they laughed, feeling far from "straight."

If she had her way, she and Jane would leave as soon as she'd performed Mabel. The festival's atmosphere left her feeling short of fresh air. Even the lodge manager, Brenda, seemed to hover. Was she spying? But why and for whom?

Barbara didn't want anyone in the group or at the lodge to know about her affair with Jane. She didn't feel safe, not with Lt. Crane in the background. And Patricia seemed possessive of everyone's time, determined that her precious gathering prove a success. *If she had her way,* Barbara fumed, *we'd all have to pick up a pass just to go across into each other's rooms!*

She even felt like a fraud performing Mabel Dodge Luhan in New Mexico. Here, Mabel was part of the historic lore of the state, and she certainly couldn't count on being the most informed person in the room about her subject as she usually was. Mabel was a goddess, a temptress, vainglorious. Pure celebrity in her time. Barbara sensed that her group looked at her like she was a privileged snob, as if they were confusing her with her character. It was perverse; she felt excluded, so *not* one of the girls. Except for Jane, of course. Around Miriam and Vivian she felt like the poor little match girl, the fairy tale her mother used to terrorize her with as a child. The girl, excluded and watching, was abandoned in the cold, freezing to death. The memory made her want to run.

Once she left the shade of the clump of trees, Barbara became aware of how the temperature was climbing. She was also very thirsty, and she cursed herself for neglecting to bring water as Brenda, who had told her about the trails, had strongly urged her to do.

She kept trudging up the path, reviewing her talk with Bettina after Jane's monologue. Her impression of Bettina was that she was the most open, the least uptight of the group. Barbara had even detected a bit of a movie-star aura. At last, she'd thought, a woman who was beautiful and smart but didn't take herself too seriously! A real player, comfortable in her own skin. But the previous night she'd seemed jittery and guarded too.

Barbara, feeling the altitude, huffed up a steep incline. And then there was Vivian. She'd been such fun in the old days, but now the good times were certainly not rolling in that court—it was clear she adored her little dumpling, Miriam. Barbara thought it intriguing that Vivian had come to portray Alice B. Toklas. Alice and Mabel had been dueling on the razor's edge all those years ago. And now, Barbara fumed, as if history were repeating itself, Vivian didn't seem to even want to be friends. Yes, she'd dropped her off at the trails this morning, but when Barbara invited her to walk with her, she'd refused.

In short, Barbara imagined herself in the middle of a rerun of Agatha Christie's novel *And Then There Were None*. Everyone seemed out to get everyone else. She thought of that old phrase of mystery jargon—*malice aforethought*. The term fit in Silver City, where Barbara was beginning to feel malice in the very air. She just wanted to take dear Jane and leave. But Jane, so responsible, was committed to completing her task as moderator.

Barbara inhaled a piercing lungful of fresh air. This brisk walk, out in nature, was just what she needed. Forget human beings for a while. *Those disappointing wretches. Yes, even you, Alec. You left me, didn't you? Like everyone else.*

"She used him, and she used him up," Miriam said. "It's a sad old story. I'd like to say that Alec didn't deserve it, but I'm afraid he did."

Miriam, Vivian, and Bettina lingered at a small table after the evening festivities had ended, sampling some food left over from dinner. Barbara had not returned from her walk, and therefore her performance slot had been filled by Miriam's keynote speech. Miriam was actually happy to have been allowed to dispatch her address without worrying about it the entire day beforehand. She tended to suffer performance anxiety, and in the rush to keep the festival on track when Barbara hadn't appeared by 5:00 p.m., she simply didn't have time for her usual dread to overtake every nerve in her body; she just had to step out.

Vivian, dressed in slim-fitting black slacks and a blue jewel-necked sweater, plucked a carrot from the platter in the center of the table. "Well, we'd like to think that no one deserves to just be eaten alive, or consumed, and then left for dead."

"God," Miriam said, slumping in her chair, "that is grisly, considering that Alec died in a car wreck."

"A one-car accident, let's not forget," Bettina said. "That's the suspicious part."

"You had a long talk with Barbara last night," Vivian said. "Tell us if there were any clues that she dropped about her dear departed."

"Well, that's just it. She didn't have much to say about him at all. I put my foot in it by blathering on about Marvin, and then I fell all over myself apologizing for taking my husband for granted when she'd just lost hers, but she didn't seem terribly interested in talking about it."

"I don't suppose she brought up the three-million-dollar insurance policy he left behind." A surge of energy shot through Miriam as she brought this up. It was fun to say such a hefty sum of money so casually.

Bettina expelled air with a *huh* sound. "Not on your life. I suppose that makes her a person of interest to the police. My question is, who else is a person of interest?"

"Because now Barbara is missing," Vivian threw out. "Can that really be a coincidence? I'm worried that she's disappeared like this. It doesn't seem characteristic at all—she has a reputation for being very professional about keeping her performance commitments, according to Patricia. Something must be very wrong. I wish we knew someone on the inside of this case."

"Well, I have been questioned by Lt. Crane," Miriam said. "So I guess that makes me closer to the fringe of the action, but hardly inside. And given that I don't know anything, that's not saying much." She gave Vivian a look of concern. "I'm very worried, too."

"Let's hope for news of her soon." Bettina chafed her palms together and leaned toward Miriam. "I felt on the inside listening to your talk, by the way. And I loved the Dorothy Sayers references in your costume. Where did you get that fabulous tri-cornered hat and cape? It was like Sayers's character Harriet Vane meets the poet Marianne Moore in a brainiac fashion shoot-out circa 1922."

Miriam smoothed the black cape studded with black pearls that she'd found in a Bloomsbury used-clothing shop eons ago. "I did spend a summer holed up in the British Museum for a month after I attended a seminar at Oxford. I saw no traces of Sayers, but I imagined her careering to class on a bicycle in her academic gown with a leather satchel of books strung across her chest."

"The locked-room mystery," Vivian mused. "I suppose that's just a metaphor for closed communities of every kind—families, work environments, anywhere people are thrown together for any period of time. If people are stuck together, resentments can percolate. It's really a miracle more people don't do away with each other when you think about it."

"Fortunately, most folks worry about getting caught," Bettina said. "That holds down the acting out of some of the rage and ill will." She yawned.

Miriam fought the urge to yawn herself before a thought brought her more fully awake. "What if each of us lives in a locked room? I mean, isn't that what our biased perception really is? Over time each of us develops patterns of thinking and feeling. We learn to filter things in predictable ways. If we don't make an effort, we get locked into reacting by rote, responding to some stimuli and ignoring others. We don't let in new ideas or experiences."

Vivian, who volunteered with a children's reading program, gave Miriam a fond look. "That's why children are so creative. Their lives, and their minds, aren't set. They try new things—paint, write, make music. Every child I've known is an artist—a Dali, say, or a budding Toni Morrison."

"Yes!" Bettina's words tumbled out in a rush. "When we get older, we tend to experiment less. We adjust the stories about our lives so our experiences reinforce who we've become." She gestured toward Miriam. "We struggle to make sense of events, to make them fit into a logical sequence—just like in a mystery, where the detective puzzles over the characters' motivations. We fight to mask the fact that so much of life is beyond our control."

"The writer P. D. James used to say that people read mystery novels not to read about murder but to see order restored. Her novels certainly had a moral center—Inspector Dalgliesh was a model of stability. And sanity." Miriam looked around the table. "I need my routines for just that reason." She suddenly wished for the peace and comfort of her own house, the touch of Phoebe's fur, the reassuring details of her schedule and her work. Here they were in a beautiful environment, but she was aware that sprinkled throughout the place were unpredictable people and possibilities she hadn't encountered before.

Unaware of her friend's darkening mood, Bettina continued congratulating her on her evening's success. "I'm so sorry Fiona had to miss your talk. I especially liked that part about the negligible odds of committing a perfect crime. It reminded me of Barbara, who seems to calculate the risks in everything she does. How did you put it? 'There are those whose goal in life is to beat the odds, without relying on them in the least.'"

The table rested in silence at this, until Vivian said, "At least someone as resourceful as Fiona is part of the search party for Barbara. And Jane accompanied them too. I didn't know she was an experienced outdoors person, but she insisted on going along." She glanced at the clock above the table. "Nine o'clock. I imagine they've called it quits for today and that they'll be back soon."

Elbow on the table, Bettina propped her head in her hand. "Hope so. You know, I keep thinking of Jane's remarks about Stein's mystery the summer she had writer's block. All those coincidences, deaths, things not working. Maybe that was true of Alec. He'd made a lot of mistakes, publicly whaled on people, had misappropriated funds, all of it. But what if none of that added up to why he died? I haven't wanted to admit this is possible. But what if the simple explanation is the right one—he crashed his car into a post? It could happen to anyone." Her voice was tentative, as if she were trying this thought on to see if it could withstand scrutiny.

"Well . . . yes," Miriam conceded. "It could. But when someone has the air of desperation about him as he did, and for it to happen on the day of his annual gala—well, it seems like blood on the dining-room floor. And now there's his wife. Barbara seems entirely too organized to simply disappear. I can't help but think that there's a plan behind this."

Miriam sat back in her chair and contemplated the cold food left on the table—the carrots and potatoes had a greasy sheen on them, leavings clinging like thin tendons. Had that really been a roast beef before they'd fallen on it, and prior to that a breathing creature walking the earth? Decline and death were just not pretty things to look at.

Twenty

On the afternoon after the day Barbara disappeared, Lt. Crane arrived at Oso Grande Lodge to co-supervise the search team.

Shortly thereafter, Miriam spotted her friend Daphne bustling into the lodge.

"How did you manage this?" Miriam inquired of Daphne, who was dressed in a black sheath topped by a shawl with purple sequins.

"We're old friends, Susan Crane and I. I called her when I heard Barbara Martin was missing." Daphne drew Miriam into an alcove under the stairwell near the art gallery, out of range of two people who were examining several shelves of antique Mexican jewelry.

Instinctively, Miriam dropped her voice. "But how did you know?"

Daphne smiled. "Some people appreciate my psychic abilities." She rearranged her shawl. "Oh, all right, since it's you, I'll confess: Vivian called me, asking if I knew this area very well and saying that I might be needed. Sometimes my skills have proved useful in locating missing persons," she said modestly.

"And Lt. Crane?"

"She's here unofficially at the moment. But you know she's still observing Barbara Martin as a person of interest in Alec Martin's death. She's worked with someone in the Sheriff's office here in Silver City before, and she called him to make sure she wouldn't be barging in." She leaned down to say softly in Miriam's ear, "I think Barbara might have been having an affair when the dean died."

"Oh. I don't think I'll ask you how you might know that." Miriam had noticed a heightened self-consciousness about Barbara of late, the aura of someone who knew she was being watched and admired by a special someone.

"Isn't it just common sense? No wonder the dean was driving erratically. He might have just found out."

Miriam wondered once again at Daphne's powers, which ranged from shrewd observation to uncanny intuition. "Do you know who she's been having the affair with?"

"I was hoping you knew."

"Me? The only person I thought she was interested in was Vivian!"

Daphne dismissed this with an impatient raise of her shoulders. "Anything is possible, but Vivian would have to reciprocate, and of course she would not." She put a hand on Miriam's forehead as if to check for fever. "You know she is committed absolutely to you."

Miriam hoped her enormous relief at hearing these words wasn't obvious. Barbara—strapping, healthy, and formidable—had brought out a long-buried insecurity that she wished she could banish to a mythical holding tank for phobias. "Male or female affair, do you think?" Miriam dismissed her own question by saying, "I think there's a clue in the character she was planning to show us, Mabel Dodge Luhan, who was bisexual at least in her early life. Is Barbara headed to Taos, an assignation perhaps? Or maybe she's discovered a rare manuscript and is going to create a huge sensation!"

Daphne grasped Miriam's shoulders. "That's it. She found something in this lodge. Something rare, a thing to keep to herself. She can't share it." The psychic fell silent for a minute and then said, "Or, whatever she's found, it's incriminating, to someone. Let's ask Brenda for the keys to her room. Perhaps we'll find a clue about where she's gone."

Miriam had no illusions that Brenda would supply the keys. The first morning she'd arrived, she'd locked herself out. Brenda had given her a new key, but not without bestowing upon her a probing look, seeming to weigh whether or not she was worthy of a second key. Miriam shook off the unpleasant sense of being scrutinized, wondering what it was about this gathering that was reawakening old feelings of inadequacy. *Don't assume, gather proof!* she heard her old mentor's voice in her ear. She nodded as she always had when he'd admonished her, and she hurried after Daphne.

Deciding to explore on their own, the two left the entry of the lodge and crossed in front of the portal festooned with bird feeders then made their way toward the cottage. Barbara was staying in the room across from hers and Vivian's, in the back of the cottage. Daphne calmly put her hand on the doorknob and turned it. "It's not locked."

Miriam peered over Daphne's shoulder. "Is the room empty? Maybe Barbara just decided to decamp."

Daphne strode over to the wooden wardrobe to the right of the king-size bed, which had a headboard also made of knotty pine. The door was carved with cursive flourishes. Inside were a few hangers strung with slacks and blouses and one stunning black evening gown. "Ah, the costume," Daphne announced, running her fingers down the creamy velvet as if her hands could breathe in the essence of the wearer.

Miriam couldn't bring herself to touch the dress herself. She peered around Daphne, feeling uneasy at having barged into Barbara's room in such a brazen way. She fiddled with a button on her long-sleeved blouse. "What do you think?"

"I think this dress feels like death."

"What!" Startled, Miriam collapsed onto Barbara's unmade bed. "Why do you say such a thing? Because you think it really did belong to Mabel Dodge Luhan?"

"Well, that I can't say. I'm just telling you what the dress conveys to me now."

"A premonition?" Miriam's rational mind grasped at an explanation.

Daphne perched on the bed next to Miriam. "I'm not sure. An intuition. I'm picking up dissonance between the gown and its current wearer."

"Something like Barbara not being comfortable with this character she's chosen to perform?" Miriam tilted her face upward, as if seeking an answer in the patterns of the wood grain in the ceiling. "Or maybe it was her own skin that didn't fit anymore."

Daphne frowned and shook her head. "If only it were that simple. I can only say that I think Barbara is in danger."

"Her disappearance has been distressing enough. But now you're frightening me," Miriam said.

Daphne shook her head. "Look at this room. Does it look like the space of someone who's going to disappear? Everything is here, waiting for her. No, something has happened."

She closed the wardrobe doors with elaborate care, leaving the gown inside. On the nightstand by the bed was an open jewelry bag. Daphne extracted a pair of black antique earrings and held them to the light. "These look like they go with her gown." She carefully replaced the earrings. "Whose room is across from Barbara's?"

"Ours is. Bettina and Fiona are in one of the two rooms in front, on this same side, and Patricia Mendoza is across from them. Patricia isn't here much. She spends most of her time with Brenda on the festival arrangements—food, fielding questions about programming from audience members, and so forth."

Daphne rose from the bed and, as she smoothed out her shawl, one of its purple sequins caught the light from the window beside the bed and appeared to wink at Miriam. Daphne's face grew somber. "If Barbara isn't found today, I will be concerned."

Twenty-One

That evening, Bettina took the stage with her "platform performance," as she was calling her event. Patricia was thrilled with this description and announced to the audience, "By using these words, Dr. Graf evokes the original Chautauqua! Early in the twentieth century, famous speakers spoke in small towns all over America in the summer, bringing arts and culture to communities far from the major cities. The events were held in tents, and the speakers stood on platforms with the audience spread at their feet. It was the original community outreach—a populist movement to educate and stimulate the general public. And now, scholars evoke some of these same prominent Americans . . . and," she gestured at Bettina, "Europeans, bringing them to life for contemporary audiences. Tonight we are treated to some insights on the influential British writer Virginia Woolf, who lived from 1882 to 1941. You're in for a treat."

Bettina thanked Patricia for her enthusiasm and propped her script on a music stand Brenda had scavenged from the storeroom at the lodge. She scanned the audience, which included about forty people from the community. Jane had advised her to concentrate on the audience and given her a mantra to recite to herself: *These people are here to see you succeed, to learn something, and to enjoy themselves. Think of teaching them, not of yourself.*

Miriam, Vivian, Daphne, and Fiona sat in the front, all casting encouraging looks her way. Jane sat in the center of the room wearing her costume, as she was moderating all the Q&A discussions during the week as Stein. As the days went by, Jane seemed to be disappearing behind her character, and Bettina really felt like she was attending one of Stein's Saturday-night salons. Jane's face did not look like Gertrude Stein's, but for now she graced the occasion with Stein's presence. It was unnerving and yet fascinating.

She glanced out at the audience again, observing that it was largely female. A thin woman was wiping her eyes—allergies? Tears at some unexpected news? One man appeared to be settling in for a lengthy nap, coerced to come by his wife perhaps. Was this an appropriate way to spend her fifties, she wondered, worrying what her audience thought of her, scrambling to find her place on the page? She'd once had a colleague who told her that turning fifty meant he never had to memorize anything again. Well, she hadn't even attempted to memorize her script. In light of Barbara's disappearance, and with the police on the periphery of the lodge, she felt deflated about the importance of "Move the Tree to the Middle," her discourse on the painter Lily Briscoe. Once Lily had that inspiration near the end of the book, she had her vision and her painting was complete. If only Bettina could find a way of making her life make sense by doing just that! Looking at the sea of faces in front of her, squinting in the dim light, she decided to put the script aside and just speak about what fascinated her about Woolf and her novel.

"I came here to talk with you about Virginia Woolf's remarkable novel, *To The Lighthouse*. The Ramsey family spends much of the novel discussing a trip to the actual lighthouse, but the trip is delayed and only happens much later, toward the end of the book, after the Great War. The lighthouse is such a thematic center of the novel for a number of reasons, not the least of which is the concept of illumination itself.

"The character of Mrs. Ramsey, who unexpectedly dies in the section of the novel called 'Time Passes,' where we also hear, 'in passing,' of shells bursting in France, is the shining force of the book. It is she who weaves together the disparate family members and guests, many of whom are self-involved, into a coherent company. And what is the source of her brilliant light? She is the traditional ideal of womanhood: she always smiles at others' witticisms and manages her cantankerous husband, Mr. Ramsey, who can't be tempted away very often from pondering his greatness. Her children adore her. She is the kind of woman whose eyes, when upon you, make you feel completely understood and totally seen. She is the mirror everyone wishes for in this life. Wise, warm, intuitively responding to each person's emotional needs, always with the perfect word or touch or look of understanding. The classic Demeter figure of fertility, she is grounded, enhancing the creativity of everyone around her. Her very being is nourishing.

"In this novel Woolf extols the beauty and preciousness of such a woman and yet explores how her very presence leads the romantically unattached, shy painter Lily Briscoe to feel that her own femaleness comes up short. Still, Lily paints. She creates, she thinks, she reflects, in spite of the frequent rantings of Mr. Tansley, a fellow guest, that 'women can't write, women can't paint!' Lily keenly reflects the life around her, the ebb and flow of feelings and frustrations; she has the ability to say what is under the surface. In that sense, she is a stand-in for Woolf herself, always acutely aware of the shifting currents of sensibility and thought.

"Virginia Woolf lost her mother when she was only thirteen, a defining event in her life, one from which most likely she never emotionally recovered. She married but did not have children. Like Lily Briscoe, she created art, she poured her passion into friendships—some of which were romantic as well—and essays and poems and novels. Even her book reviews were brilliantly insightful. On the surface she was a very different woman from her mother as well as from Mrs. Ramsey, whom we assume was modeled upon Woolf's mother, Julia Stephen.

"We see Mrs. Ramsey performing the ideal of femininity. Yet Woolf herself wrote how a woman can only come into her own when she kills the 'angel in the house.' The angel is the ideal of womanhood that keeps us tending to others rather than claiming our own lives. How do we reconcile this admiration she has for the traditional woman alongside her determination for women to have freedom to write and speak out and create the lives they uniquely must have?

"The voyage to the lighthouse actually occurs in the last pages of the novel. Thinking of the small boat landing, Lily sees her painting cohere for the first time. The lines, the colors—greens and blues—fall into place. The lighthouse landing illuminates her creativity: she draws a final line and experiences the triumph and exhaustion of completion. She has moved the tree to the middle, as she says, and the painting is complete. 'I have had my vision,' she thinks. The lighthouse, the family, the landing, the aura of Mrs. Ramsey, the intelligence of Mr. Ramsey, all the life that had trooped through this place on the Cornish coast, all of it coalesced into her vision.

That is how art works—a stray line is brought into focus almost by accident. The vision comes, and with it the right word or brush stroke—that is the true landing."

Bettina stopped, not sure where to go from here. She glanced over at her script. It was time to read some actual words of Woolf, she thought. She hoped she wasn't just blathering on. She glanced up at the audience in time to see Miriam's face radiating approval. And yet surely her friend expected more from her, some grand denouement or gesture, to bring each member of the audience to an epiphany. If only she could extend Lily Briscoe's metaphor of finding the key to the creative puzzle so that every person in the room could move the tree to the middle for herself!

She felt deflated, even though the faces in the audience seemed to be tipped toward her, absorbed in what she was saying, soaking in language as a sunbather might the rays of the sun. Bettina smiled, thinking of how grandiose an image that was, placing herself at the center just as the sun was in the solar system. What would Mr. Tansley have said at the very thought of such an assumption from a woman?

But at that moment, Lt. Susan Crane appeared in the back of the room. She made her way discreetly to Jane, leaned down, and whispered in her ear.

At this, Jane immediately rose. Jane projected her robust Stein voice, but Bettina noticed a slight tremor underneath. "I'm very sorry, but we'll take just a ten-minute break right here. So sorry to interrupt, Dr. Graf. I'm sure you're all enjoying this as much as I am," she added, and then she made a beeline for the front of the room, where Lt. Crane had joined Miriam and Bettina and the others.

"Barbara Martin has been found," Lt. Crane said in a controlled voice. She wore comfortable clothes—black slacks, a white blouse buttoned to the neck, and a short, tweed jacket. Bettina shifted uneasily from foot to foot; she resisted the impulse to take off her shoes, as the straps of her Mary Janes were cutting into her instep.

"Oh, thank goodness," Vivian said, clasping her slender hands together and then twisting her gold wedding band.

"Well, not entirely," Crane said. "I'm afraid she's seriously ill."

Bettina took a step backward. She grasped Miriam's arm. "Was it dehydration? Sunstroke? Fiona was so worried about that."

Beside her, Fiona nodded. "I'd hoped we'd find her much sooner."

Susan Crane's face was pale with tiredness. "Hydration is the least of her problems. We actually found her in a stand of trees near the parking lot. She'd already come out of the woods. We're not yet sure what happened. She was unconscious when we called the ambulance. In addition to sunstroke, we've found bruising on her face and neck. She appeared dehydrated, and the investigator from the coroner's office thinks she had possibly been drugged. The police here are treating this as attempted murder at the moment."

Jane quickly broke in. "Is her condition treatable? How serious is it?" As Lt. Crane shook her head, Jane headed for the door. "I'm going to the hospital."

Crane attempted to detain her. "I don't think they'll let you see her right now—"

But Jane rushed out of the room.

Puzzled, Bettina whispered to Miriam, "Did you know that those two were so close?"

Miriam leaned toward Bettina. "I don't know anything, and this proves it. With this news and Jane gone we'll have to call off the rest of the evening." She then addressed Lt. Crane. "This is atrocious! And if, well, if we're talking about such an attack, the perpetrator is very bold, isn't he? I assume it is a he? To attack her there where some other car could drive up at any time?"

"We don't know. She could have been drugged earlier somewhere else and then dragged to the parking lot. The perpetrator clearly wanted the body found."

Miriam looked as if she were trying to visualize the attack; her face went through a series of contortions. "Someone was stalking her. And then attacked her. We don't know whether or not her assailant intended she would die of exposure before she was found. That could have happened. Or she could have died of a heart attack or some other condition after being attacked in such a way, yes?"

Bettina confronted the lieutenant before she could answer. "We were so sure she was involved in her husband's death. But surely we can't assume that now, can we?"

"You mean the same person was responsible for Alec's death and this attack on Barbara?" Miriam's pecan-colored eyes didn't blink. "You realize what you're saying, don't you?"

"I don't know what I'm saying," Bettina sputtered. "This is all so shocking."

"If we think that the same person attacked Alec and then his wife, it makes all of us suspects." Fiona sat down on the stool that Bettina had put in the stage space.

"I couldn't possibly comment on that," Crane said, and she began to make her way toward the door.

Daphne stepped in close to Miriam. "The costume," Daphne murmured. "We need to see if it's still hanging in Barbara's closet."

"But why?" Miriam demanded. "That seems the last thing to worry about."

"Not at all," said Daphne. "I'm certain there's a clue in the fact that Mabel Dodge Luhan was the public face Barbara wished to present here. Mabel, the ultimate insider and game changer. Friend of so many of the literati of the time: D. H. Lawrence, Gertrude Stein, Carl Van Vechten, Emma Goldman. The list goes on and on."

Bettina thought back to the conversation she'd had with Barbara the night of Jane's performance. She hadn't seemed brash and bold and secure, like Mabel. More than anything, she'd seemed hungry . . . for something. Or someone.

Twenty-Two

Vivian immediately went to bed. "My head is killing me," she said, sliding between the crisp sheets. "Go ahead and read if you like. The light won't bother me. I just have to shut my eyes and think about nothing. As if that were possible."

Miriam pulled the bedclothes up to Vivian's chin and kissed her. "I'm so sorry about your head. You've taken ibuprofen already?"

But Vivian already was floating away from her into sleep, her forehead creased with worry lines. Miriam gently stroked her spouse's face to erase them. She undressed and put on pajamas and slippers, then she settled herself at the small desk in the corner of the room. She checked her phone—Daphne had checked on the dress and reported that it was still hanging where they'd seen it earlier—then she opened her notebook and began to write.

We've assumed that Barbara was involved in Alec's death. Does this attack on her change that? If Daphne is right, and Barbara is having an affair, then Alec could have crashed entirely on his own, inattentive and desperate. But for both of them to have been victims of violence so close together, and poor Barbara drugged and left to die of exposure! I read somewhere that poisoning indicates great rage and often intimacy between the killer and the victim. Susan Crane gave us no details of course, but . . . What if someone right here in the lodge were responsible? If this were a novel, I'd suspect the character most adversarial to the one that Barbara was playing. But that would be Vivi as Alice B. Toklas, and that is impossible.

She tapped her pen on the knuckle of her left thumb. When that became irritating, she doodled a series of owl faces in the margins. She'd seen a great horned owl at dusk the night before, sweeping with its massive wings across the field leading up to the lodge and landing in a tree. Owls were seen in Native American culture as existing close to the spirit world, on the margins between life and death.

Who stands to inherit Barbara's three-million-dollar life-insurance policy from Alec if she dies?

She put her pen down again. Here she was, clinically imagining this poor woman as already dead. Had she no feeling? But, then, she knew Barbara only in passing, having had very limited interactions with her. Still, Barbara was part of their academic community. Since childhood Miriam had feared being selfish and uncaring. So many people had told her that most only children were. Guilt, like a tiny seed, wormed its way into her throat and lodged there. Somewhere, someone must be terribly sad about what had happened to Barbara. And then she recalled Jane's odd behavior. Well, of course—the affair that Daphne had mentioned! Jane had been involved with Barbara all along.

Daphne had confided to her that the police suspected that Alec had found out about the affair right before his fatal crash. Miriam wrote, *"The Dean's Revenge,"* and then circled those three words twice. She'd thought more than once about how that horrible awards dinner she and Darryl had attended had served as Alec's revenge against several in the university community whom he thought had stood in his way. He'd hurled the insults in front of a captive audience. But what if Alec's revenge had also been directed at his wife? How could events have been set in motion on the morning of his death that led to Barbara's life being threatened? She had to talk to someone right away. The soft, puffing sounds emanating from the bed indicated that Vivian was not available.

Bettina surely would be up prowling about. She foraged for her robe in the wardrobe and grabbed a bottle of single malt. Provisions in hand, she went out into the living room that adjoined all four of the suites.

She was right. At the first tap on the door of the room adjacent to theirs, Bettina opened the door, her green eyes alert and focused. "Miriam, thank goodness! Come in. I was going crazy in here by myself. How could anyone sleep after this news?"

"I thought maybe Fiona would be up with you."

"There's an exception to every rule. Fiona is dead asleep—"

"Ach. Vivian too. Out cold."

"Let's just take that bottle of single malt you're carrying outside on the patio. Here, these two glasses will do fine." She picked up a throw from the foot of her bed and threw it over her shoulder.

The patio door squeaked as she slid open the door, and the two women slipped out into the quiet night. The moon and its near star Jupiter glowed through a light cloud cover. A breeze wafted the dry scent of grass and piñon toward them through the clear air. They sat down on a wooden bench on the covered portal and listened for a moment to the fountain murmuring near the pond close by. Above them were heavy pine beams; in front, where it opened to the gardens, the portal was supported by two larger wooden columns. The warm texture of the wood in other circumstances would have made the area feel snug and safe.

Miriam wrapped her robe tightly about her as the evening had begun to cool down. She poured them each a few fingers of Glenmorangie and launched in. "Daphne told me that Barbara may have been having an affair. And now, from Jane's consternation tonight, it appears she and Barbara are in a relationship. I don't know, but it's certain that Alec was very troubled before he died. His drinking had gotten worse and more public, and the scandal about the embezzlement was roaring through every hallway on campus like a Texas gulley washer down a dry wash."

"There's a low water crossing here too, separating us from the main area of town," Bettina said mildly, unrolling the sleeves of her light-blue pajama top. She arranged the throw she'd taken from the room so that it covered both of their laps. Her wavy, auburn hair stood wildly around her head, and she brushed it back from her forehead with one hand and raised her glass of single malt to her lips with the other. "I completely agree about Barbara and Jane. We were blind not to see it sooner. But go on. So, sex and money are involved as always. Not just Alec's malfeasance—don't forget that insurance policy he left behind."

Miriam looked around them as if the trees and waving seedpods jutting up from the grasses harbored invisible lurkers. Satisfied that they were truly alone, she said, "Daphne has an 'in' with the police. There's some evidence that Alec may have lost control of the car because of something Barbara said to him during a cell phone call at the time of the accident."

"I'm listening, but do you really not know what this 'in' is? I'd say she and Susan Crane are an item."

Miriam's train of thought rushed on and left the rest of her brain behind. "What?" She rubbed her forehead. "No. That's not in character for Daphne, and she would have confided in me if it were true. Besides, I think Susan Crane is spoken for. Have you noticed she's wearing a ring on her left hand? You're such a romantic, you always think everyone is having an affair, or wants to have one."

Bettina pursed her mouth in a prim way. "I do think I have insights about such things. I can accept being wrong just this once. But you weren't finished. I know you have a theory. Spill it."

"It's not very formed. But here it is, for what it's worth. We know that Alec was getting increasingly desperate about the embezzlement coming to light. That plus the awards dinner put him one memo away from being deposed as dean. And then, apparently, he had personal problems—his recent marriage was on the rocks. What if he killed himself? Smashed into that post deliberately?"

"Well, that would invalidate the life-insurance policy."

"Exactly. Maybe dying broke—in debt, actually—felt like a way to take revenge on Barbara. Leave her humiliated in the wake of the scandal and without any inheritance from him."

Bettina raised both hands above her head and stretched. "Oops," she said, noticing a plump breast peeking through a gap in the fabric of her top caused by a missing button. "I must invest in new pajamas. But I only wear them when I have a roommate at a conference, which is almost never. Fiona and I thought it would be such a lark to catch up during this time, but it's not looking exactly like the cozy and hilarious weekend we'd envisioned. But back to Alec and Barbara. What if Alec found out about her affair with Jane and committed suicide, but before he killed himself he hired someone to attack Barbara?"

Miriam poured them each more single malt. "But why here? And why now? Why not arrange for the assault closer to his own death? He seemed at the end of his resources, like a man who barely knew what he was going to do the next day—not at all like a man able to plan his wife's demise months in the future."

Bettina shifted so that her legs were crossed under her, which gave her a meditative appearance even though her thoughts appeared to be leaping ahead. "Well, he may have arranged to have Barbara followed before he decided to off himself. Or maybe it was an accident and he didn't *plan* to die ahead of time. He knew she was coming to this festival, so perhaps he hired someone to make it look like Barbara died of exposure or had a heart attack . . ."

"But what about the bruises on her throat?" Miriam's mouth took on a determined cast. "Good Lord. So complicated. It all seems a bit of a stretch." She sat up straighter. "Wait! Crane said that Barbara may have been drugged. I read somewhere that Mabel Dodge Luhan attempted suicide twice. Maybe Daphne is right, and there is a connection between Barbara and her character. Neither of Mabel Dodge's attempts were successful, obviously, as she went on to have her salad days in Taos."

"Funny expression, 'salad days.' What does it even mean?" Bettina asked.

"Ha! I happen to know its derivation, as I sat in on Professor Lester's Shakespeare class the other day. It appears in Shakespeare's *Antony and Cleopatra*. Cleopatra says, 'My salad days / When I was green in judgment, cold in blood . . .' The term usually refers to the heyday—and indiscretions—of youth. But Mabel was actually more mature, in her forties, when she moved to Taos." She straightened her glasses. "From the waning end of my fifties, forty is young. The term also connotes a green time in one's life, fruitful and so on. That was certainly true for Mabel in Taos."

"How did she attempt suicide?" Bettina asked.

"Well, I know one time Mabel took a large quantity of laudanum. Susan Crane said that Barbara had been drugged. Perhaps our mysterious perpetrator used a sedative to make her groggy and easy to deal with."

The two women sank into a morose silence accompanied by the thin wail of several young coyotes in the hills beyond.

Bettina remembered the joy she'd felt when she'd received her invitation to the New Mexico festival. "This isn't turning out to be quite what I expected—a pleasant gathering in a beautiful setting of like, or at least convivial, minds."

Miriam responded with a throaty, rumbling sound. "You remember that old Steve Allen show *The Meeting of the Minds*, where all those actors would dress as characters in history and have stimulating conversations?"

"That was before my time, but that program came up when Patricia was talking about the Chautauqua revival. She gave me a few videotapes of the show to watch. I liked how irreverent it was."

"I don't believe any of those characters ever murdered one another. But they did have feisty discussions."

Bettina sat up very straight. "You really think someone at the lodge tried to kill Barbara?"

"The Locked-Room Mystery," Miriam said in a gloomy voice. "You know, Alec was supposed to accompany Barbara to this event. Remember? She told us that at the Corner Café that day."

They once again slumped into silence. Bettina leaned back on the bench, her creamy throat exposed to the sky. A few moments later she turned to Miriam. "Here's a thought. What if Barbara was drugged, and the dosage was intended to be fatal because her character Mabel once attempted to die that way? What if someone is playing some kind of giant game involving the history of the characters chosen for the festival?"

"Good grief. Who else died or tried to die in a suspicious way among the characters? Let's see, Stein died of stomach cancer, Alice B. Toklas of old age, thank God, Victoria Woodhull of heart disease in her late eighties, Wharton of heart attack and stroke, Virginia Woolf of suicide . . ." Here Miriam stopped. "Bettina, you and Fiona must be very, very careful. What if there is a killer here and he or she is able to make things look like one thing but really . . ."

"Whoa. Slow down, Miriam." Bettina chafed one of Miriam's hands between both of hers. "Don't let your imagination run away with you completely. I'm convinced that this all has to do with Alec's death. Barbara must know something she hasn't told the police."

Miriam's brow puckered, and she shivered in the chill night air. "I don't know. Something is very wrong here. I blame Patricia; she's the one who asked for certain characters to be presented here. And then there's my talk about the Locked-Room Mystery. Here we are, trapped in this lodge together."

"But, dear one, we're not trapped. We can leave at any time. It's not like one of those Agatha Christie mysteries where the guests are all gathered at a house and a storm cuts off the power and causes a flood so that no one can leave."

Just at that moment, a jagged flash of lightning sizzled close by, followed by a horrendous roar of thunder. Huge raindrops began to spatter near their feet. They moved their bench back farther under cover. "Funny you should say that," Miriam said, her teeth chattering.

"I did mention the low water crossing too," Bettina said. "I didn't mean to tempt fate."

"That's it, fate!" Miriam exclaimed, tearing her attention away from the sudden downpour that ensued. "Alec crashed doing a very routine thing, going to the store. Barbara almost died taking a walk in the woods. Both of those acts could be just random, like in Stein's *Blood on the Dining-Room Floor*. But they make me suspicious. Someone has to benefit."

"Well, Alec's death means that Darryl has one less finalist for provost to contend with," Bettina offered.

"This isn't funny, my red-headed friend," Miriam said. When she caught the twinkle in Bettina's eyes, she broke out laughing.

"You sounded like Hercule Poirot just then." Bettina poured another inch into her glass.

"I did, didn't I? Maybe composing the Locked-Room Mystery lecture has invoked Dame Agatha's spirit. But if so, who among us would be next do you think?"

Bettina shifted uncomfortably. "Well, given all this talk about suicide, we'd have to say the person bringing Virginia Woolf to this gathering is next, and we both know who that is."

Twenty-Three

From the *Fresno Tribune,* June 10, 2001:

"Ivory Power in the Ivory Tower?"
By Sally Hawkes

The piercing of the dot-com bubble occupies most people this close to Silicon Valley, but for a cadre of faculty in the English Department at Fresno University, the deflating of spirits and morale trump Wall Street. Campus pandemonium has erupted over the search for a Dean of Liberal Arts. The upshot of the event was that, as is customary, a committee of full professors was appointed by the University Provost to select a new Dean in the wake of the retirement of the current Dean, Robert Harkins. The committee had six members, each from different departments in the College of Liberal Arts.

The mission handed to the committee was to select five finalists from both around the country and within the university, although the Provost charged that "home" candidates could number no more than two of the five. Provost Stanley Carpenter, still burning from criticism regarding his own promotion from Dean of Liberal Arts to Provost in a search five years ago, attested that he wanted the best candidates in the nation for this search, insisting that home-field contenders would not have an inside track. The two in-house candidates were Jane Auckler and Alec Martin, both professors of English.

The student newspaper ran an editorial contesting the demographics of the committee: appointed to the search were one woman, no people of color, and five white men. The committee, according to member Carol Grey, professor of English, fielded more than fifty candidates for the position. "The finalists were all accomplished; that wasn't the problem," Grey said. "It's just that it came out at a meeting that one of the committee members was formerly married to one of the candidates and neglected to mention that little detail. Another was coauthoring a book with a second candidate. Objectivity in judging the candidates was in serious doubt. It was beginning to look like a farce."

Gray's bombshell announcement was that "the committee voted unanimously for Jane Auckler. That was on a Friday. But on the following Monday, the Provost declared Alec Martin the next Dean. Rumor has it that a prior arrangement—a favor owed? payment for loyalty to come?—existed between the Provost and Alec Martin. The worst of it, from the faculty's point of view, is that Jane Auckler resigned after the announcement. We felt we'd lost a valued colleague in addition to being utterly betrayed by Provost Carpenter—who had enticed each of us onto the search by telling us that he was prepared to honor our recommendations."

Fiona logged out of the article she'd been reading in the library of Western New Mexico State University and pushed her chair back. One of the wheels of the chair squawked loudly, and the woman on the computer next to her turned a startled face her way. Just then Bettina arrived, as arranged.

Bettina looked comfortably mussed in a navy V-neck pullover and blue jeans. She sat down at the table opposite Fiona and immediately announced, "Good news. Patricia told me that she's checked with the hospital, and Barbara is mending nicely."

"That is good news," Fiona said.

Looking around the library, Bettina asked, "Any luck?"

"Hang on." Fiona rose and approached the desk to pick up the printout of the article she'd just read, and she returned with a couple of pages. She handed them over to Bettina and resumed her seat. "Remember you told us that Barbara said that Alec had taught with Jane and reported her to be difficult politically? Well, somehow Barbara neglected to mention that Alec finessed Jane out of a deanship seventeen years ago."

"And Jane finessed him out of a wife." She nodded at Fiona's raised eyebrows. "Miriam and I have concluded that the two are having an affair." Bettina pushed up the sleeves of her sweater, revealing plump, freckled forearms. She scanned the article and returned the pages to her friend.

Fiona felt a prickle on the back of her neck. She was beginning to see their little gathering at Oso Grande as even more incestuous than she had feared. "Yikes. I wonder if Patricia had any idea of this connection between Jane and Barbara."

"The dean fiasco in California or the affair? No matter. I doubt it in either case. I think those two women are very good at keeping secrets."

Fiona absently folded the sheets of paper into smaller and smaller squares. "And good at keeping secrets from each other as well? I wonder. I mean, here's Jane having an affair with a woman married to her archenemy."

"Might Jane have been using Barbara to get back at Alec?" Bettina looked uncertain. "Although Jane's panic when she heard that Barbara had been discovered in a bad way seemed real to me."

"How can we know that? I do wonder how Jane can trust Barbara, given the past. And then, Barbara married Alec."

"Well, poor taste in husbands has never been much of an obstacle in affairs of the heart that I've noticed."

"Cynic." Fiona flicked the intricately folded wad across the table and into Bettina's lap.

"It might actually be a prerequisite for having an affair for most women, as a matter of fact."

Fiona gave Bettina as blank a look as she could muster.

"Ouch! Are you thinking that I was referring to Marvin when Darryl and I had that . . . dalliance? Marvin excepted of course." Bettina put a hand on Fiona's arm. "I'll always be sorry about that. I never wanted to hurt you. And, Marvin, well, you know I can't live without him."

Bettina looked so guilty and miserable that Fiona relented. "I can't say it doesn't matter because it does. But Darryl and I are doing well, so I think we've all weathered what happened between the two of you. You know, it's really none of my business—if only I could be that sensible and believe that. But, anyhow, you can stop apologizing." She bit her lip, her forehead crinkling, thinking how Bettina was a friend whom she would forgive almost anything. She wasn't sure why; perhaps because she was simply so honest about her appetites. Changing the subject, she said, "But, Bettina, hasn't the wind been knocked out of the sails of this festival? Shouldn't we cancel, lick our wounds, and go home?" Fiona slumped back into her chair.

"I don't think we can. Not now. Daphne is here, and Lt. Crane. I'm not sure they'd let us leave. Not until this assault on Barbara is cleared up, any-how."

An unfamiliar wave of claustrophobia swept over Fiona. Her eyes swept over the loaded bookshelves and the bank of computers in the research room. She wondered what percentage of her life she'd spent in libraries. "Let's get out of here, at least. I feel so stuck. And to think I'd been look-ing forward to this as a break from routine. I'm missing Darryl, and I find myself thinking, 'Give me routine, please!'"

Fiona allowed herself to be tugged out of her chair by Bettina.

"Look, Fiona, let's go for a walk. An easy one, just around the grounds of the lodge. Miriam told me there are scores of bluebirds that perch on the fence by the field on the way in. You need some fresh air."

"I feel like I need a helicopter rescue. How did I let myself get talked into doing this, this *performance*? I don't even like public speaking! I know, you don't need to tell me that I'm fortunate to have small classes."

The two walked out of the library—so modest compared to the grand modernist edifice of the Research Center on the Austin University campus that she and Bettina frequented—and down the hill onto the main street, where Bettina had left the rental car. The street had very high curbs. Its length was studded with period brick buildings, most of which had under-gone renovation, many turned into restaurants or galleries. Still, the mod-ernization was uneven, and Silver City's downtown retained its flavor as a turn-of-the-last-century mining town.

"Vivian's lunch event with Jane today seemed effortless," Fiona said as they walked. "I never knew that Vivian could negotiate so well—what a great idea to have a dialogue between Gertrude and Alice instead of going solo. That was her idea, right, not Patricia's?"

"It was her idea, and I say smart thinking, too." Bettina lengthened her stride to keep up with Fiona's. "But of course it was so fitting to have Stein and Toklas do an event together. Patricia saw the value in mixing things up as well at the festival. But stop worrying. Whatever you do will be terrific. And there's plenty of distraction with Daphne and Lt. Crane soft-shoeing around, investigating God knows what. That's the real show."

"Thanks, I think."

They waited at a corner as a vintage pickup, repainted a resplendent cherry red, throttled through the intersection. Fiona continued, "It was so touching today when Vivian, as Alice, said, 'Gertrude's home has always been the English language, but for me, home is always Gertrude.' She brought me to tears."

"I think Vivian feels that way about Miriam, don't you? Maybe that's why that moment was so moving."

Fiona nodded, but she couldn't help but think, what was home but your place among those you loved?

As they walked, Fiona wondered why she was dreading her turn at the microphone so much. A long-forgotten memory surfaced, of her mother demanding that a teenaged Fiona perform for her women's hobby club, and her feeling of slight nausea at the prospect. A stint in drama club made her more comfortable. But these days just meeting a new class at the beginning of a semester gave her performance anxiety. Maybe in her forties she was getting phobic about meeting audience expectations. Even though the general public thought that there was nothing that professors liked to do more than lecture, Fiona knew that she was not alone among her colleagues in experiencing occasional stage fright.

They stopped at a cozy coffee shop for decaf lattes. While they waited at a small enamel-topped table for their drinks, Fiona fiddled with a napkin, shredding it into a pile. "With all that's gone on, I haven't told you how much I liked your lecture. I always mention Woolf's notion of the "angel in the house" to my students, but I'm not sure they get it."

"Thanks. How can these young women understand the pitfalls of being 'nice girls' when one of their primary relationships at eighteen or nineteen has been as a daughter striving to meet, or try to meet, the expectations of their parents? There are many rewards for behaving well."

Fiona had an impulse to laugh at her friend's earnest tone and couldn't help but say, "How would you know about behaving well?"

"Beast," Bettina retorted. "Seriously, you can't know as a young woman how society is out to get you, wanting your time, your energy, and your focus to help other people, all the while ignoring your own needs. If we knew then the head winds we'd face as professional women, we'd have run screaming back to our dolls! Or trucks, or whatever you played with. But I'm glad you liked my talk. It wasn't exactly what I'd planned . . ."

"That's just what made it feel so passionate and right," Fiona said. "I admired how you just *talked* to us about something you'd thought a lot about. The irony of this 'platform performance' business is that you have to be really, *really* good to make a canned performance or lecture sound authentic. And just muttering unrelated remarks sounds unprepared and pathetic. What you did was just right. I can't believe I have to follow you and Jane and Miriam. I think I'm getting ill—surely that would get me out of having to perform?"

Bettina expertly applied two fingers to Fiona's wrist and checked her pulse. "You're in excellent shape. Finish your coffee. Or, hell, let's take it with us."

They exited the coffee shop and slid into their rented Ford Explorer, then drove to Alabama Street, making, it seemed to Fiona, far too many turns on their way. How could such a small town, just plain "Silver" to the natives, be so confusing? They sped through a residential neighborhood on the outskirts of town. A couple of sleepy horses turned their heads their way as they passed.

In three miles they came to the gravel road leading to Oso Grande. The glancing September light was glorious, its soft sheen glazing the tops of the grasses as they drove onto the property. Scrub oaks lined the road, their fall orange colors contrasting with the green of the junipers and pinions.

They reached the end of the fence, where the lodge was in view. The rails of the fence were empty. "No bluebirds," Fiona said glumly.

Bettina slung the car into a too-tight parking space and engaged the hand brake with a jerk.

"Bettina, there are only two other cars here. Why did you have to squeeze us between them?"

"An old campus habit. I see a parking spot, and some inner sonar screams, 'Can you ace the space?' Sorry."

Fiona wedged herself out of the car by sucking in her stomach and sidling sideways in a crooked fashion. She turned her ankle in the gravel trying to avoid the filthy bumper of the car next to them. "Damn!"

Before they reached the porch of the cottage, Daphne and Miriam hailed them. Daphne was holding a black dress beaded with jet seed pearls at arms' length, fostering the illusion that the dress marched ahead of her.

"Oh, good," Miriam said upon catching up with Bettina and Fiona. "We need both of you right now."

Fiona groaned, seeing the walk she'd been looking forward to vanishing in the distance. "If it requires any thinking, I can't help." She put her full weight on the ankle, relieved that it seemed a bit tender but okay.

"Just your presence, dear Fiona. Come along," said Daphne. She was dressed in a long, blue skirt and a purple sweater; vitality fairly sparked from her person. "Brenda has set up a table for us in a storage room near her office where we won't be disturbed. We can lock ourselves in, in fact." Daphne flourished an ornate wrought-iron key that Fiona thought might have been forged in the 1400s, buried in some secret, crumbling bunker, and dug up a mere fifty years ago.

"A reading, of course," Miriam confided to Fiona. "Daphne has Barbara's costume to provide a physical artifact of Barbara's presence. The police haven't come up with anything about the attack, so we're going to try to unearth a clue."

Fiona knew better than to argue with any of Daphne's plans. The woman was eccentric, and her energy wavered between contemplative one moment and electric the next. She was unpredictable, but uncommonly insightful. Fiona didn't know her nearly as well as Miriam did, and her logical mind balked at times at the psychic's methods, but she decided to go along. "I guess if Victoria Woodhull consulted the spirits, we can too," she conceded.

Finishing her coffee, Bettina tossed the cup into a trash can as the group trouped through the double French doors and into the dining room. Miriam stopped to get a cup of tea. "Anyone else?" she asked.

"Yes, please," said Daphne. "And Miriam, would you go get Vivian? Five is an unstable number, perfect for our purposes."

Bettina shot Fiona a mischievous glance. "Why is that so perfect?" she whispered. "I'd give anything for some stability or logic or for . . . well, for Marvin. He'd know just what to do. If this keeps up, I'm calling him to come here."

Daphne swept her little entourage through the kitchen, where Brenda waited.

"Thank you for finding a space where we can meet undisturbed," Daphne said.

Brenda inclined her dark head and stretched her lips in an uncommon smile. "I am so glad to help you, Daphne." Her solid frame of average height looked small next to Daphne, whose Junoesque figure topped out at six feet or more.

Bettina cupped a hand around Fiona's ear and whispered, "I have a hunch Daphne has recently done a very in-depth tarot reading for her, one to Brenda's liking."

"Would you like tea or coffee?" Brenda offered, leading them down a short hallway where the room waited.

"Thank you so much, but Miriam is bringing me something," Daphne said, groping in her pocket for the oversize key that she handed to Brenda. Brenda obliged by opening the room and returning the key to Daphne.

"I encourage you to lock the door from the inside." Brenda looked over her shoulder and touched the luxuriant hair at the back of her neck with a nervous hand. "It feels like the lodge is overrun at the moment." Annoyance spread over her features. "The police. And then there are the festival audience members, who are always coming early for the evening performances and clattering through the gallery. I think you'd be happier with privacy."

Daphne inclined her upper body in a short bow. "I can't thank you enough."

Brenda grasped Daphne's hand. "And I feel the same way. We shall talk later?"

"Absolutely."

Fiona watched this exchange, mystified. Brenda had always seemed so removed, even disinterested in their group of participants, yet now she appeared almost devoted to Daphne's comfort. The psychic had even more talents than she'd suspected.

Miriam and Vivian arrived just as the three of them had seated themselves at the table. The table itself, the wood so old and worn as to be almost black, was square, so Miriam and Vivian had to scrunch together on one of its sides. Conveniently, the small room contained a coatrack; on one of its arms Daphne arranged the black dress that was Barbara's Mabel Dodge Luhan costume.

Seeing the dress hang there empty, Fiona felt a wave of anxiety. "Has anyone heard when Barbara can get out of the hospital?"

"Jane is with her, and the last report I had was that she is doing much better. She's no longer dehydrated, for one thing. I'm not sure when they'll release her. But let's commence," Daphne said, unwrapping her cards from a purple satin cloth.

It was all Fiona could do not to jump up and call the hospital. How could they all sit calmly and focus on the cards when their colleague had been attacked and then abandoned, bruised and battered, on the trail? She tried to catch Bettina's eye across the table, but her friend just put a finger to the middle of her bottom lip.

"Patience." Daphne's voice was a low murmur. "I'm using the traditional, more patriarchal Rider-Waite deck today, as I think what we seek is about agency in the world. Now, I want each of you to shuffle these cards. Think about Barbara as you do so. We're asking for some indication of her general well-being, of course, but also inquiring about clues as to the influences surrounding her. Are there, for example, forces gathering around her that wish her ill?"

Dutifully, each woman took a turn at shuffling, each in her own way. Bettina began by slopping the cards in front of her and smearing them about the way a five-year-old attacks her finger paints; she then straightened the heap back into the deck once more and lined up the edges. Vivian took the deck with nimble fingers and shuffled like a poker player, flashing the cards first one way, then the other, and each time the halves meshed perfectly. Miriam's hands were too small to handle the cards easily—she used the shaking method Fiona's grandmother had mastered, letting a sequence of cards from one hand slot into cards held in the other. This ponderous approach took some time, so that by the time Fiona got the cards, she splayed them together so ferociously that they spewed out over the table.

"Concentrate," Daphne growled, scooping up the cards. She indicated that Fiona should cut them with her left hand. "Into three piles, please." She paused for a moment. "All right, all of our energy is here, in this deck." Casting a quick eye at the piles, she chose the middle stack and turned over the first card.

"The subject of our reading is the Queen of Pentacles," she announced. "Wealthy, surrounded by color and growth, she reflects the Empress from the Major Arcana. Creativity and fertility are hers. This, my friends, represents Barbara in all her fulsome vitality. A handsome woman of great resources, both material and financial, she is secure in the world. I might add that she is in the prime of her life." She regarded each of them at the table. "Such is her vitality that even while she has been attacked, she is still very much with us."

At this mention Fiona felt the temperature in the room drop several degrees. She slipped her arms into the sweatshirt she'd slung over her shoulders when she went to the library and zipped it up.

"The atmosphere, what surrounds her," Daphne continued, covering the Queen partially with the next card, "is the Ten of Swords. Sacrifice." On the card was a figure lying on its face on the ground, ten swords stuck into his back. "Our subject has had a great loss. I think this refers to the dean's death and the more recent assault on her person. However, from defeat comes victory. There is calmness beyond her—note the quiet sea and the sunlight over the mountains—but the atmosphere of the matter is colored by pain and sorrow."

Miriam touched the atmosphere card. "Can the card also refer to risk? Someone must be exposed in an unknowing way when stabbed in the back."

"Good point." Daphne levitated her hand above the card as if to feel its temperature.

Bettina rushed in. "Barbara's affair with Jane, a woman who lost a deanship to her husband some years ago, was a very risky move. As Miriam and Fiona and I have discussed, we were blind not to see their connection earlier. I don't know if Alec found out about it before he died, but to him it must have felt like a revenge move on Jane's part."

"What's this?" asked Miriam.

Bettina gestured toward Fiona. "You tell it."

"I was doing some research in the library today, trying to find history on Jane's academic career," Fiona began, "and found an article about a skewed dean's search committee back when Jane and Alec were faculty at Fresno University. Both of them were insider candidates for an open position of dean of Liberal Arts. Jane was the unanimous choice of the search committee, but the provost bypassed her and named Alec the dean. Jane resigned her position in protest."

"Is it possible that Barbara didn't know this when she met Jane and they started their affair?" Vivian asked, her hand tightening into a fist on the table.

Daphne pursed her lips. "I suppose it's possible, but surely she would have found out soon after the affair began. Or, let me put it this way: I doubt Jane would have disguised her animosity toward Alec when talking to her new love."

"Why do you think that?" Fiona asked. She was always amazed how other people seemed to know how affairs should be conducted and would dissect them in a logical fashion, when from the inside one just blundered toward love, or at least lust, and hoped for the best.

Miriam lifted her tortoiseshell glasses from the top of her head and put them squarely onto her face. Fiona recognized her friend in full professor mode. "It's too good a secret to keep, that's why. It's the kind of thing that would have electrified Barbara, because the fact of the affair shows that she was tired of her husband. Alec was drinking heavily, making a public fool of himself, embezzling funds. He was a very sullied prize."

"Yes," Daphne agreed. "One of the bonds between the two women most likely became their disregard of Alec. It's hard to say which woman despised him most at that point. Miriam, you know Jane the best of anyone here. Does she carry grudges? Might she have sought Barbara out precisely because she was Alec's wife?"

"Jane is a professional acquaintance, not a close friend. I've always experienced her as open and honest. But she is also ambitious about her career. I'm sure the setback at Fresno was very painful for her. Still, I can't see her starting a relationship as a revenge move." Miriam looked soberly at the faces at the table. "It isn't in character from what I know of her. But . . ."

"But?" Bettina echoed. "Love and war, Miriam, love and war. People don't always come across at their best."

Miriam sighed. "That is certainly true. And the same could be said of Barbara. She may have felt at war with her husband. We simply don't know. She is not the kind of woman to tolerate public humiliation, and Alec had become an agent of just that. She's every bit as ambitious as Jane. More, perhaps. No, they both had something to prove when it came to Alec."

"Let's continue," Daphne said. "The cards are guiding us and leading us to a more intuitive understanding of what has happened." She turned over a third card. "What crosses her—the three of swords." In the card, a red heart was pierced through by three swords under a stormy sky. "On the surface, complications of the emotions. Sorrow over a faithless lover, perhaps. Yet the card contains the dawn of something new amid the turmoil. This card crosses the sacrifice card we've just looked at. Its energy runs counter to the atmosphere, but not against it. Turbulence of the heart. That certainly fits."

"The crossing card position in the spread is always hard for me to understand," Vivian murmured. "It crosses, but its energy is not necessarily *against*."

"Exactly," Daphne affirmed. "The cards are just two energies juxtaposed—think montage or collage. Now let's look more deeply. The faithless lover is Alec. The new dawn is Jane. There is a clearing away of a possible betrayal. If approached with honesty, affairs of the heart, no matter how tempestuous, can be dealt with and overcome. It's possible that the death of Alec was the clean sweep the card can indicate. After all, he caused pain to both his wife before he died and to Jane over a decade ago. He was a man who left detritus in his wake. The number three signals growth and expansion and refers back again to our Empress, the number three in the major Arcana. So we have two references to her already, as our first card, the Queen of Pentacles, brings up her lushness as well. Together, the cards indicate a creative time, one of great possibility."

The colorful images whirling in front of her made Fiona uneasy. Daphne's mention of betrayal struck her. Alec had betrayed both Jane and Barbara, the former in her career, the latter in her marriage, by his ruinous behavior. Yet Barbara had also betrayed Alec. Fiona remembered her father reading fairy tales to her as a child and telling her that betrayal was something everyone must experience in their lives, for if we truly trust or love, we expose ourselves to it. Eventually betrayal would come, and the key was not that it happened but how one chose to deal with it. "Is it part of growing up?" she remembered asking him. "Feeling betrayed is a part of living, and so the growth you gain from it, the 'growing up,' can happen from time to time no matter how old you are," he said with a wistful smile. "I'd like to spare you from pain, Fiona, but I know that I can't protect you from all the hard things in life."

Her reverie had caused her to miss some of what Daphne was saying about the next card, one she placed under the first three cards and called the "foundation of the matter," an ornately robed and crowned male figure on a throne, imperious and strong. "The Emperor is stable, logical, and judgmental. As a table has four legs, the number four anchors us in life. The masculine mind in its splendor, the Emperor allows us to be successful in the world. This card makes me think that masculine agency is at the heart of the matter."

Vivian cast a blank look at Miriam and then reached out a long finger and nudged the card. "In the tarot we all have both masculinity and femininity, isn't that right? So does this mean that Barbara must develop this side of her? Or that by being with Jane, she is shoring up that side of her persona?"

"I'm not sure yet," Daphne said, hooding those spectacular eyes of hers, one the sky blue of a snow leopard and one amber like a tiger's. "Does anyone have other ideas?"

"You know very well it's all about power," Miriam said softly.

Daphne bestowed a beam upon Miriam as if she were her favorite pupil. "Exactly. Barbara is a powerful person. We all know that. But this makes me wonder if she's not coming into even more power and wealth and stability."

"But she's lying in a hospital bed!" Bettina said. "Surely her battery needs to be plugged in, and right now."

"I think if you called the hospital," Daphne stated, "you'd find that she is almost completely recovered."

Bettina brandished her cell phone. "I'm going to call right this instant."

They all waited as Bettina's call was routed from the hospital operator to the floor nurse and finally to Barbara's room. "Jane! . . . We're all so worried . . . Can you—she is? That's terrific news. Do you need one of us to come and drive you? . . . You have to wait until the discharge nurse comes back? We'll be there in an hour . . . hugs to both of you." Bettina turned to Daphne. "How did you know?"

"The cards. It couldn't be clearer. Barbara is a very strong woman, getting stronger I'd say. Let's just lay the rest of these out and see if anything else is of interest."

Daphne quickly filled in the other positions that made up the reading called the Celtic Cross. "The immediate past is the Knight of Cups, the roller coaster of Alec's mania. The crowning card, either the best that can happen or a possible influence, is the Queen of Swords, a strong woman but a sorrowful one. Hmm. Storm clouds are gathering—something to watch there. And then the immediate future, the Two of Cups—a secret will be revealed from the unconscious."

Before Fiona could protest that she wanted more details, especially about the sorrowful queen and the storm clouds, Daphne laid down four cards in a vertical column, bottom to top, and rattled off the cards and a quick interpretation for each: "The Ace of Cups, the gift of the self—perhaps her new life with Jane; the Four of Pentacles, holding on too tightly, especially of resources, when there's really no reason to; the Two of Wands, a new venture . . ."

The seer pounced on the next and last card. "Ah! Here's what we're looking for, the High Priestess, the keeper of the ancient secrets, the witch, the ultimate female intuitive. Is this Barbara's own energy or someone around her?" She leveled her disconcerting gaze on each of the four of them in turn.

"Well, we know that it's you," Miriam said to her. "Who else could it be?"

"It could be the combined synergy of all of us," Daphne declared. "Plus Jane and Barbara of course."

"And let's not forget the magic of Oso Grande itself," Bettina added. "Just watching the moon rise over the mountains makes me feel transported."

Daphne raised her chin, her face radiating peace. "Exactly. We're all here, interdependent, radiating out our individual energy into the collective spirit, the *ne plus ultra* of womanly power. The secrets will be revealed right here, among us."

Fiona looked around the table at each of them and, lastly, at Miriam. "The locked-room mystery. No one can come in, and no one can go out. Our gathering is a variation on that, isn't that what you're saying? All the clues are here, if we could just see them and make sense of them."

"How exciting," Vivian chimed in.

"And terrifying," said Bettina.

Twenty-Four

Lying in her hospital bed, Barbara wavered between humiliation and fear. She hadn't even been able to take a simple walk in the woods without embarrassing herself—she hadn't asked anyone knowledgeable like Brenda or Fiona about the trails and conditions, her shoes were pathetic and inadequate to the rocky, unstable footing, and she hadn't even brought water even though she'd been instructed to do so. Then she'd exposed herself to real danger and ended up as the victim of a predator.

Jane kept asking her what she remembered of the assault. But all she could remember was a thread of a conversation. She'd been sitting under a tree when she heard a voice asking her if she needed help.

"Yes," she'd said. "I'm afraid I've lost my way."

"Do you want the Gomez Peak trail?" a deep male voice asked.

The sun had been shining directly into her eyes. All she could make out was someone blond and tall with a close-cut beard. The sun lit his hair so that it looked like he had a halo.

She had attempted a laugh. "I have no idea. Can you point the way back to the parking lot? And do you have any water?"

The man, tall and limber, had leaned over and offered her a blue metal bottle. She'd taken a swig, and that was all she remembered before she'd blacked out. Some time later, groggy and aching, she was aware of being loaded into an ambulance. People milled about, but her vision blurred so that she saw only outlines and wavery shapes. Pain ripped through her head, her ankle felt broken, and her face swelled with bruises. All she wanted was to go home, and that meant to be with Jane. Austin didn't feel like home any longer, and not just the city; she wanted to be as far away from Austin University as was possible.

Once her senses returned in the hospital, she said to Jane, who sat beside her, "Let's go back to California. We don't have to live together if you don't want to."

"Honey, shhh. Here, drink more water." Jane's hand rested, firm and reassuring, on her forehead. "We'll find out who did this to you and then we can leave."

Barbara's mind stumbled on those words every time: someone had done this to her. She'd felt safe at the lodge, though she was aware she wasn't exactly popular with the other performers, except for Jane, of course. Everyone was perfectly polite, but she knew that her viewpoint was outside the political norms of the rest of the group—she knew little about feminist criticism, and she wasn't using it as a lens on the life of Mabel Dodge Luhan. Instead, her performance showcased the glamour of Luhan's life, the travel, the friend to famous artists, the grand hostess. But this friction had been nothing. If Alec were alive he'd laugh until he fell down at her use of the word *politics* for matters he'd label *hen-peckery*. "Darling," he'd say, "unless full body armor is required, it's not real politics." She'd always thought he inflated AU as an arena—professors squawking in their playpens instead of making real decisions. At least that was her view before Alec died.

"Jane, can you find out where everyone was at the lodge when I was hurt?"

"Sure, but I think we've accounted for everyone."

"What about Brenda and Patricia?"

"Heavens." Jane spoke carefully. "I must have seen Brenda in and out of the kitchen four times as I was helping Miriam rehearse in the dining room. Patricia, hmm. Don't know. But this is her festival! She's devoted to everyone's well-being. I can't imagine she has a hand in this."

"Agh, my head. Let's get a nurse in here. Do you think I can leave tomorrow?"

Jane patted her hand, but Barbara noticed that she appeared distracted. As she clenched her jaw, she looked like an avenging angel.

A little frightened by her expression, Barbara grabbed her lover's arm. "Don't grind your teeth, honey. It's over now, and I'm okay."

But Barbara felt anything but okay. The doctor told her she'd sprained her right ankle, strained the thigh and calf muscles, also on her right side, and that she suffered from a mild concussion. A lump bulged on her forehead where she'd been coshed by something. She tried to feel grateful that things weren't worse, but misery flooded her entire being.

Miriam and Bettina volunteered to get Jane and Barbara. Fiona had gratefully faded to her room for a nap, while Vivian and Daphne were headed to find Lt. Crane for the latest update.

Miriam held on to the handle above the passenger window as Bettina took the wheel. "Why are all my friends such terrible drivers?" she asked. Bettina did not seem to think such a statement merited a reply.

When they arrived at the hospital, they could not find the alcove where the patient pick-up was located. They drove around, past Emergency, past Out Patient parking, and found themselves making an elliptical loop from one parking lot to another.

"I give up. I'm parking right here." Bettina took the designated space of Chief of Surgery.

Miriam squirmed at this. "We don't want to get towed."

"Ha. If you want to get results, pretend to be someone, I always say." Bettina shoved her door shut with a satisfying crack and headed toward a side entrance.

Inside they found an information desk. A thin man with bleached-white hair told them Barbara's room was 313. "That sounds like a lucky number," Bettina said.

An elevator at the end of the corridor stood open and empty as if waiting for them. "Don't they have sick people in Silver City?" Bettina looked down the hallway at a single nurse strolling by.

Miriam found she couldn't join in the levity. Her nerves felt stretched tight with anxiety; she felt that all of them were somehow at risk. She'd never been at an event before where one of the participants had been assaulted. "Come along," was all she could manage as she took Bettina's arm.

When they reached 313, a tech was wheeling a trolley with various tubes of blood sticking up along with what looked like a month's supply of gauze. "Excuse me," the young woman said with a fetching smile as she breezed past them.

Jane looked up from a magazine, her furrowed brow clearing when she saw Miriam and Bettina. "Oh, good, we feel like we've been in quarantine forever," she said.

"I'm sure you do," Miriam said. "Do you know when you can leave?"

Barbara opened her eyes. She was sitting almost upright in the adjustable bed. "I think tonight or at the latest tomorrow morning. Jane tells me I've been here only two days, but you know how time goes so slowly in these places. You're both a happy sight, I'll tell you that." She grabbed Jane's hand. "If it hadn't been for my darling Jane, I don't know what would have happened to me."

Miriam managed a neutral look at Bettina, who blinked rapidly at her friend at hearing this evidence of intimacy. "Lucky you to have her then," Bettina said cheerfully.

Barbara closed her eyes for a moment. "As you may have figured out for yourselves, Jane and I haven't been completely honest about the closeness of our relationship. It seems foolish now to pretend that we didn't know each other before. And with Alec gone, it doesn't really make sense to hide the fact that we're together."

"Of course," Miriam said, noticing that Jane had gone very still during this speech.

Jane disappeared behind the door and reemerged with two folding chairs. "Here you are, you two. Sit down. Fill us in on life in the real world."

"The real world hasn't been particularly great. Has Lt. Crane been here?" Miriam asked.

"Twice," Jane said. "We've spoken with her over and over again about the same things—which we don't know anything about, so her questioning just wears us both out."

"Talking when you don't know anything is fatiguing," Miriam agreed, thinking that many people she knew needed to remember this fact. No wonder she often came home after meetings craving a nap. Not every mention deserves a thought, as Vivi once said. She observed Jane closely, but she didn't see anything secretive about her reaction to the reference to Lt. Crane. Her relationship to Barbara must be putting her firmly in Crane's sights, yet she seemed her usual calm self.

"I don't suppose the lieutenant has made any headway on who did this?" Bettina raised her head, pushing her hair behind her ears. She sounded almost wistful.

Miriam wondered if her friend wanted to believe the attack on Barbara had nothing to do with their festival. "Who told you about the trails you took to begin with?" she asked.

Instead of Barbara's usually rosy color, her skin looked papery and pale. "I think it was Brenda. But there was nothing mysterious about it. I think Vivian heard her mentioning them too. We were standing outside by the side porch to the lodge, watching the hummingbirds on the feeders. Vivian was close by, I know, because I asked her to drive me over there."

"But how did you think you'd get back to the lodge?" Bettina asked.

Barbara shut her eyes. "I was feeling depressed that morning, to tell you the truth, and I didn't much care. But I had my cell. I'm sure I'd have called Jane. She also has a rental car."

As Bettina nodded, Miriam thought better of mentioning that most likely there wouldn't have been any cell service to make a call from the mountains. She wondered if she could ask why Barbara was feeling depressed when Jane leaned over and picked up the pitcher of water. She filled Barbara's glass and then straightened up a pile of magazines so that the edges lined up perfectly. "Tell us what Daphne thinks about all this."

"She orchestrated a tarot reading right before we came here," Bettina said.

Miriam squeezed Bettina's arm with a look of caution. Bettina promptly ignored this. "It was pretty fantastic. Lots of turbulence in the first cards. But then a foundation of stability. What did you think, Miriam?"

"I think we should ask Barbara if she feels up to hearing our explorations into the psychic realm."

"Please, continue," Barbara said, some color coming into her face. "This is the most interesting development since I woke up in this place. I know everyone wants to know what I remember, but honestly, I was talking to a blond young man, and the next thing I knew I was waking up in pain with the EMT guys hovering over me. The thought of stability sounds terrific at this point."

"Well, the reading centered on a woman of power and wealth," Miriam said. "As Bettina said, many good things came out of the sacrifice and sorrow of the early cards." She fidgeted in her chair, took off her black fleece sweater, and half rose to pour herself a glass of water, using one of the Dixie cups that were stacked by the pitcher. "I can't help but feel uneasy. I feel risk in the very air. Daphne's reading was fascinating as always. But the codes of that language sometimes pass me by. I was not, as Bettina was, reassured. Barbara, I am concerned about you. Did you know of someone who wished Alec ill? Is that what this is about? And could this same person be targeting you?"

For a moment Barbara looked stunned, her handsome face slack. "I wish I knew." She grasped Jane's hand. "If it weren't for Jane, I wouldn't be functioning at all. To have lost Alec so suddenly . . . then the odd way that he died, all the uncertainty, the police hovering over me. Even the insurance policy that Alec left me. It's all a shock. I feel more in the dark than anyone."

Bettina broke in. "Miriam had this terrific idea the other night—that we might be targeted on the basis of the characters we're portraying here in Silver City. For instance, someone drugged you. It turns out that Mabel Dodge Luhan tried to commit suicide by taking laudanum at one time."

"Wasn't that sort of both of our ideas?" Miriam tried to recall the conversation with Bettina the night Barbara was found. At the time, aided by the Glenmorangie, their deductions had sounded brilliant, but she had no idea who had come up with what. On second thought, even bringing up the suicide attempt seemed inappropriate.

"Well, now that you mention it, I think Daphne first brought it up. It doesn't matter. The thing is, is the attack on you linked to Alec's death or aimed at our festival?"

Miriam touched Bettina's arm. "Does it have to be one or the other?"

Jane's voice was firm. "I agree. It could be utterly random. You went out the other day for a walk with nothing with you—no wallet or credit cards. But the person who attacked you may have assumed you were carrying money. He may have wanted to rob you. Maybe he's done it successfully before with other tourists."

"Mugged in the mountains?" Barbara sounded dazed. "I never thought of that."

Miriam pounced on this. "It's possible. This brings me back to your performance, Jane. 'Strange things happen in the country,' you said when talking about Stein's *Blood on the Dining-Room Floor*. Random acts happen that our minds try to make sense of. We're looking for a pattern. What if there isn't one?"

Miriam paid close attention to Jane and Barbara's reaction to this theory. It was merely an idea tossed out as she and Bettina chewed over events. No matter that random things did and could happen, she still believed that Alec's death was at the heart of the attack on Barbara.

They were interrupted by an orderly who poked his head around the door. "Mrs. Martin, the doc says you're free to go if you're ready."

Back at Oso Grande they helped Barbara to her room, leaving Jane with her. The late afternoon was mild and still. Miriam and Bettina found Fiona sitting outside in the sun on the portal at the rear of the cottage, reading through a black notebook.

"Are we disturbing you—do you need to rehearse?" Miriam asked, indicating the open script in front of Fiona.

Fiona shaded her eyes as she peered up at her friends. "Please disturb me and pull up a chair. I suppose the Chautauqua isn't getting canceled? I was hoping I wouldn't have to do this."

"I'm afraid it's going on as planned even though Barbara is not in any position to perform. She's going to rest in her room tonight and not attend Patricia's event. But I can tell you it's possible to live through the performance thing," Bettina said. "How can we help?"

"I guess just look interested and sit in front."

Miriam noticed Fiona's tangled blonde hair, as if she'd been raking her hands through it, and thought her friend looked in pain.

As Bettina brought over two chairs and offered one to Miriam, her phone rang, a kind of jazzy tune Miriam couldn't place.

"I'm going to take this. It's Marvin." Bettina left the portal and headed toward the front of the cottage.

After Bettina was out of sight, Fiona turned to Miriam. "Tell me how Barbara is doing."

"Amazingly well. The woman has the constitution of an ox. But I can't imagine she'll stay here now. She must think this place is cursed." Miriam leaned back in her chair and studied a cloud pattern above her head.

It resembled a flying saucer, the round mushroomy kind envisioned in 1950s fiction. At the thought of doing anything, her chest felt empty and her shoulders ached. What she really needed was a good sleep. She was accustomed to spending her days in a much quieter rhythm; she found the unceasing stimulation of this trip exhausting. She pulled Bettina's chair over to use as a footrest and closed her eyes.

"Headache?" Fiona asked gently.

"Bone tired," Miriam replied. She closed her eyes, the saucerlike cloud drifting across her field of thought. Really she should go back to her room and lie down, but rising from the chair felt like an impossible hurdle . . .

Bettina returned, fairly vibrating with excitement. "Marvin is coming. When I told him about Barbara's assault, his old Marine Corps antennae went up. He insists we can't be here without him."

Fiona's voice brightened. "I've already called Darryl. He said he'd fly into El Paso, rent a car, and be here in the morning."

Bettina stabbed at her phone and then slipped it into the front pocket of her jeans. "I was just going to text Marvin to book the same flight, but he's already sent a message that he's on it. They think they'll be here by noon."

Miriam felt bathed in a wash of relief. "Reinforcements. Wonderful." Maybe the new arrivals could shed light on the events here. "Anything new going on in Austin?" she asked. Even though she'd been gone only four days, her life there felt like the distant past. Strange how intense experiences stretched out time even while they heightened the present moment.

Bettina's forehead creased in thought. "We didn't talk about the weather, so I assume it's still hot. Marvin was interviewed on the local gardening show and was pleased to report a bump in commercial sales. But, you know, something he said about plants got my attention. You know how we always say that every part of a yard can be used, you just have to find the right plant for each spot, one where the plant is at home?"

At Fiona's nod, she continued. "Well, that seems like what's happened to Barbara. This environment is alien to her. She doesn't flourish here. Or, to put it another way, it's like she's trying to relax lying in a bed of nettles. It isn't going to work."

"Or someone is committed to making her feel that way," Fiona broke in.

Miriam thought this over. She had felt for some time that all of them were precariously planted in this enchanting place. And yet none of them had left. If they were prisoners here, it was because that's what they had chosen to be. Carl Jung had pointed out this curious fact of human nature many decades ago, something to the effect that the cage we're trapped in is always of our own making. Alec had found that out as he increasingly became more bound by his own machinations. The manner of his particular escape, in his case by leaving this earth, was still an open question. Its unraveling would presumably provide the answer to the strange sequence of events since his death.

Twenty-Five

That evening Patricia's Victoria Woodhull performance proceeded with the refreshing jolt of a sudden shower in the desert. Jane introduced her by saying, "Victoria Claflin Woodhull was born, the seventh of ten children, in rural Ohio in 1838. Her father was a con artist who used his two daughters, Victoria and her sister Tennessee, as clairvoyants to make money. The two women escaped their abusive father and their background by becoming celebrated medical clairvoyants. Their fortunes turned when they became the confidantes of the industrial magnate Cornelius Vanderbilt. They became the first women to open a brokerage firm on Wall Street after Woodhull made a fortune in the Gold Panic of 1869. Woodhull rose to the vanguard of the early suffrage movement by campaigning that the fifteenth amendment of the Constitution implied that women also should have the vote. She declared that women should have control of their bodies and their sexuality. So threatening to the existing order was Victoria Woodhull that she was called names like 'Notorious Victoria,' 'The Free Lover,' and 'Satan.' Her fellow suffragists called her 'The Woodhull' in admiration, as she was such a force of nature. The first woman to address the US Congress on the suffrage issue in 1871 was not Elizabeth Cady Stanton or Susan B. Anthony. It was Victoria Woodhull. Her speech was a sensation, and she then ran for president the next year."

Patricia looked elegant in a high-necked white blouse with a black jacket and long skirt. She wore a white tea rose at her throat. She stepped up to the podium and spoke forcefully from Woodhull's speech to Congress in 1871. "Women constitute a majority of this country—they hold vast portions of the nation's wealth and pay a proportionate share of the taxes . . .

"The American nation in its march onward and upward cannot publicly choke the intellectual and political activity of half of its citizens by narrow statutes. The will of the entire people is the true basis of republican government, and a free expression of that will by the public vote of all citizens, without distinctions of race, color, occupation, or sex, is the only means by which that will can be ascertained . . ."

In a section of the performance on her childhood, Patricia reenacted for the audience the moment the young Victoria saw for the first time a spirit called Demosthenes, after the great orator in ancient Greece, who guided her for the rest of her life. The spirit rose out of the water, telling the girl how she would become a great orator and live in a fine house. "He taught me to speak, and his words flowed through me. I saw myself standing in front of an oak lectern, addressing a great crowd of people. I clutched the podium in fear, my heart pounded in my ears, but then my mouth opened, and words poured out. Women wept, and men threw their hats in the air. Around me the air was filled with the sound of people clapping and cheering. For me, Victoria Claflin. For me."

"I didn't know Patricia could act like this. If this were the original Chautauqua," Miriam whispered to Bettina, "the tent would be billowing out at its sides with all this energy."

"I'd say levitating," Bettina replied, inspired by hearing this early female pioneer but glad for the fortieth time that she was finished with her own presentation. The room felt as humid and warm as a tropical greenhouse in a botanic garden. She excused herself to Miriam and slipped out of her chair at the end of the row.

Outside, the clear, cool air enveloped her skin. Mosaic panels like small gates but in varying sizes were arranged near the door to the lodge. Bettina seemed to remember that a new artist was being featured that week in the lodge's gallery. The brilliant colors of the mosaics, some containing images of birds like roadrunners and blue jays, complemented the potted flowers.

She wandered on a gravel path that led from the portal into the garden and struck out for the pond. A few minutes later she sat on a bench, listening to the bullfrogs booming. The sound reminded her of her son Carl's frequent belching sessions with his friends when he was in the second grade. Thank goodness Marvin was on his way tomorrow. He was so solid, so masculine, and yet she could count on him not to make feeble jokes about an overabundance of estrogen at the festival, a tactic she'd observed Alec use at committee meetings if there were more than two women present.

A late-roosting dove rustled in a ponderosa pine tree, but otherwise the night was still. She stood and studied the sky for clues of what the next day might bring, but the darkening mountains offered only silence. A quarter moon cast only faint illumination.

Ahead of her loomed an indistinct shape in the circular pebble-lined paths of the labyrinth to the west of the pond. Bettina took a few steps and observed a compact figure slowly circling into the labyrinth's center. A woman, she thought, as she noted how she put one foot in front of the other with an almost metronomic precision. The figure bowed its head. Bettina moved closer and was jolted out of the twilight by sobs.

A few moments later Bettina saw that it was the manager, Brenda. She held a large cross in her hands, and as she drew close to the center of the labyrinth, she held it before her like a talisman. Once in the center, she sat down on the ground.

Bettina turned, not wanting to disturb her, but the motion alerted the woman. She straightened her spine and called, "Who's there?"

"It's Bettina. I'm so sorry to be a nuisance. I'm just out for a walk." She feared her few words were jarring, so quiet was the evening.

Brenda got up stiffly and bent over, arranging the cross between two rocks. She didn't seem disturbed by Bettina's presence.

Bettina realized she hadn't been alone with Brenda since the first day, when she had arrived and been given a brief tour of the lodge. "It's very peaceful here."

"I come here often," Brenda said, making her way back down the labyrinth's path until only one ring of stones separated her from Bettina.

"I've been wanting to walk this since I came," Bettina said. The labyrinth's paths beckoned, an oasis of simplicity, seeming far away from the jangle of their event, rehearsals, presentations, and the underlying tension of the Barbara Martin issue. She wanted to ask about the cross when Brenda began to moan, her voice a low rumble.

Bettina fumbled in her jacket pocket for a Kleenex. She found one, all neatly folded, and took a step closer to the woman, who by this time had buried her head in her hands. "Can I help?" She handed her the tissue, which Brenda accepted.

"No one can help. Not even God."

In spite of the woman's distress, Bettina felt a soothing quiet lapping around them.

"It's my son," Brenda offered. "He died five years ago today."

"Oh, I'm so very sorry." Bettina folded her hands together as if in prayer. The possibility of losing one of her children haunted her. What Brenda had endured was unendurable. She was about to ask if Brenda wanted to talk about it, when the other woman spoke, her voice muted with tears.

"There are many spirits here." She looked sharply at Bettina. "One is an ugly spirit. You must be careful. We must all be very, very careful."

Before Bettina could ask why, Brenda said, "Benjamin was not a bad boy." She dabbed at her face with the tissue.

Bettina imagined a young child in a hallway shaking with terror, and long arms enfolding him more and more tightly until he couldn't breathe. "What happened?"

"A tree collapsed on him during a thunderstorm. Very close to here, behind the pond." Brenda's mouth twisted as she turned to face the pond, her head slightly bent. "He was a man, thirty years old, but he was my only boy."

Hadn't Bettina read once that lightning in New Mexico killed more people than in any other state? Or maybe high winds were the culprit.

Brenda said, "Sometimes, at night, walking here, I can feel his breath on my face."

Bettina's hands flew to her own face. A presence nestled next to her, a rush of air, an ache of loss. "Does being out here so near to where he died bring you any comfort?"

Brenda nodded. "I am happiest when I feel him near me. All of the old family are gone. My father died soon after Benjamin. A stroke. But I know it was the grief."

By this time the two women were slowly walking in the direction of the pond, toward a bench made from the slabs of tree trunks that faced the water's edge closest to the main lodge.

"This place is peaceful," Bettina said, "in a way that I didn't expect. The pine and oak trees, the mountains nearby, the pure light, the clear dry smell of . . . of nature itself. I find my mind being scoured of all the things that don't matter." She sat down on the bench and watched the wings of insects graze the surface of the pond. Brenda also sat, her silence heavy but not forbidding.

Bettina was about to ask more about why the woman had told her to take care when Brenda's strong fingers gripped her arm. "Listen," she said.

Bettina stopped breathing. Across the pond was an old barnlike structure, gray in the moonlight. The gentle rush of night air sighing through the leaves seemed to pause and settle around them. Even the croaking frogs in the pond were quiet. In the silence came the distant click of a key turning in a lock. Bettina found her voice after a moment. "What is that place used for?"

Brenda shook her head. "It's full of pots and soil. Only the gardening staff uses it. And also my husband, Manuel, who is in charge of the grounds." She dipped her head in a shy gesture, and Bettina wondered if this was a recent marriage. "But they work here only in the day. That sound. I've heard it before. It is the spirit."

Bettina considered. "Someone might be hiding something in that shed. I'm not saying that there isn't also a spirit here. The lodge is old, many people have lived in it, and now others stay for a time and move on. But that key turning sounded real." She plunged her hand into her jacket pocket and brought out her phone, fumbling to find its flashlight function. "You stay here if you like, but I'm going over there."

Brenda looked stricken. "I'm coming too."

Leaving the bench, the two women crept around the rim of the pond, trying to tread softly on the gravel path. At a rustling sound coming from underneath a stand of thick rabbitbrush, they stopped. The shed was now directly in view. The dark closed in around them. Cautiously they made their way around the perimeter of the structure. Even in the dim light Bettina noted the peeling paint and the sloping roof. The shed's walls curved inward, clearly headed for collapse.

Bettina found it eerie to be out hunting spirits when only a few hundred yards away stood the lodge, with its audience still most likely in thrall at Patricia's answers to questions about Victoria Woodhull.

By this time the doorway to the shed was in view. The door gaped open. Bettina motioned to Brenda that she should remain in place while she went around to the other side of the door. Once planted on either side of the opening, Bettina directed the beam of her phone into the building. She had an impression of dust and clutter before the stillness was broken by a shout of "Give her space!" from the lodge.

They hurried back, the shed forgotten, skirting the pond and hurrying up the flagstone walk and through the portal into the main entrance of the building. In the performance space, a group spilled around Patricia, who was grasping her right ankle. She managed a grim smile when Miriam and Vivian knelt beside her.

"What happened?" Bettina asked, slightly out of breath from rushing across the yard.

"I guess I tripped."

"It seemed like your ankle just collapsed." Vivian turned to Bettina. "She'd just finished the question-and-answer session and had taken a bow."

"I think the long skirt caught on my heel," Patricia said.

Jane still stood on the stage, where she addressed the crowd in a reassuring voice. "She's going to be fine, folks. Thanks so much for coming out this evening." She spoke to a few members of the audience as they filed out. Two women lingered for a moment. "There must be something we can do," one of them said, clearly reluctant to leave.

"Everything is fine," Jane repeated.

Brenda assumed the role of proprietor and ushered out the remainder of the spectators, murmuring a few words over and over to those lingering. Bettina couldn't quite hear what she said, but the manager's low voice was soothing and conciliatory. Daphne, who had been lingering after the performance to see if she could help, accompanied a group of women out of the space so Brenda could go back to her duties. The psychic was in her element as she swept them out of the room, vivaciously soliciting their reactions to Victoria Woodhull's amazing journey from medical clairvoyant to presidential candidate.

Still on the floor near the fireplace, Patricia, her usually confident voice shaking, announced, "I'm going to try to stand."

Fiona held her firmly on one side while Jane half lifted her from the other. "Let's just stand, pivot, and sit in this front row of seats for a minute."

Patricia wobbled a bit but made it to her feet. Bettina watched her face as it moved from a fearful expression to a neutral one.

"What do you think?" Jane asked as Patricia was seated in a chair. She'd

168

taken off her shoe and was carefully moving her foot in half circles in both directions and wiggling her toes.

"I'd try some compression on that right away," Bettina ventured, coming closer, noting the swelling around the anklebone. "And elevation."

Patricia nodded, her eyes shining under the lights. She seemed to be fighting tears. "I think it's going to be all right. I'm just so glad the performance is over. Woodhull was such a regal, graceful person. I can't imagine standing for the entire time, and attempting her erect posture, with a bum ankle."

"You wouldn't have been able to do the movement in the section where she meets the spirit Demosthenes," Fiona said. "The vision she had about her future was so poignant."

"It was a lovely audience." Patricia sounded wistful. "I hope I didn't ruin the overall impression with my fall."

"Of course not. You were wonderful. In a way your fall was a metaphor for the downfall Woodhull experienced after being briefly imprisoned for her views and after losing the election," Miriam said staunchly.

Bettina imagined Miriam as a high school sports coach, drumming enthusiasm into her team with her fists in the air. Her friend, infused with an indefatigable belief in human potential, had supported her faculty similarly when she'd been their department chair.

"Thank you for that. Let's see how much I can trust this leg." Patricia rose and, declining offers of help, took a few ginger steps and then a more confident one. "I think some ice and I'll be fine." But on the third step pain pinched her mouth, and Fiona and Jane rushed to grab both her arms.

"Why don't you go lie down?" Miriam urged.

"Yes, Patricia, I think you're a little in shock from the tumble you took. And you had all that adrenaline from the performance, too. When that drains away, it can leave you pretty flat." Jane spoke in a comforting tone. "Let's just go to your room. Fiona, can you follow with some ice?"

"Thank you," Patricia said, her face against her white blouse taking on a grayish cast. "I think I do need to settle down. I'll see you all at breakfast."

Bettina caught Brenda's eye as the others filed out, Miriam carrying Patricia's books and the script that she used in her performance, Fiona bringing her lace-up black boots along with the white rose that had come dislodged in the fall. She hoped someone would check on Barbara, who was resting for the evening in her room. Brenda drew near and began to clear the chairs.

"Should we go back outside?" Bettina felt compelled to whisper, as if someone might overhear even though they were the only two left in the room. Had she imagined the click of the lock in the shed? Dust had streamed in front of the beam from her flashlight. She recalled tensing, anticipating the whisper of a bat's wing or the shuffle of a rodent along the floorboards. Then the shout from the lodge had wiped everything else away.

Brenda shook her head. "I think we should leave it for tonight." She cocked her head as if listening. "It's very quiet there now. If something or someone wanted to speak to us, they are gone now."

How could she be so sure? Bettina absently began following Brenda's lead, folding the chairs and stacking them against one wall. "Have you heard someone there before?" she asked, standing directly behind Brenda.

The woman hesitated, aligned the stack of chairs neatly, and then swiveled around with the compact movement of an athlete. Her dark eyes were unreadable. "I often hear things," she said. "I have all my life. There are things you don't choose." She took a breath as if to continue speaking. But she said only, "And now, I think Dr. Mendoza is right. We should all settle down and get some rest." She bowed with an enigmatic expression and headed for the kitchen.

Bettina was at a loss for what to do next—read for a while, ask Miriam if she wanted to have a drink, go outside herself and explore . . . She shivered at the last thought and went to the far side of the large room to sit in an armchair by the fireplace.

Brenda's story about her son came back to her. He had been only a few years older than her son Carl was now. She didn't want to imagine the pain of such a loss. Yet the fear of that possibility was always present for her as for any parent, hovering at the edge of pride or pleasure in the child as the years went by. In spite of her dignity and wisdom, Brenda seemed an achingly sad figure.

Bettina rested her head in her hands. She wished she too could "settle down" after the evening's events, but the weather-beaten shed with its spirits and secrets held sway in her brain. Like Brenda's lowered head as she spoke of Benjamin, she suspected it would hover in her dreams throughout the night.

Twenty-Six

Outside the door to their room, Vivian told Miriam, "I'm going to go help Fiona and Jane make Patricia more comfortable. I'll meet you back here in a bit. But I don't know what happened to Bettina."

"I'll go back and find her. Maybe she's helping Brenda with something. We all left in such a rush." Miriam retraced her steps back across their cottage patio and into the lodge in search of Bettina. She found her still in the great room, standing at a large window and staring into the night.

Miriam thought her friend appeared dazed, her normally high spirits absent. She moved over to the window next to her. After a moment, she asked, "Where were you at the end of Patricia's performance?"

Bettina's pale face turned toward Miriam. "I'd gone out for a breath of air and happened on Brenda in the labyrinth. She told me this is the anniversary of her son's death."

"Oh." Miriam felt her own mood plummet. "I wondered where Brenda had gone. She's usually everywhere during these events, in her quiet way orchestrating everything, the food, the audience's needs, managing the staff so that everything is delivered in a whisper of quiet." Miriam sat down on one of the sofas near the fireplace. "It's very sad that she lost her son."

Bettina slid into the opposite end of the sofa. "She does often seem invisible."

"Who do you think she really is?" Miriam wondered if she was being unfair to the lodge manager, but she often sensed something hidden and unknowable about her. The mention of her dead son made her suddenly more human.

Bettina blinked. "You don't think she's who she says she is? Why do you say that?"

"What you've just told me is the first personal thing I've known about her. How did her son die?"

"She said a tree fell on him in a storm when he was thirty."

Miriam shook her head as she took in this sobering news. Life's beginnings and endings seemed to move in an endless, exhausting rotation. Bettina's head was bowed forward as she massaged her face with both hands. Her daughter Clare had been ill with a chronic infection the last year. "Are you worried about Clare?"

"No," Bettina said, "not so much. She really is much better now. I was just thinking how Brenda seemed almost hostile when I met her, and tonight I realized it's because she's just so quiet most of the time, so self-contained. She appears when she's needed, like a magician's apprentice. But of course she's a real person with fears and difficulties of her own."

"Yes." Miriam hesitated. "You know we must tell Lt. Crane what Fiona discovered about Jane's history with Alec. It simply can't be a coincidence that she and Barbara would meet and end up together, can it?"

Bettina propped her hand under her chin. "I believe Fiona has already told her about the political hijinks at Fresno."

"But the insurance policy. Barbara will inherit, and she and Jane will have a rather large windfall. It's too convenient."

"But not illegal," Bettina said, twirling a wavy strand of her hair around her ear with an absent air. "Unless they can be found to have caused Alec's accident. Which would mean his death *hadn't* been an accident. I can't imagine that Crane isn't working on that possibility right now."

"But her investigation," Miriam said, "seems to lack imperative. To me, it seems glaring that these two women get together and that the impediment in the way—a husband—dies suddenly and leaves an enormous amount of money to his wife. Not to mention that the lover in this case had reasons to dislike said deceased husband. I feel we're sitting on a thin crust that's about to crumble beneath us."

"I feel that too. And yet, so far, we don't know that either Jane or Barbara has done anything that constitutes a crime. More important, I don't see how that would involve any of us. Do you?"

Miriam began to sense unease in the air, and indeed all the lights but one had been turned out in the corridor outside of the great room they occupied. She thought of Vivian, hopefully safe in their room. "What do you mean?"

Bettina sat up straight and pulled her shoulders back, as if her upper back ached. Her long-sleeved black top hung loosely; Miriam wondered if her friend had lost weight since they'd been in New Mexico.

After a moment Bettina replied, "Well, these accidents, or incidents, keep happening. Now Patricia has fallen. It seems there's a pall hanging over all of our heads. And just tonight Brenda told me that there was an evil spirit about the place and that I should be careful. Wouldn't you think if Jane and Barbara had gotten what they wanted that the rest of us might be safe?"

"But things like Patricia falling and Barbara being attacked might have nothing to do with Alec or the relationship Jane and Barbara have."

"*Blood on the Dining-Room Floor,* you mean? Random acts. But why then do I feel so personally at risk?"

"Maybe because of what Brenda said to you?" The silence closed around Miriam, and her own sense of risk grew. The great room of the lodge, with its iconic art and bulky furniture, at this hour unpopulated, was a hulking and menacing presence. "Let's go to our cottage and have a drink. It's too quiet in here." The fireplace, in shadow, caused Miriam to imagine a draft. "Brrr. This room is so warm when it's filled with people."

Bettina stood up, gesturing at the chairs she and Brenda had stacked against the wall. "All right. I suppose someone is going to come and put away these chairs before tomorrow. Are you hungry? Why don't we go into the kitchen and see if we can find any of that grilled chicken that was served tonight and take it back with us." She had already gone through the dining area and pushed through the adjoining door into the kitchen.

Miriam started to follow when she heard a hoarse gasp. She hurried into the room to see Bettina bending over a shape on the floor.

"Oh my God, call 911," Bettina said. Brenda was lying on her back, perfectly straight and still as if someone had laid her out for display.

Miriam knelt down beside Brenda and put her head to her chest. "She's breathing. Regularly." She took the manager's hand and rubbed it between both of hers. "Brenda," she said quietly but urgently, "wake up. Can you hear me?" She touched Brenda's forehead. It was cool but not clammy.

"Ohhhh." Brenda's head moved from side to side. She opened her eyes. "I think I'm going to be sick."

"Quick. A bowl." Miriam pointed toward the shelves that flanked the refrigerator.

Bettina hurried and pulled a metal bowl from underneath a group of nesting bowls with a clatter. "Here. Let me help you raise her shoulders."

With a groan Brenda shook her head. "No, the feeling has passed. It's my head." She rubbed the back of her skull. "A knot. A big one."

Miriam touched the swelling on the manager's head. "That's nasty. Did you faint?"

Brenda eased herself into a sitting position with Bettina's help. "I must have slipped. I was stacking the platters that were used tonight." She pointed up and toward the wall, where large cookware and trays were stored along with serving dishes. "I remember thinking the floor was slippery. I looked down and saw a puddle. I turned toward the sink to get a sponge, and that's all I remember."

"I'll get some ice." Bettina turned the corner where two large refrigerators stood and returned with ice in a soft cloth. Her face was calm and focused as she carefully put it to the back of Brenda's head. "Can you hold this in place, or do you want me to?"

"I've got it. If you'd help me into a chair, that would be good."

Miriam waited while Bettina went out to the dining area and came back with a chair with arms. "Let's get you into this."

"Thank you," Brenda said as they eased her into the chair. She managed a half smile. "First poor Patricia, and now me. A night for falls." Her laugh was brief.

"Look," Miriam began, "let us help you up and get you somewhere you can rest. Do you need us to drive you anywhere?"

"If you would just hand me my phone. It's on that counter. I'll call Manuel. My husband," she added. "We live on the grounds. He'll be right over."

Miriam, surprised that Brenda had a husband who was most likely part of the lodge's operations, secured the phone and passed it to Brenda. She had assumed the lodge manager was alone. But why? Perhaps because her presence was so ubiquitous, she appeared to have no time for a private life. Nor could she remember Patricia saying anything about a partner.

"I think we should wait until he arrives," Bettina said.

"No, please. You've been most helpful. Go on, I'm sure you're both tired." Brenda turned a warm smile on Bettina. "I told you earlier about the spirit. It seems to be very active lately. Or angry."

As they made their way to the cottage, Bettina said, "I meant to tell you—when I was outside with Brenda, we heard a key turning in a lock of that dilapidated shed at the edge of the woods. Maybe that was Brenda's husband, Manuel, in the building. But Brenda seemed as nervous as I was about who or what could be in there. We crept over there to investigate, but then we heard the commotion in here after Patricia's fall, so we left."

"That is strange." Miriam had noticed the old shed on several occasions when she'd been walking the grounds. Something about its advanced stage of decrepitude made her want to take up sketching. She decided that she would do that very thing if this interminable Chautauqua ever ended.

The two women entered the cottage and joined Fiona in the room she shared with Bettina.

"I was about to come and get you two," Fiona said. She sat in an easy chair, a glass of white wine on the table next to her, wearing white flannel pj's with blue fish cavorting on the fabric. She took off a pair of half glasses and put down her script for the next day's performance.

"Lord," Bettina said, plopping into a matching chair. "I hope we last until tomorrow, when Darryl and Marvin get here. It wasn't enough for Patricia to sprain her ankle—we just left Brenda, who fell in the kitchen and knocked herself out. Or at least that's what she said."

Fiona absently folded and then opened her eyeglasses. "Good God, not her too! How can these things keep happening?"

"I was just telling Miriam that earlier I was out in the labyrinth with Brenda and we heard what we thought was a key turning in the old shed out there." Bettina rummaged through the shelves of a cabinet and brought out two glasses and a bottle of Scotch. "I hope you don't mind if I have a glass of your wine," she said to Fiona. She tipped some wine for herself into one glass and then passed a measure of Scotch in the other to Miriam.

"But by the time we were going to explore the place, we heard the commotion in the lodge."

"A night of poltergeists?" Fiona asked, her open face brightening. "That's much more interesting than studying this talk or speech or whatever it is. That is, if Brenda's okay. I'm so rattled by this," she indicated the black binder she'd put aside when they'd arrived, "that I didn't even ask right away."

"A sore bump, but I think she's all right. Did you know she was married?" Miriam asked and frowned. "Manuel. I wonder if he's the person I've seen wandering about the grounds with tools."

"Many people are married," Bettina said mildly.

Miriam playfully tossed a pillow at her friend. "You know what I mean! She just seems so solitary."

Bettina caught the pillow and put it behind her back. "Thank you, dear. What are we to make of this latest 'accident'? Maybe there is a spirit, or, as you put it, a poltergeist, or . . ."

"Or, we should be getting nervous, you mean?" Miriam drank her Scotch with a meditative air. "Scotch always helps my nerves, fortunately. Have you seen Vivian?" she asked Fiona.

Just then there was a knock at the door and Vivian entered. "I knew there would end up being a party or get-together after all this excitement. I'll have some wine if I may."

Fiona obliged by pouring her a glass of Chardonnay. "It occurs to me that when Darryl and Marvin arrive we'll need another room," she said. "I don't suppose anyone thought to ask Brenda about that." She looked at her three friends.

"As a matter of fact, I have," Bettina answered. "Marvin and I can stay on the second floor of the lodge, on the pond side, and you and Darryl can have this room."

"Thank goodness for new energy," Miriam said. "But when they hear what's been happening here, they'll probably want to move into town somewhere."

Laughing, Fiona said, "But they can't. You have put us into the locked room, and of course we are all stuck here until we figure some things out."

"I put you into the locked room?!" Miriam huffed. "It doesn't work that

176

way. We are simply here in a place that appears to be functioning as one. I didn't plan it."

"Pity you didn't," Bettina said, winking at Vivian. "We might have been better prepared."

"All humor aside," Vivian said, "I'm going to be happy to be home I think. Beautiful as it is here, I need more predictability and less drama."

"We have only two more events. Fiona's Wharton and the farewell party. Then we are finished."

"Miriam, 'finished' has an ominous sound. Let's just say our task will be complete." Vivian paused. "Doesn't the 'locked-room mystery' mean that someone in the room is the perpetrator and the rest potential victims? A No Exit situation?"

"The term really refers to a seemingly impossible crime," Miriam explained. "For example, the only door to a room is supposedly locked from the inside, and yet a murder happens within it. Only the corpse is there. How did the murder occur? I'm thinking about the term more loosely— more like the traditional Gothic novel, where a small group of people is trapped together, and we assume that one of them is the perpetrator. A closed situation or community." She thought of academia, especially her own department, with its low turnover.

Fiona weighed in. "That's like Christie's *And Then There Were None*. When I was a kid I always thought a 'locked-room mystery' meant a last-man-standing kind of a thing. So either the killer or the hero survives, but not both."

Miriam reasoned that much of life was seen this way—presidential elections, sports events, multinational corporations gobbling up smaller companies; there was always a winner and a loser. It was king of the hill rather than everyone gaining. "What if Barbara had died?" she blurted out.

"That would have been awful," Bettina began, "but why worry about that now when she is so obviously safe?"

"I'm thinking about what Vivi is saying about everyone but the perpetrator being at risk. What if Barbara's having been found and then recovering so nicely is not what someone had planned?" Miriam saw the faces of the others digesting this thought in characteristic fashion, Bettina taking a swig of her drink, Vivian leaning back with a carefully blank expression, and Fiona jumping up and pacing.

"I just don't see how anyone benefits from getting rid of Barbara." Fiona sounded exasperated. "I wish I did. It would be different if, for instance, she had put in her will that the three-million-dollar life-insurance policy and whatever else she has would go to Jane on her death." She stopped pacing and turned her startled face toward them. "Jane," she said again. "Maybe she *is* the person who would inherit the insurance . . ." Her mouth closed around *insurance* as if she'd swallowed the word and found it sour.

Bettina spoke up, wonder in her voice. "That's a 'for instance' all right."

Twenty-Seven

Deputy Sheriff Brent Ransom of the Grant County Sheriff's Office invited Lt. Susan Crane to participate in a preliminary interview with Jane Auckler. The meeting took place in Silver City on September 28. Ransom was interviewing anyone who might have information about the disappearance and attack on Barbara. The three of them sat around a round table in a small, carpeted conference room.

Ransom, a powerfully built man with a solemn face, leaned back in his chair and folded his arms across his chest. He picked up a chipped coffee mug and took a drink. "Thank you so much for coming to speak with us, Professor Auckler. Lt. Crane has a few questions she'd like to ask you about your connection to Barbara Martin. This will only take a few minutes of your time."

Jane nodded and folded her hands tightly in her lap. "Good. I have commitments today. And very little time."

Lt. Crane rested her hands on the table. She noticed that Jane avoided looking at her directly but instead appeared preoccupied with studying the institutional beige walls of the small room. "Let me come right to the point. How would you describe your relationship with Barbara Martin?"

"We're good friends." Jane spoke quickly. She blinked rapidly and offered nothing further.

Crane adjusted her wire-rimmed glasses and smiled. "My understanding is that you're closer than that."

Jane's mouth tightened. "We're close friends, yes."

"I'll let that go for now." Crane stood. "Coffee? Water?"

"Just water, please."

Crane stood and retrieved two bottles of water from a table near the door. She stepped back to the table and pushed one toward Jane and took the other for herself before resuming her seat. "Where were you on the morning of Dean Alec Martin's garden party that took place in Austin on May 5 of this year?"

Jane opened her water bottle slowly, as if trying to recall. After taking a sip and putting the bottle down, she drew her phone out of the small bag that she'd hung on the back of her chair. The silence stretched as she scrolled through the phone. "Let me just check my calendar. Classes would have still been in session then. Ah, let's see . . . I believe I took my cat to the vet that morning. Um, yes, here it is. I had an appointment with Dr. Clark. It's quite a drive for me, but Sparky won't go anywhere else . . ."

Crane slapped the table with one hand. "Professor Auckler, let's stop this. You were in Austin, weren't you?"

"No."

"I'll give you another chance on this." Crane enunciated slowly. "You were in Austin on May 5 of this year."

Jane sighed loudly, as if the statement held no consequence. "All right. I can't imagine what difference it may make, so I may as well tell you. Yes, I was staying at a B and B in Austin for two days."

"And did you go over to Alec and Barbara Martin's house that morning? Or was she with you at your guesthouse?" The lieutenant's blue eyes were steady.

For the first time, Jane's voice rose. "I had nothing to do with Alec's car accident. Nothing." She lifted her bag off the chair and put it in her lap as if she were about to depart.

Ransom cleared his throat in the ensuing silence. The room remained quiet except for the creak of his chair.

"Interesting that you bring up the accident," Crane said. "Did you see Barbara Martin that morning at her house on Hemphill Avenue?"

In an almost dreamy voice, Jane said, "We had had dinner the evening before."

Crane found the woman's unwillingness to focus maddening. "And did Barbara Martin spend the night with you at the guesthouse?"

Jane's long fingers twisted the button that secured the top of her handbag. "I can't imagine what relevance the location where Barbara Martin sleeps might have to Alec Martin's unfortunate accident."

"I'll be the judge of that, Professor." Crane's voice sharpened. "The fact is that the last call on Alec Martin's cell phone came from Ms. Martin's phone. I think you were there with her when she made that call, either at the B and B or at Ms. Martin's home. As that is the last communication the dean had, it is very relevant. Anything that happened that morning concerning the dean is of the highest importance."

"It's all such a misunderstanding." Jane abruptly stood. "And it's ridiculous that I should have to defend myself just because I may have seen the dean's wife that morning. To my knowledge, visiting a friend is not yet a crime."

"Professor Auckler, the activities of Barbara Martin on that morning are crucial. Surely you must see that. Were you not with Ms. Martin on the morning of her husband's death? And did you not speak to Mr. Martin on Ms. Martin's phone?"

"I may have used her phone." Jane's voice turned sulky.

Crane waited. "'May have' or you did use the phone?"

Jane sat down, her lips twisting in frustration. "Yes, I used her phone. Very briefly."

"What was the nature of your conversation with the dean?" Crane inquired. When there was no answer, the lieutenant continued. "Did you not choose that opportunity to tell him you were having an affair with his wife?"

Jane's hand trembled as she lifted her water bottle then set it back down without drinking. "I did not call Alec Martin. He was not someone I ever spoke to. Or rather, I hadn't spoken to him in over a decade."

"I am losing my patience with you, Professor. We believe that phone call is key to Alec Martin's accident. He was upset after his conversation with you. Or did his crash occur *during* the phone call with you?"

In a loud voice Jane hurled her answer at Crane. "I didn't call him. Alec Martin was a fool. And if he answered his phone that morning, I say *if* . . . well, who would do that while driving in a congested area, making a sharp turn or whatever it was that he did out of that parking lot? He was a poor driver."

Crane waited as if digesting Jane's diatribe. When she spoke, her voice was soft. "We believe he only answered that call because he believed that it was from his wife. But it wasn't his wife, was it? It was you. And you told him that his marriage was over."

"His marriage *was* over. He didn't need me to tell him that."

"Was this phone call Barbara Martin's idea?" Crane tapped one finger on the table.

"I won't discuss this further," Jane said coldly. "I don't keep track of the calls Barbara makes. And she gives me the same courtesy. Please keep Barbara out of this."

Crane stood. "As you are so obviously in this together, I'm afraid that's not possible."

Twenty-Eight

"And did Brenda seem to be doing all right when you saw her this morning?" Marvin asked, his blue eyes resting with relaxed attention on Bettina's face as she recounted the events of the past four days.

They were sitting on wooden chairs on the small patio off their room on the second floor of the lodge. The musical ripple of water running into the pond below them and off toward the shed softened the dry air. The chill of morning had led to a temperate, sunny afternoon.

"She was in the dining room at breakfast, still looking a little under the weather, but she assured me she just had a mild headache."

Bettina leaned back, letting the sun warm her face. Unburdening the happenings at the lodge made her aware of how on edge she'd been.

"And Patricia?" Marvin leaned forward to kiss his wife on the lips. "I'm relieved to find you in one piece after all that's happened here."

"We could have certainly used you last night." Marvin had been a medic in the Marines. His steadiness was like a balm to Bettina, making everything appear manageable rather than a hopeless muddle. "Patricia is limping a bit, but the woman's irrepressible. She thinks, in spite of all the mishaps, that we should go on with Fiona's presentation tonight."

"And your audience has held steady?"

"Hmm, haven't thought much of it, but now that you mention it, it seems about the same. But Jane has been masterful in keeping any unpleasantness out of view."

"Still, Silver City is a small town, isn't it? Maybe the buzz about Barbara's being lost and found has increased your program's allure."

"*Allure?* You've been obsessed with marketing your business for too many years! You're starting to sound like, well, I'm not sure what. A smooth operator I guess."

Marvin tilted back his close-cropped head and let loose a rumbling laugh. "That's high praise from you, the original smooth operator. Let's go for a walk." He held out his hand and raised Bettina from her seat. "The mountains agree with you. You look sleek as a big cat."

Bettina put her arms around his neck. "In a while. We don't need to meet the others until four." She kissed him. "Let's take a little nap first." She led him toward their bed. "I've missed you."

As Barbara rested after her discharge from the hospital, she basked in Jane's cool competence. She felt utterly helpless and completely cared for. She liked to put her head in Jane's lap and let her stroke the hair back from her forehead. Barbara's father had done that when she was upset as a child. He'd died when she was only ten. He'd been the love of her life. Until Jane. She couldn't help but compare Jane to Alec, whom she now saw as a control freak requiring constant support. She realized that for most of their relationship, she'd acted as a bolster against what he called the tides flowing against him.

"Are you sure you don't mean you're up against the Ides, as in March . . . you know, Caesar . . . that kind of thing, dear?" She'd pointed out one day. His face rumpled in that prudish way she'd come to dislike, as if he'd drunk something horrid like cod-liver oil or eaten lima beans because his mother had insisted.

She pushed Alec from her mind. Never speak ill of the dead, her mother had always said. Trouble is, she'd never explained how not to think ill of them.

There had been a moment's unpleasantness after Bettina and Miriam's visit in the hospital. As soon as the two women had gone, Jane had snapped, "Do you think it was wise coming out to those two so flagrantly?"

"I'm tired. Tired of secrets, of pretending. Anyone with half a brain can see that I'm hardly the picture of a grieving widow. I'm proud of our relationship."

Jane regarded her with a steady stare. "I thought you were still worried about being under suspicion."

"I've had so much else to be worried about. And, you should know by now, you can't pretend around those two. They knew already. I'm proud to be with you, Jane. You'll see, this will all blow over soon."

Jane nodded curtly. "I hope you're right."

On the afternoon preceding Fiona's Edith Wharton performance, Barbara woke from a nap in Jane's room. Jane sat at the room's small desk, answering email. When she saw that Barbara was awake, she joined her on the bed and began to massage Barbara's back.

"Jane, dear, how many more days do we have to stay here?"

"You know as well as I do that this festival lasts two more days. I wish we could leave, but I don't see how, not as I've agreed to do the MC duties."

"Mmm," Barbara said. "If we can just stay like this, I might be able to make it through two more days."

She laughed, soft and low. "I do love you, Barbara. I love it that you're greedy for everything—life, love, pleasure." She kneaded the tight muscles around Barbara's neck.

"Where shall we go when we leave here?" Barbara felt like she was floating. "Let's go on a trip. A long, long trip."

Jane's hands dropped away. She stood and began to pace the length of the room. She opened the small refrigerator, closed it again. "Barbara . . ."

Barbara heard an unfamiliar tension in Jane's voice. "What is it, sweetheart?"

"That police . . . person . . . Lt. Crane. I'm afraid she spoke with me earlier today."

Barbara propped herself up on one elbow, wincing at the pain in her ankle. "Oh. God, poor you. She's persistent, isn't she? I can just imagine her with her nose to the ground, holding her magnifying glass and scrutinizing every speck of everything. It's ridiculous. What does she want?"

Jane stopped pacing, but the energy in the room had shifted, as if the engine that was Jane's usual vitality had stalled. "I'm afraid she knows I was in Austin the morning of Alec's accident. And the night before."

Barbara groaned and pulled herself into a sitting position. She patted the spot next to her, and Jane perched, stiffly, at the edge of the bed. "I suppose she was bound to find out." Barbara reached over awkwardly and put a hand on Jane's shoulder. "That's not good, is it?"

Jane stiffened at the touch of Barbara's hand. "No. She asked me in fact if I used your phone to call him that morning when he was in the car."

"Why would she think you made that call?" The tipping-over sensation she'd experienced in the mountains while looking down into a canyon overcame Barbara. "It was my phone. And what's so unusual about a wife calling her husband?"

"Nothing," Jane said. "Except, I suppose, when the husband crashes his car and dies immediately after—or was it during?"

"But she's accusing you of making the call? I hope you said you most certainly did not."

"I'm afraid she thinks you and I were together the morning Alec died. And that we planned to call him, upset him, and, well . . . she can't think we planned that he would crash. Many people get phone calls when driving and don't die as a result."

Barbara chewed on the skin around her thumbnail. "The problem is that I told Crane that I was with Alec at breakfast that morning, which was true. But I didn't tell her that as soon as Alec drove away, you arrived. The fact is that of course I *was* with you." Barbara tried to laugh, but she couldn't manage it. "It's that fucking insurance policy, isn't it? If that weren't in the picture . . ."

Jane turned to face her lover. "It's very much in the picture, Barbara."

"Yes, well, and I'm going to need a chunk of that insurance policy to pay back the money Alec 'borrowed' from university accounts. God . . ." Barbara groaned. She wished this would all go away. *Fat chance of that.* She allowed herself to wallow for only a few moments, then she gathered herself firmly, one legacy from her resolute mother that had always served her. "Of course she knows about the call. Alec's phone registered that last call from my cell. Well, there's nothing we can do about that."

"She's hoping to shake my confidence," Jane said. "By asking me if I made the call, she's looking at a premeditated provocation. Alec was having a breakdown already. What would it take to push him over the edge?"

Barbara stared at Jane's agitated face, her short hair accenting her strong cheekbones. She sensed that this desperate person had hidden underneath

Jane's mask of calm all along. Attempting a steadfast tone, she said, "He was over the edge. That's a given."

"We helped push him over." Jane's gray eyes were unfocused. "I helped. I did make that call. And I did tell him his marriage was over."

Barbara struggled for calm, but her headache had roared back. "Yes, but I had told him that very thing the night before, when I left the house to go meet you. I told him I wanted a divorce. It's not a crime, Jane, to want a divorce. We didn't do anything."

"We didn't help him. He was crumbling. Do no harm, as the Buddhists say. We can't say we did the kind thing."

"Jane, I wanted a divorce. Don't take this on. You had a history with Alec, and it wasn't a good one. You wanted me to leave him. That doesn't mean you wanted him dead."

Jane was silent. Then she said, very quietly, "Doesn't it?"

A couple of hours later Bettina and Marvin arrived in the dining room for dinner and Fiona's presentation of Edith Wharton. They slipped into seats next to Darryl and across from Miriam and Vivian. The heavy mahogany table glistened with polish, a handsome set of silverware, and Spode china. Large plates of prime rib, asparagus, and roasted potatoes settled in front of each guest along with arugula and goat-cheese salads. Bettina reached for the basket of jalapeño corn bread for which she'd developed an affection during their time at the lodge.

"Are you nervous?" she asked Darryl, who looked sharp in tailored linen pants and a soft-blue shirt. On his right little finger was a large turquoise ring. Bettina had helped Fiona pick it out for him at one of the shops downtown.

"Nervous for her, yes. And I'll be almost as relieved as she is when it's over. Fiona heard that a library group is discussing Wharton's novel, *The House of Mirth*, and that they're coming to hear her tonight. We had to work through a minor heart attack about that news! Fiona's worried that she'll disappoint them. She's so used to critical academics that she doesn't realize that these people are just genuinely interested." Darryl fiddled with the silverware by his plate and then looked directly into Bettina's eyes with an engaging smile.

Bettina took note that he looked marvelous in his early fifties. She had to improve her mental toughness around her own aging since she'd turned fifty. After all, as she could recall from her leisurely afternoon in bed with her husband, God knows Marvin's vitality seemed in good form at fifty-five.

Marvin leaned in. "We discussed this on our drive over here. It's hard to be support staff when you and Fiona acted so put upon by this assignment."

"You mean we were reluctant about these presentations? Yes . . . but challenged too. And we very much wanted to come to New Mexico," Fiona said.

Bettina laughed. "Yes, when it comes to attending conferences, I'm afraid for academics it's very much location, location, location."

Patricia, leaning on a cane to support her sprained ankle but otherwise seeming energetic, introduced Jane a few minutes later. "It is an odd stroke of literary history that at our festival Gertrude Stein will be introducing Edith Wharton. These two literary lions, both living on the Left Bank of Paris in the early decades of the twentieth century, do not seem to have actually met. They couldn't have been more different: Stein, the champion of the new and experimental, whose family were German Jews recently arrived in America, and Wharton, a daughter of Old New York, backed by centuries of British and Dutch ancestry and considered an exemplar of traditional style and polished prose."

Moments later Jane commanded the podium. "The nearest detail I can find out about their meeting is that they may have attended, on different nights, one of the first scandalous performances of Stravinsky's *The Rite of Spring*. It was the hottest ticket in Paris, the cacophonous music causing a veritable riot!

"Edith Wharton was the first American woman to win the Pulitzer Prize for fiction and the first American to be awarded the French Legion of Honor for her tireless work with refugees and children in need during the First World War. Her charities in service to the homeless and the disadvantaged were but one aspect of this generous citizen of the world. Few people know that her 1897 book, *The Decoration of Houses*, which she coauthored with the architect Ogden Codman, is still in print today and remains a standard for early twentieth-century modern houses. Please welcome Dr. Fiona Hardison, who will tell us more about this illustrious figure, the highest-paid fiction writer in America in the 1920s and the author of more than forty works."

Dressed in a simple navy-blue jacket and skirt with an ivory blouse, Fiona assumed her place at the lectern. "I'm calling my lecture, 'Edith Wharton, Inside the House of Fiction.' Wharton was happiest most of her life within that house of her own making. From the time she was a small child she began what she called 'making up,' creating stories before she could read from books she held upside down. But much of her fiction came from what she saw as the challenge, almost the impossibility, of being a woman in the world she came from, that of late nineteenth-century New York. She said, 'I was a failure in Boston because they thought I was too fashionable to be intelligent and a failure in New York because they thought I was too intelligent to be fashionable.'

"Wharton was a woman of her time but also one who imagined a different world. Someone once called her and Theodore Roosevelt 'self-made men.' 'It's true,' she said in response. 'We were born, only three years and three blocks apart, into the same tight, privileged world of Old New York, and we both rebelled against the complacency of a point of view that found politics too dirty for gentlemen and letters too unsuitable for ladies.'

"Her path to become an author was shocking to her family, who found 'authorship to be something between a black art and a form of manual labor.' She gravitated, as did Stein, to men of genius, calling the novelist Henry James and the art critic Bernard Berenson, for example, particular friends. When she began writing in earnest in the 1880s and 1890s, there were few female literary models to follow." Fiona looked up at the audience and added, "Wharton was not the kind of political pioneer that Victoria Woodhull had been, yet she wrote again and again of the social strictures that strangled women's lives and potential."

Fiona went on to address Wharton's creation of Lily Bart in *The House of Mirth*, a creature so perfect, she wrote, that all of society wanted to collect her. Once collected and domesticated, however, she would soon lose her illusion of unattainability and no longer be the rare creature they so desired. She pointed out the irony that a commodity once obtained loses its luster, or at least its ability to inspire lust and longing.

As she listened, Bettina's mind seized upon what now seemed an old idea of women as commodities. Had Alec "collected" Barbara because of her beauty and accomplishment? Wharton had never wanted to be commodified, and she chafed just the same at her limited role when she first married Teddy Wharton. The oppressive status of a wife in the privileged classes and her family's resistance to her dreams of becoming a published author led to breakdowns in the early years of her marriage, which took place in 1885. Teddy Wharton had not shared his wife's passion for literature, culture, and conversation.

No wonder Wharton had been captivated by the joke about her and Teddy Roosevelt being "self-made men." The phrase became a drumbeat in Bettina's mind as she attended to Fiona's pleasant alto voice. It reverberated with the very project they were all in Silver City to do, which was to construct an identity beyond their own persona. How many women had craved or emulated the veneer of maleness? Bettina's mind seized on the lodge manager, Brenda, who had initially appeared to be a heavy, masculine presence. Looming large was Gertrude Stein, who had gravitated toward male privilege in her life, referring to herself as "husband" in relationship to Alice as "wife." Writing under the guise of Alice's autobiography, Stein proclaimed herself a genius alongside male geniuses like Pablo Picasso and Alfred North Whitehead. Jane had joked about how Mabel Dodge had once described Stein as having the head of a Roman emperor.

Bettina had been impressed by how supremely comfortable Jane appeared in the role of Gertrude Stein. How much of Jane was self-made? And did being self-made give the maker a sense of privilege, a feeling of being outside the norms of those who conformed more blindly to society's dictates?

Jane was imposing; she could command an audience and quiet a room. Daphne had turned over the card of the Emperor in the tarot reading the other day. What had the psychic said? Something like, "Masculine agency is at the heart of the matter." Bettina didn't yet know exactly what that meant in terms of the mysteries surrounding them at the festival, but certainly Jane was in center stage at Oso Grande and in Barbara's heart. She didn't outwardly seem to share her chosen character's childlike delight in play. However, Bettina suspected that in her relationship with Barbara she might be sensuous and creative. Jane wore the mask of the celebrated Stein persona with ease at the festival—Jane was formidable, capable, and wickedly smart, just like Gertrude Stein.

Twenty-Nine

That evening, after Fiona's Wharton, Miriam fussed in her room, changing into a pair of comfy black knit slacks and a green and gold striped turtleneck. She sat down with her notebook to scribble a few notes before joining Vivian and the others for a drink. She'd been mulling a question that was one she often asked her students to explore: What is the organic logic of the story? For the events at Oso Grande made a story, she just couldn't yet see its full shape or its consequences.

Right after dinner, Daphne told me that she'd found out that Barbara—or Jane, using Barbara's cell—had made a call to Alec as he was driving, in the minutes before, and possibly during, his crash. She refused to tell me how she knew. "It's obvious," she snapped when I pressed her. "The dean was driven mad, pardon the pun. And by his own hand. But he was urged on by the news that his situation was in even more of a shambles than he thought. Collapse follows capitulation. Always. His death may as well have been pre-ordained."

I've learned to accept Daphne's extraordinary resources of information.

Distraction may have been fatal, but in a brutal way Alec's crash saved him. He hadn't had to face the humiliation of a charge of embezzlement or the heartbreak of his wife's defection. The crash saved his pride. Its puzzling circumstances meant his death rippled outward, covering more and more ground, affecting more and more people. His insurance policy possibly ensured his revenge: the fact of that money made Barbara an object of suspicion. Even if she inherits, she will owe him her security.

Miriam paused and drew a circle around "owe" and "she inherits." Barbara would inherit Alec's legacy; his death will always be connected to the money—that was the dean's revenge. Fiona had raised the possibility that Barbara may have already named Jane the inheritor of her fortune. If so, Jane had a motive to outlive Barbara. Again, this could put Barbara at risk. Were these kinds of hazards more of Alec's revenge? She tapped her pen on the page. *Revenge = Torment. If Barbara wants to be free of Alec, she might have to renounce the money. But would Jane let her? Maybe Jane considers the money payment for the setbacks in her career, which in her view benefited Alec.*

She closed the notebook. But did people turn away three million dollars in real life? Would she?

Alec had been needy, and prideful, and grandiose. And intelligent, she had to give him that. At least at the beginning and middle of his career. She opened the book again.

> *There's a part of Barbara that tears at my heart. She is angry and vulnerable, charming, and now, in love. I remember the pain of being dogged by suspicion over Isabel's death. I knew I was innocent, but being suspected by the police isolated me. Suspicion is suffocating. Crushing. Terrifying.*
>
> *Barbara has latched onto Jane. Perhaps she once grasped at Alec in the same way? He failed her, so she looked elsewhere. BARBARA WANTS TO BE SAVED.*

At the word "saved," Miriam's hand drew away from the page as if the paper had stung her. Barbara was such a performer. Her public self was very commanding. But what about her private one? Was it true what they said about actors, that they are more comfortable within a role than without because they don't know who they are at the core? Or that they lack confidence in the person they really are? Too convenient, of course. A stereotype. But still. Miriam thought of the empty black dress in the room where their group did the tarot reading. Empty, limp, hanging there waiting to be filled out by a living, breathing body. The role waited for her. She drew a circle around "Barbara wants to be saved." The words sounded again and again in Miriam's mind like a mantra, and so they assumed the ring of truth.

Miriam knew the pitfalls of wanting someone else to come to the rescue.

The fantasy of the prince galloping to their aid had trained women to scan the horizon for a savior. Few found their white knight, and others were horrified by the strings attached, the high price of what seemed like liberation but which then turned into restriction. *The life you save may be your own*, she wrote, and closed the notebook again.

So many threads had come together about Barbara and Alec, while others unraveled in the same instant. Miriam wished she could think more clearly. Barbara, she hazarded, was in danger. To think she had once worried that Barbara was interested in Vivian! That seemed eons ago. No, Jane was at the center of Barbara's constellation, the gravity of her star pulling Barbara ever closer.

Miriam rose and put her notebook in her computer bag. As she was about to leave the room to join Vivian, there was a mild tap at the door. She answered it to find Susan Crane, looking very put together in a crisp outfit of a belted khaki tunic and matching slacks. *As if she were going on safari*, Miriam thought, which might be appropriate for investigating crime. She couldn't help but think that their little gathering was hardly big game, however.

Crane settled her round glasses more firmly on her nose. "I thought this might be welcome about now," Crane said, extending a bottle wrapped in a paper bag. "Daphne insisted I bring you something you would like."

Inside the bag was a bottle of Glenmorangie. "Why, thank you," Miriam said, mystified. "I thought the police are not supposed to drink on duty."

"That's certainly the line from every crime series I've ever watched. But this is more of a social call. I'm here to ask you for some advice. Do you have a few minutes?" The detective's eyes behind her wire-rim glasses were the rinsed blue of the sky after a summer rain.

Miriam wondered if it had been difficult for Susan Crane to approach her so casually; the woman appeared reserved behind her very competent exterior. "You'll have some with me?" Her curiosity obliterated her former eagerness to join her friends. "Just give me a moment to text Vivian so that she knows I'll be even later than I am already."

"I'd be happy to join you."

In a moment, message sent, Miriam scrambled to get glasses and pry a few ice cubes from the small fridge in their room. These she put into a bowl that she deposited on the small table near two chairs with arms. She motioned Lt. Crane to a seat and perched opposite her. She put a single ice cube in each glass and poured a small measure. "How can I help?"

Both women sipped from their glasses. Susan Crane's usually sober face creased into a smile. "This is good. If it's an acquired taste, I fear I've already acquired it."

"The damage is done?" Miriam leaned back contentedly. "If only we could just relax and worry about things like single malts and what walk to take and how much better tonight's sunset was than last night's. I told Vivian this morning how we have to come back here when we have no obligations and just enjoy this beautiful place."

"No argument from me, Professor Held." Crane crossed her legs, revealing slim ankles and a pair of brown and white lace-up shoes that reminded Miriam of her favorite saddle shoes in junior high. Somehow the shoes made Crane feel like an old acquaintance.

"Remember you were going to call me Miriam. I haven't been a professor all of my life, and I hope I won't remain so until the end of my days! My mother became an artist in mid-life. It was so exciting to see her change from being just my mother driving me to school in our battered station wagon to this figure who had openings at galleries and dressed in glamorous, slinky black outfits."

Crane's blonde eyebrows lifted. "Might I say the same of you in a year or two?"

"Ha. Well, I don't think I'll become a painter—although being in New Mexico I hear the clarion call. Art seems to be everywhere, starting with the clouds cloaking the mountains. But you know I have thought about writing mystery novels."

"What's stopping you?" Crane raised her glass and pointed at the bottle of Glenmorangie and, at Miriam's nod, poured a couple more fingers into each of their glasses.

Miriam had a moment's panic, thinking of all the times when she had asked students that very question when they said they intended to write or meant to be more prepared for class. She mulled the question over a bit. "I don't honestly know. I have started a story now and then." She sipped her drink. "I can no longer say I have no material. Which reminds me, you said you wanted advice about something, Lt. Crane?"

"Susan, please. It seems to me we went through this dance before about our names when your former chair was murdered. We can almost say we go way back." The lieutenant grimaced at her own remark, as if concerned she had invoked the spirit of a harrowing time in Miriam's life. She recrossed her legs. "It's about Jane Auckler and Barbara Martin."

Miriam's attention sharpened. What at this event wasn't about Jane and Barbara? She felt swamped, in fact, by the minutiae of dissecting the movements of these two women who seemed to be consuming all the attention of everyone all of the time. What had she just spent the last twenty minutes doing before the lieutenant arrived? The two women had invaded her diary, her thoughts, her conversations. She realized that she couldn't remember the last time she and Vivian had talked about something other than this wretched festival, and at the center of it all was the duo of Jane and Barbara. "Of course," she said.

Crane leaned forward and put her glass down. "Suppose you saw clearly how a crime had been committed, one that masqueraded as a simple accident. Speaking hypothetically, of course. And you saw how two people had conspired so cleverly and so seemingly innocently that they were far from where the crime took place. And yet . . ." She picked up her glass again and rotated it along its bottom edge, making slow circles. "And yet, everything points back to them as having motive, means, and opportunity. They are not only the source of malice, the reason a man died, but everything points to them as benefiting from this person's death. Well, that's too mild. It's clear that they put the crime in motion and watched as if observing a boulder slowly winding its way down a mountain and crashing on someone standing below. Would you call it murder?"

"The foolproof crime," Miriam murmured. "One committed, it seems, without an effort—an accident, a trick of fate."

"Exactly. A trick of fate. But one orchestrated very carefully."

Miriam felt as if she were hearing a version of her lecture read back to her. She nodded with a sense of rising excitement. "So, tell me. If you knew that a man was on the edge of a nervous breakdown, too distracted to drive, and while he was driving you called him and said just the words that would complete his collapse, are you liable for what happens to him?"

"I see we understand each other," Crane said, an unhappy look on her face.

"Very difficult to prove of course," Miriam replied. "Unless . . ."

"Unless?"

"Unless one could put into play a situation where these two people felt forced to act again. To defend themselves. Or to cover up their involvement. Or possibly to prove that they were not perpetrators but innocent bystanders."

"Ah." Crane stopped fiddling with her glass and left it on the table. She adjusted the belt buckle on her tunic and folded her hands in her lap. "Construct a locked-room mystery? Put the essential ingredients into a closed space, shake, heat, and . . . presto chango?" Crane lifted her hands wide, palm up, as if inviting magic into the room.

"Something like that," Miriam said. The lure of intrigue coursed through her like a tantalizing burn. She hoped it wasn't just the single malt. She didn't think so. "You know, my father was something of a philosopher. He was fond of quoting a British biologist named Haldane from time to time, something to the effect that the universe is not only queerer than we suppose but queerer than we can suppose." Miriam looked over her glass to see a pensive look pass over Crane's face. "In other words, anything can happen, even magic."

"You don't happen to know how we might provoke such a situation, do you?" Crane asked. She was sitting very still, her head cocked to one side.

"Well, the universe offers endless possibilities. But of course it's unpredictable."

The two women drank in silence a moment.

Crane nodded. "That's what those '50s crime writers were so good at, making the implausible plausible. Or was it making the plausible implausible? I'm thinking of *The Talented Mr. Ripley*."

"About a killer. And a liar. But Ripley had courage And imagination." Miriam raised her glass and inclined it toward Crane. "Let's drink to that."

Barbara and Jane returned to Jane's room after Fiona's presentation. Barbara kicked off her black flats and flopped down on the bed.

"I'm exhausted," Jane said, removing the brooch from her costume in front of a mirror on the door of the bathroom. "Thank God we have the party tomorrow and then we're out of here."

"I couldn't agree more. It's all too much. Where should we go?" Barbara watched as Jane examined her face critically in the mirror, pressing her fingertips against the dark circles under her eyes.

Jane turned from the mirror. "You're right that we should both go back to California. Why don't we just take the luggage we have and go? You can get someone to forward the things you want from Austin later."

Barbara plumped a pillow behind her back. "I love it. Perfect. I don't care if I ever see Austin again. I think I'll just sell the house. Donate all the furniture and Alec's clothes to charity."

"Well, wait," Jane said. "I love the armoire in your bedroom."

"It belonged to Alec's mother." Barbara gave Jane a startled look. "They were very close," she added, and the two of them dissolved into giggles. "I don't know why, but that seems hilarious!"

Jane bent forward, laughing. "When I think of the two of them, I think of Anthony Perkins and the mother in the rocking chair in *Psycho*."

"How can you say that—you've never met Alec's mother!" Barbara found Jane's sense of humor wicked, almost over the top sometimes. Still, she couldn't help but laugh along with her. "How did you know she was just like that—passive, inert?"

"And dead?" Jane sat down at the end of the bed.

Barbara wiped away tears. "I needed that. We've been under too much stress. Maybe we should skip the party, pack up, and leave."

"I don't know if I can do that to Patricia."

"Why? You've been fabulous. You've held this whole thing together."

Jane began to massage Barbara's feet. "No. I promised her I'd stay 'til the party. It's just one more day. Please, Barbara."

Barbara realized that Jane rarely ever said please. Or thank you, for that matter. For a moment Jane looked smaller, with almost a pleading look on her face. Barbara thought of Alec and shivered.

"What is it?"

"Oh, nothing," Barbara said, aware of Jane's finely tuned sense of other people's moods. She pushed away the image of Alec and instead smiled and held out her hand. Jane grasped it. Too tightly? Barbara had a shocking thought. *What if it's my fate that everyone I love changes and becomes dependent on me? What if I'll never find an equal partner?* She looked at Jane, at her strong, shapely body, her large hands, her bold features. The feeling passed.

"Do you think you can just disappear when you leave Austin?" Jane asked.

The question struck Barbara as odd. "What are you saying? Not tell my friends or family where I'm going, you mean?"

Jane stared at her with a peculiar expression, a hard look, as if deciding, "Yes, I want that one," or, "No, she's not for me."

Barbara fought the urge to turn around to see if someone was standing behind her. "That's not exactly my MO. Not my style at all."

A muscle twitched near Jane's mouth. Tension radiated from her in waves, as if she could barely contain her temper.

Barbara sat straighter in the bed. "What's going on?"

Jane twisted the silver ring on her right hand. "I have to confess something."

"Oh?"

"I hired the blond young man who gave you the water that knocked you out."

Time seemed to slow. Barbara sat very still. "What? I don't believe you! Why would you do such a thing?"

Jane's shoulders slumped. "I wanted you to feel like you needed me." She rushed on. "When I went to the hospital, I felt like I was saving you. You were so vulnerable, so happy to see me. It felt wonderful."

For the first time Barbara saw what an actress Jane was. Struggling first with fear, then anger, she didn't trust herself to say anything. She parsed what she heard, wondering who the woman in front of her might be who'd risk that her partner might die of exposure so that she could rescue her. *What if it had been too late . . . ?* She fought the urge to get up off the bed and disappear out the door. *My God, after all the years I've spent with controlling men . . .*

Barbara chose her words very carefully. "Jane, did you want Alec out of our way? Is that what you were telling me the other day? Is that why you called him that morning?"

Jane's expression was earnest. "I was just doing what we both wanted. That's all. I knew you wouldn't be able to do it. I have a hunch the steering wasn't working properly in his car either."

"You mean, you . . ." She pushed away the thought of Jane deliberately disabling Alec's car. She couldn't take it in.

"No, no . . . well, yes, but I didn't have to do much of anything. Not really. He had an older Nissan. Practically ancient. You know how people who love those Japanese cars think they can last forever. But they can't. They break down."

Jane had gotten up as she said this and moved to the counter, where she kept the wine and the bourbon. Barbara couldn't see Jane's expression as she poured a stiff Maker's Mark for each of them. She brought a glass over to Barbara. "We deserve this," Jane said.

"I'll say." Barbara took the glass and took a deep swig. Jane's confession about tampering with Alec's car and orchestrating the attack on the trails threatened to blow her mental circuits. The fog she'd felt since the concussion cleared; her mind was working furiously. She wanted to bolt, but she needed to defuse Jane before she did anything else. "Come, lie down with me for a few minutes," Barbara said in as soothing a voice as she could manage. She hesitated. "Jane, I'm quite capable of taking care of myself. Before Alec I managed quite well."

Jane didn't respond. As she lowered herself onto the bed, she said, "I'm so tense." She took another drink from her glass and waited. Then she said, in a small voice, "I know you're wonderfully able without me. I guess sometimes I'm awed by how powerful you really are."

Barbara braced her glass against her stomach to hide the shaking in her fingers. "Are you serious about hiring the young man to attack me?"

"Of course not," Jane said with a dazzling smile, but her eyes had a glassy sheen. "But it's true that I loved being there for you. Don't worry. I have no idea who that man might have been." She placed a hand on Barbara's cheek and stroked it tenderly.

Jane's touch pitched Barbara into confusion. Jane's mood wobbled from moment to moment. Barbara sifted through explanations for Jane's behavior and came up with nothing. Jane seemed depressed, and Barbara assumed mania could follow. Jane's ping-ponging moods set off a danger warning deep in Barbara's gut. But she had to keep Jane with her until she could find Lt. Crane.

Barbara's thoughts careened from one possible strategy to another. She froze. All she could see was Alec behind the wheel, the power steering failing . . . his face stricken. And then the crash . . .

Jane placed her glass on the nightstand decisively. "Here's a thought.

Let's get out of here and spend our last night somewhere else. That way we'll feel some distance from this place and be poised to head out the minute our duties are over."

Barbara worked to sound enthusiastic—"Delicious!" Any action was preferable to sitting in this hotel room. She tossed down the rest of the bourbon and limped to the door as quickly as she was able, hoping Jane wouldn't follow her. "Wait right here. I'll be right back with my luggage," she told Jane as the door clicked behind her.

Thirty

Vivian and Miriam slept in the morning after Fiona's performance. By midmorning they were the only people lingering in the dining room. Miriam thought the lodge uncommonly quiet, absent its usual morning bustle. She woke thinking about her conversation with Susan Crane, and in spite of her good night's sleep, she felt a stirring of unease. Over the past few days she'd learned that if nothing was happening, something was about to.

They finished their scrambled eggs, scones, and fresh fruit, brewed a third cup of tea, and paged through a few magazines they'd brought from their room.

"What should we do this morning?" Vivian stowed an issue of *The Nation* back into her bag.

"I think a walk," Miriam said. "Let's see, I thought I brought the trail map down with me . . ." She looked around her place setting and checked her bag: no map. She moved her plate aside to find a note folded once beneath it. On the front fold in capital letters was the word "Private" and Miriam's initials, "M. H." When she lifted the flap, she read: "Please meet me in the shed at 11:00." The typed note was unsigned. Miriam sighed.

"What is it?" Vivian asked.

Miriam showed her the note. "Do you recognize the printer this may have come from?"

Vivian shook her head. "It's written in Helvetica, a common font." She reached into her bag to check her phone. "11:00. That's in an hour and a quarter." She thought a moment. "I would say take it to Lt. Crane."

"Umm."

"Miriam." Vivian's voice sounded a warning note. "If you refuse to act sensibly, I'm coming with you to the shed."

"I was counting on it. I have a feeling about this, Vivi, that it's a mistake to take it to Susan Crane. Not yet anyway." She tapped the table with her fingertip. "You don't think this note was meant for someone else, do you?"

"Bettina's description of the shed does not make it sound in any way like a place for a romantic meet up, if that's what you mean," Vivian said. "Okay, we'll have it your way about not telling Lt. Crane. For now."

The two women immediately went into town, as Miriam had forgotten to bring decent walking shoes. After making the rounds of a hardware store, a mountain sports store, and a deli, they emerged with a heavy, oversize flashlight, two sturdy pairs of hiking boots, a small daypack, and cheese and fruit and almonds in case they missed lunch.

They went to their room to put on the canvas pants they often wore for birding. "Do we look like birders or hikers or burglars?" Miriam asked as she put the snacks and some water into the daypack. "But this flashlight doubles as a weapon. And I didn't really have appropriate footwear for an encounter with an unknown person in a shed that we know is dilapidated and probably filthy." Miriam imagined large spiders gnawing at her ankles. The boots offered at least some protection, she hoped.

"We're prepared for just about anything," Vivian said with satisfaction. "And we wanted to try out a trail or two before leaving here, didn't we? So the boots really are essential equipment."

"I might slow you down on the trail, but Fiona would take you, I'll bet. I'm not sure about hiking at altitude. This festival seems to have taken the starch out of any athletic ability I might have once had."

Vivian laughed. "We could just amble in the mountains and check out the birds. Brenda told me there are Williamsons Sapsuckers and Pygmy Nuthatches in the park at the entrance to the trails Barbara went to."

"That sounds like much more my style." Miriam had been so preoccupied with events at Oso Grande that she'd forgotten one of the lures of the place originally had been going on long birding rambles with Vivian. At dusk on her first night at the lodge, she'd spied Evening Grosbeaks during their last foray at the feeders, the females looking rakish with their cream eyebrows against their brown faces.

They left their room after changing, noticing that housekeeping was cleaning the room in the cottage near theirs where Fiona and Darryl were staying. In the main lodge they climbed the stairs to the second floor and knocked on the door of Bettina and Marvin's room. No one seemed to be about, so they assumed the foursome had gone into town. The quiet atmosphere Miriam had noticed earlier only seemed to deepen as the morning wore on.

At a few minutes to eleven o'clock, the two women crossed the grounds to the shed. The building listed toward the ground, looking as derelict as ever. Miriam cautiously turned the doorknob—she feared any display of muscle would send the structure into disintegration—but it was locked. "Well, now what?"

"I guess knock?" Vivian hazarded.

Miriam pounded on the door and then listened. She heard something inside and was seized by anxiety. "Listen. Do you hear that?" She rattled the doorknob once more.

"You know that feeling, that electrical sensation right before a thunderstorm?" Vivian asked, her face pale.

"Only too well." Miriam looked around the grounds, hoping to see Brenda or her husband, Manuel, but she saw nothing except a pair of chickadees flying among the pine trees, their black and white heads winking in the sun.

"Here, give me that." Vivian took the oversize flashlight and rammed the blunt edge against the knob, and then, using both hands, she proceeded to slam the instrument as if it were a mallet at the edge of the door where it met the jamb. Soon after, the door swung open.

"Fantastic!" Yet Miriam held her breath and didn't move, fearful of what she might see. She imagined one of her friends tied up on the floor.

Vivian tugged at her sleeve. "Take your hand away from your eyes, Miriam. There's no one here!"

"What?" Miriam took a step inside the shed while Vivian switched on the now-dented flashlight and swept it around the musty room lined with old shelves and crumbling terra-cotta pots. Worn hedge clippers and spades stood in one corner flanked by a new-looking rake and shovel.

In the middle of the floor was a white sheet of paper, again with Miriam's initials on it. "Do we dare touch it?" Miriam asked.

Vivian brushed past her and picked it up. On it was typed, "If you want to see your friend Bettina Graf alive do not call Lt. Crane. Speak to no one. Take the trail that leads past the pond and follow it just over a half mile to the first fork."

A freezing sensation gripped Miriam's throat at the thought of Bettina in danger. "Oh my God!" She grasped Vivian's hand.

"When did you last see Bettina?" Vivian's voice was small.

"Last night, when we all had drinks. I guess we broke up around midnight. You were there."

"I know." Vivian cleared a short bench of potting supplies and slumped onto it.

"This is ridiculous! It's like a treasure hunt." In her panic, Miriam flailed through the room, disrupting spider webs. "There must be something else here."

"We have to find Marvin," Vivian said.

"Well, here." Miriam took her phone out of her pocket, scrolled to her favorites, and called Marvin. "The simplest methods are the best." Unnerved, she listened to it ring. Mercifully, Marvin picked up.

"Marvin, what a relief!" Miriam said. "Is Bettina with you?" She squeezed her eyes tightly shut, hoping for an affirmative.

"No," he said. "As a matter of fact she was supposed to meet me at the Blue Dome Gallery in town a half hour ago. She had some things to do this morning and then was going to catch a ride from the lodge with Brenda. I was hoping this was her calling now."

"Oh, no."

"What do you mean?" Marvin's voice was almost too low to hear.

"Can you meet us, *right now*, back at the lodge?" Miriam opened her eyes to see Vivian whispering something that she couldn't make out.

"Darryl and Fiona are in town with me, but I don't know where they are. Should I find them or just take the car?"

"You must come right now. Don't even stop to phone them. Please. We're afraid someone has lured Bettina into the mountains. We're at the old shed not far from the pond."

"I'll be there in a few minutes. Don't move."

Miriam lowered her phone. The musty odor of the shed was over-powering. "Let's go outside at least. He's coming right away."

They went outside and sat on the ground, their backs propped against the shed. "I wonder if there's a staff meeting going on or something." Vivian put her hand on Miriam's shoulder and whispered, "Why is there no one anywhere?"

Turning a ten-minute drive into a four-minute one, Marvin skidded into the drive, vaulted out of his rental car, and came running to meet them. Miriam showed him the note and explained about the earlier summons she'd received at breakfast.

"This could be a prank, but what if it's serious?" Marvin asked. "Let's go."

"I think you'd better go and see if you can find Lt. Crane," Miriam said to Vivian. "We'll go up the trail."

Vivian looked reluctant. "Maybe we should wait until I get some help. You don't know what you'll find up there."

"There's no time," Marvin said. "Get the lieutenant, and tell her where we've gone. Please."

"For God's sake, be careful, you two." Vivian lingered a moment, watching them set off for the trail a few hundred yards away, and then she headed straight for the main lodge.

The two walked in silence for a few minutes until Marvin spoke. "Bettina has been filling me in about all the strange happenings around here. There are too many coincidences if you ask me."

"Well, these notes indicate someone is planning ahead. The fact that we don't know where Bettina is coupled with the orchestration of the notes does seem to raise the bar on things. Although Barbara's attack had us all terrified . . ."

Marvin's jaw set in a tight line. "I'm just glad I'm here. I wish Bettina had told me all of this sooner."

"Have you met a groundsman named Manuel?" Miriam's voice wobbled a bit as she struggled to keep up with Marvin's brisk pace. Deep chested and muscular, he powered ahead.

"As a matter of fact, I did just this morning when I was taking a walk around the property," Marvin said. "I liked him. Big too. Wish he was with us right now in fact."

The increasing altitude seemed to stimulate Marvin's stamina and determination to reach his wife. Abruptly, he broke into a run. Miriam found herself comforted by his agile frame in front of her. Moments later, he tripped on a tree root and sprawled across the trail. "God damn it!" he barked, holding his right knee.

Miriam scrambled to catch up to him. "Are you all right?" She held out her hand.

He grasped it and, weaving a bit, hauled himself upright. "You should have seen the guy running the other way," he muttered.

Miriam wished she could laugh, but her throat was too tight. Marvin gave her a wry grin. "Let's go." He limped for a few steps but then managed to regain his stride.

"We're almost to the place where the trail forks," Miriam said, dreading what they'd find there. What if the note was a sick joke telling them to go to this spot if they wanted to see Bettina again but really luring them into some kind of trap? She felt again the cobwebs brushing her skin in the decrepit gardening shed and wiped at her face. The place had been mushroomy with mold. Gruesome.

They reached the fork right below the first saddle and stopped. "Now what?" Marvin said, his sturdy torso tensed, his hands folded into fists as if ready to deck someone.

"Listen." Miriam thought she heard a thin wail, like a hungry kitten. "Did you hear that?"

Marvin answered by going off the trail and into a thick stand of scrub oak. "Bettina!" he shouted. He repeated her name while swiveling in all four directions, then he disappeared into the brush.

Crashes, a thud, and then a loud "Shit!" marked his movements. After a minute Miriam no longer heard Marvin flailing about. Even the birds kept their silence. Miriam looked about uneasily. How could she be certain that someone wasn't still lurking nearby? "Marvin?" she managed to croak.

Miriam was about to brave the brambles when she heard, "This way. I've found her."

By the time Miriam threaded her way through, Marvin was removing a gag from Bettina's mouth and untying her wrists. Bettina's eyes looked glazed. "Thank God you two are here," she said. In a gray T-shirt and tights, she looked dressed for a walk.

Bettina's hands and feet had been tied with rope. Her hair was a swirl of twigs and leaves. Marvin took a knife out of his pocket and cut first the cord from his wife's wrists and then from around her ankles.

Bettina sat up, shaking out her hands as if to restore feeling. "I wouldn't have believed this if it hadn't happened to me," she said.

"Tell us," Miriam said.

Marvin crouched down beside Bettina and put his arm around her. She rested her head on his shoulder. "I ate breakfast alone this morning, and under my plate was a note saying that if I wanted to know what happened to Barbara Martin on the trails I needed to go to the shed at ten o'clock."

"I found a note to go there at eleven," Miriam erupted. "I'm sorry, please go on."

"Jane was waiting for me in the shed. She looked upset. 'Barbara's missing again,' she said. 'Can you help me find her?'

"I told her, 'Of course, but I just got a note about Barbara's accident on the trails.' Jane shook her head impatiently. 'Never mind about that now,' she said. 'Come with me.' I should have told someone right away." Bettina cast an apologetic look at Marvin. "But she made it seem so urgent. I took the bait—she needed my help—and away I went.

"So she took me up this trail, and when we got to this fork where the trail goes right and up to the saddle, she asked me for some water. I gave her my bottle, and she must have put something in it, because after she gave it back I took a drink, and right away I started feeling really woozy. That's the last thing I remember until I woke up a minute ago in the brush. She must have carried me over and hidden me there. I consider myself fit, but there's no way I could carry someone the way she did. She's a little taller than I am and very strong. When I woke up I found that she'd tied me up and put this scarf as a gag around my mouth and left me here."

"Did she do this as a distraction, do you think?" Miriam asked. "Staging your capture to throw us off the real track?"

"Miriam, I feel like my life has been threatened! It doesn't feel like a distraction to me," Bettina huffed.

"I see what Miriam is saying. What is Jane really up to, and is Barbara at risk?" Marvin said, at the same time gently touching Bettina's head. "Where does it hurt, sweetheart?" he asked.

"Oh, I'm fine! Just humiliated at being taken so off guard. A fine detective I'd make." Bettina fumed as she brushed dirt from her leggings.

Miriam drew out her phone. "Vivian was supposed to find Lt. Crane. I'm calling her to see what's happening down at the lodge." The call did not go through. "There's no service up here," she mumbled, thrusting the phone into her pants pocket.

"Honey, can you walk?" Marvin rose and gently urged Bettina up from the ground.

Bettina flexed her knees. "Yes, but Jane threw my shoes into the brush. If we could find them, that would be a big help."

Marvin and Miriam scurried around in ever-widening circles to find the missing footwear while Bettina continued rubbing her ankles and wrists to restore circulation.

"Got one!" Marvin called, holding up a red sneaker. "And—" sounds of rustling—"here's the other." He clapped the shoes together as soil and filaments of forest floor rained down from the soles.

"Make sure no spiders have crawled inside," Miriam said, still sensitive to memories of webs and crawly creatures.

"The poor creatures would now be deaf," Bettina said, watching her husband smacking the shoes together once more.

Marvin carefully stuffed the gag and the rope into a pocket to hand over to Lt. Crane.

After Bettina stopped to stretch her calf muscles, the three of them made their way down the trail. "I feel incredibly stiff," she said.

"I'm sure you do," Miriam said. "You're doing fine—I'd be crippled after what you've gone through. Walking should help."

After they had trudged single-file down the slope for a few minutes, Miriam asked, "Do you think it's true that Barbara is missing again?"

"I can't imagine what Jane is up to," Bettina replied. "She has seemed so overprotective of Barbara. Until now, she seemed entirely sane and logical. But then to attack me . . . it doesn't make sense."

"Something has changed for Jane." Miriam wondered how much to reveal and then decided she'd end up telling her friends anyway. "We've found out that Jane was in Austin visiting Barbara the night before the dean was killed, and she was at their house the morning of the crash. She most likely used Barbara's cell that morning to call Alec as he was driving out of the grocery-store parking lot."

"So the phone call is implicated in Alec's crash?" Marvin said. "I wonder if that constitutes manslaughter."

"How could it?" Bettina stepped carefully around a clump of tree roots on the path. "People get distressing calls all the time. If someone is foolish enough to answer the phone when they're negotiating a precarious turn of the road, how can that be anyone else's fault?"

"Well, when the *someone* calling is having an affair with the deceased man's wife and has a past grudge against *said deceased*, inquiring minds want to know." Miriam laid a hand on Marvin's shoulder. "We found out a few days ago that Alec fraudulently got a deanship in California that Jane wanted desperately. She resigned in protest. That was more than fifteen years ago, but I suspect the loss has rankled more as the years went on. And then Alec stood in the way of her relationship with Barbara."

By this time they could see the pond near the gardening shed, and Vivian and Lt. Crane and another officer were waiting there. Daphne, wearing a long, belted tunic, watched their small party approach as she conferred with Brenda. The manager's dark hair gleamed in the sun; next to her was a large man Miriam assumed was Manuel.

As Marvin and Bettina followed more slowly, Miriam rushed over to Vivian and Lt. Crane. Crane introduced her to Sgt. Joe Mason, his body as lean as a runner's. Miriam had noticed him accompanying her ever since she'd arrived at Oso Grande. "Have you seen either Jane or Barbara? Bettina was knocked down and tied up on the trail by Jane, who said Barbara is missing again."

Crane frowned. "Why would Jane threaten Bettina in this way yet leave her unharmed? And leave a note for you to find her? All she's done is call attention to herself."

"She kept all of you occupied for some time," said Brenda sensibly, her long face somber. Miriam noted how the manager's hands were folded calmly in front of her; she sensed a quiet, steadfast core in the woman that she had previously mistaken for secretiveness.

"You mean she used me as some kind of red herring?" Bettina asked, having caught up to the group with Marvin. "To keep everyone's attention off where Barbara might be?"

Miriam put an arm around her friend's shoulders. "You're very lucky. I think Jane is thinking on her feet. She may have intended to use you as a hostage and then decided against it."

"I don't think so," Crane said crisply. "Jane Auckler knows exactly what she's doing. She wants us to think she's flustered, grasping at straws, maybe desperate. These notes suggest she's improvising. Perhaps even poking fun at us with them, playing with our hopes and fears because we don't have any information. But she's very much in control of this show. We have no way to find Barbara without her. When is the last time anyone saw her?"

No one had seen Barbara that day. "She was at Fiona's performance last night," Bettina offered. "We hadn't seen her at one of our sessions since the first night, when Jane did her Stein. I thought she looked very well."

Manuel came out of the shed, waving a piece of white paper. "This was in the corner where I stack the planter trays," he said. "Whoever put it there knows I go into the building every day." Miriam wondered how the man could locate anything or otherwise function in the disordered ruin of the shed.

The note was typed as before, but this one was addressed to Lt. Crane and Miriam. It read, "Go to the storage room where the tarot reading was held. Bring no one else. If you don't appear by 1:00, it will be too late."

"It's 12:45 now," Crane said. "This assumes Jane could calculate exactly how much time it would take from the time Miriam and Vivian found the first note to find Bettina, bring her out of the foothills, and discover this note. It's too close—it requires a perfect execution, almost a rehearsal, of the events. I'm beginning to think these 'times' she mentions mean nothing. But we have no other leads. We've no choice but to go."

Marvin, following the conversation closely, asked, "Was Jane present for the tarot reading?"

Daphne stepped forward. "No. She was in the hospital with Barbara."

"Then how does she know the reading was held in the storage room?" Marvin pressed.

"I'm afraid I told Jane about it," Daphne said. "She had heard about the reading and appeared to be very interested in our conducting one there."

With a startled expression, Brenda said to Crane, "The key to that room has been missing since early this morning. I meant to tell you."

Crane briefly conferred with Joe. Clearly impatient to move, he gestured toward the back of the lodge.

"All right. Miriam and I will go to the storage room. Joe will give us a two-minute lead time and then follow, going through the back door by the kitchen, next to Brenda's office and the storage room. He'll stake out the office."

"I'm going with him," Marvin said, his head set forward in an aggressive posture. "You might need more help."

And more muscle, Miriam thought. "I have my weapon," she said aloud, brandishing the sturdy, if dented, monster flashlight she and Vivian had purchased.

"This is insane," Vivian said. "You don't know what you're going to find. I don't think either Miriam or Marvin should take the risk."

Brenda and Manuel immediately surrounded Vivian, each gently taking an arm, and drew her onto a bench.

Miriam noted Vivian's set face and ramrod posture as she fumed between the manager and the caretaker. She knew Vivian was finding this investigation extremely irritating and frustrating. Her spouse was fiercely independent. Miriam would have to somehow make it up to her for being relegated, literally, to a backbench during the proceedings. Miriam gingerly planted a kiss on the top of Vivian's head as she passed by, imagining she felt her wife's hair sparking with electricity underneath her lips. "We all have to trust Lt. Crane, honey. I'll be right back."

Staring straight ahead, Vivian said, "For God's sake, be careful." She grasped Miriam's hand and squeezed it.

Miriam and Lt. Crane skirted the labyrinth and the pond as they made their way to the front door of the lodge. The afternoon was unseasonably warm. Dry grasses along the edge of the path tickled Miriam's hands as she walked, and the air seemed devoid of humidity. She realized she was extremely thirsty and regretted not taking a bottle of water with her. She'd left her pack with Vivian.

She contemplated what a perfect "locked room" the storage room made. It had no windows and only one door, which opened onto a short hallway across from Brenda's office next to the kitchen. The small room was as dark as a vault. She tried to imagine hiding places in the room, but all she could recall was the large, dark table they'd all sat around during Daphne's reading, shelving around the walls, and the coat tree in the corner that had held Barbara's costume. The space had more closely resembled an extra-large walk-in closet than an actual room.

They glided into the entry, through the great room, which held only a large, round table for the final festival participants' dinner that evening, and into the small dining area by the kitchen. In that space even the art on the hand-plastered walls, usually so bold in its design throughout the lodge, appeared tentative and hushed, as if waiting for something or someone: a simple pencil drawing of a horse alone in a field, a watercolor of a stream making its way alongside a road. *Liminal zones*, thought Miriam, places where people were not here or there but on the way to becoming.

They trooped into the kitchen, then Crane and Miriam moved into Brenda's office. That room had two doors, one to the hallway leading to the storage room and one opening to the kitchen. As they walked in, they heard the slightest shuffling of feet as Joe and Marvin positioned themselves behind them in the kitchen.

Lt. Crane put her ear to the door of the storage room. "Silence," she whispered. She waved Miriam forward. As Miriam laid a hand against the cool, wooden door and listened, she too could hear nothing stirring inside.

Slowly, Crane extended her hand and cradled it around the doorknob. Her face creased in strain. Impatiently she brushed strands of hair off her forehead with her other hand, then she tensed her arm and turned the knob. The door swung open.

The storage room loomed in front of them like a black pit. If quiet could make a sound, the room echoed with emptiness. The detective moved ahead. Behind her, Miriam was startled to see a gun in Susan Crane's hand leveled into the center of the room. The detective slapped the wall with her other hand and flipped the light switch. A fluorescent light in the ceiling cast its unrelenting glare on the table and shelves. Canned goods and old appliances—a small fan with a bent blade, a toaster, a tiny microwave— lined the shelves. The table was dust free and empty. Nothing was on the scuffed wooden floor but an old pair of boots neatly lined up to the kickboards to the right of the door.

"Look!" Miriam pointed at the coatrack. Barbara's Mabel Dodge Luhan costume hung from one curved arm, limp, its black seed pearls glinting in the harsh light.

The two women edged forward. Pinned to the right shoulder of the gown was a white note with a single word typed upon it: "Goodbye."

Thirty-One

Bettina, Vivian, Marvin, and Joe Mason crowded into the storage room behind Miriam and Crane. "What does it mean?" Bettina asked, holding tightly to Marvin's hand.

"Joe, Jane Auckler's room is upstairs. I'll get the keys from Brenda and meet you up there." Lt. Crane wheeled around, secured her gun in a shoulder holster under her jacket, and left the room with Joe following her.

As the rest of the group made their way through the kitchen and into the dining room, Marvin's phone buzzed. After glancing at the screen, he said, "Darryl and Fiona. I forgot all about them. They're stuck in town." His face flushed as he groped in his pants pocket for the rental-car keys.

"I'll go with you," Vivian said, and the two rushed out into the foyer and through the double entrance doors.

Bettina watched them go, overcome by a light-headed sensation. Her wrists burned from the cord Jane had used as a restraint. "I think I need to sit down for a bit," Bettina told Miriam.

"It's all that adrenaline," Miriam said, taking her friend's arm. "When that drains away it leaves you weak as a kitten. I'll just get you to a chair and then get you some tea and something to eat."

Miriam maneuvered Bettina into the great room and into an overstuffed chair with arms. Retreating to the set-up near the kitchen, she poured two cups of tea and set them on a tray. She selected an apple from a basket on the table and put the fruit with a knife on a small plate.

Placing the tea and the plate on the table next to Bettina's chair, she sliced the apple up into quarters and removed the seeds. "You need to have a bite of something."

Bettina dutifully took one slice of apple and drank two sips of tea. "Better," she said. "I'm afraid I'm a little shaky." She waved Miriam toward the leather sofa adjacent to where she was sitting. "Go ahead, sit down. Don't worry about me. I just need to rest a bit."

She noticed Miriam hesitate, seemingly gauging Bettina's every breath, before perching on the edge of the sofa closest to her. "Really. I'll be fine," Bettina insisted.

In the preoccupied silence that followed, Miriam got up, stood in front of the unlit fireplace, picked up a small, stone horse from a shelf on the wall filled with small seed pots and Zuni fetishes, replaced the horse, and then sat down again. "Good Lord. You know, Mabel was the only one of our characters who actually lived in New Mexico, and yet she never showed up at our gathering. Does anyone else find it strange that we never got to see Barbara actually wear that dress?"

"Hell, yes," Bettina said. "But it's put on quite a performance anyway, don't you think?"

Miriam pushed her empty teacup away and eyed Bettina, who finally nibbled on the chunk of apple in her hand. "How's your head?"

"You mean the headache from whatever knocked me out or in general?" Bettina rotated her neck in an attempt to ease tension. "It's gone, but I feel nauseous. My nerves are screaming, and that's the worst of it." Her memory was a bit fuzzy about exactly how Jane had managed to administer the drug in the bottle of water. Had she turned her back on Jane after giving her the water? She recalled feeling apprehensive around Jane as they'd hiked up the trail. The woman had exuded mania. Instead of her usual measured movements, she'd waved her arms and pumped her fists, talking too much and too fast.

Bettina's throat tightened as she relived the alarming moment when Jane loomed over her. "I don't know when I've felt so vulnerable," she said. "And to think I just walked right into her hands like I did. She wasn't acting like herself, but I disregarded all the alarm bells going off in my head. My nerves were prickling with tension, yet I struggled to appear relaxed." She fought tears of anger. "How could I have been so gullible?"

Miriam's forehead rumpled in concern. Rising to sit on the arm of Bettina's chair, she took Bettina's hand and slid her cup closer to her. "More liquids are in order, I think. You've had quite a shock. I hope you're not pushing it too hard. Maybe you should get checked out?"

Bettina waved her hand impatiently. Talking about the episode only made her feel queasy again. "I'll be okay. A few sore muscles, that's all."

Miriam hesitated, patted her friend's shoulder, and resumed her seat on the sofa.

Aware that Miriam continued to monitor her closely, Bettina said, "I'm very worried about Barbara. Where could she be?" She wished she had something concrete to focus on, anything but the helplessness of being tied up and left beside the trail. She uttered the first words that came to her, absurd though they were. "Where's Miss Marple when we need her to say 'curiouser and curiouser'? Oh, I think Alice said that when she was bewildered in Wonderland, but who cares? It's Miss Marple that we need."

"I don't know what to think." Miriam's face was pale and immobile. She turned the palms of her hands up and looked at them. "I feel we've missed something terribly important. I didn't know Barbara was in such trouble. Did you? And because of Jane of all people! She's been so attentive to Barbara."

Bettina suspected that Miriam too felt an odd affection for Barbara. The woman, once so supremely confident as to appear unapproachable, now seemed like a waif who desperately needed their aid. "No, but then, I trusted Jane. She seemed straightforward, committed to the project at hand. A brick. We didn't know her history with Alec or about the cell phone call before Alec's death. But when Fiona suggested that maybe Barbara had made Jane her beneficiary on the insurance policy, that changed everything."

"I don't understand why they've gone or why Jane pulled that hoax this morning by attacking you, knowing you'd be found. But you're absolutely right about the money. If Jane is in line to inherit everything, Barbara is truly in danger." Miriam, chin in hand, stared at the floor, her voice bleak. "I wish I smoked. I need to do something."

Miriam's distress immediately made Bettina sit straighter. She felt her resolve return. "Alec's motives the day he died are a mystery. It could have been suicide for all we know. So much of his old life was over."

"But whether or not they made that cell phone call, they're in the clear about Alec . . . unless there's something else we don't know." Miriam's voice was flat, and her face had a faraway expression. Bettina recognized the signs of her friend's mind churning.

"I think there are things we don't know," Bettina said slowly. "It's looking more and more like Jane has something to hide. Who was behind the assault on Barbara, for instance? Afterward, Jane played the hero, taking care of Barbara's every need. The picture of the solicitous lover. But what do we really know about Jane?"

Lt. Crane entered the room from the back of the lodge. Bettina noticed a new energy in her stride and focus. "Both of their rooms have been cleared out. Joe is calling every hotel and bed and breakfast in Silver City now. We'll find them."

"That's assuming they want to be found," Bettina said. "What do you have there?" She pointed to a pair of black-onyx antique earrings.

"These were on the nightstand in Jane's room. I believe the earrings are part of Barbara's Mabel Dodge Luhan costume. They're also a clue—a 'bread crumb'—that Barbara left for us. Daphne told me that black onyx is known as a 'protection stone'—it transforms negative energy. I very much think that Barbara wants us to find her."

Joe discovered that two women matching Barbara and Jane's description had checked into The Pines, a lodge in the woods on the way to the Gila Cliff Dwellings deep inside the Gila Wilderness. Bettina and Miriam followed Lt. Crane's car in their rented Ford. Crane had alerted Deputy Sheriff Ransom, who was also on his way. The narrow, primitive road, heavily trafficked with tourists, its gravel surface corrugated with use and marked by deep ruts, proved to be very slow going. Fortunately the vistas of mountains and tall pines distracted them from the rough ride.

When they arrived at the rustic, three-story log structure—it had taken them forty minutes to go ten miles—they parked in the tiny car park out front and waited for Lt. Crane to give them instructions. She came over to the driver's side and motioned for Bettina to lower her window.

"You two stay here. We think she's on the top floor. I'm hoping Barbara will be here unharmed. If she is, she might need some support, and some friends."

Bettina raised an eyebrow at Miriam, who steadfastly ignored her; instead she focused on the detective's face. Crane continued, "I'm hoping you can take her back with you after I interview her. I also want you to call me immediately if anyone comes out the main entrance or the side doors of the building. Joe and I are going in now."

Bettina said hopefully, "Maybe I should station myself in the hallway in case anyone comes down the steps?"

"Leave that to us," Crane said.

The two detectives split up, Joe going into the side door and Crane into the front.

Bettina and Miriam waited for five minutes. "I can't stand to just sit here in the car," Bettina complained. Overwhelmed by agitation, she couldn't ignore the urgency she felt about Barbara's situation. The others hadn't seen what Jane was capable of, but she had.

"You've already been injured once today. I think it's best if you follow Crane's instructions," Miriam said in a low voice.

"How can you be so calm? Normally you'd be raring to go like a filly jumping a fence!" Bettina resisted the impulse to take Miriam's pulse. "Are you all right?"

"My stomach is churning from that lurching road. I'm not calm at all. How could anyone be in this situation?" Miriam crossed her arms tightly as if to ward off a chill. "Look, we have no choice but to wait. And hope Barbara is all right. Jane's attacking you has changed the equation. Nothing about this situation has gone as I thought it would. I'm completely out of my league here, and so are you, in my very humble opinion."

"I don't care. I'm going in. Crane mentioned the top floor. This place doesn't look big enough to have more than two rooms up there. And why is our lieutenant so low-key? Why isn't she involving the local police?"

"How do you know she's not?" Miriam protested.

Bettina eased herself out of the car and then bent down to look at Miriam. "Keep your phone on."

Miriam lifted her hands in the air. "I think you're making a mistake. Lt. Crane is trying to keep this very quiet. Possibly both of them are perfectly well and will go with her willingly."

Bettina shut the car door with exaggerated slowness so it would make no noise. "Suit yourself. I'll be right back."

The lodge was only a short walk away, perhaps fifteen yards. Bettina crossed the car park, hurried up the side steps as fast as her aching body allowed, and opened the glass-fronted door. Inside she found a dim hallway and a stairway. She was about to climb the staircase when she heard a scream. Was it from inside or outside the building? *Good Lord, Miriam's out there alone!*

She immediately retraced her steps and ran back to the car. "Miriam!" she called breathlessly.

"What is it?" Miriam's voice rose in alarm.

"Are you all right?"

"I'm perfectly fine. What's wrong?"

Bettina leaned in the open passenger window. "Did you hear a shout or a scream?"

"I didn't hear anything. I think you'd better sit down here and wait." Miriam's pale face was a map of worry as she looked up at her friend. "Please, stay here."

"No, I'm fine. I was afraid . . . never mind. I'm sure I'll be right back." Bettina, relieved, made her way back to the side door of the lodge. This time she climbed two floors to a short landing and opened another door to the third floor.

She'd been right about the two rooms. One door stood open, and Bettina gingerly moved toward it. A shallow pool of light in the open doorway glazed the brown carpet with gold.

Puzzled, she stopped just short of the door, waiting to hear Crane's confident voice. Instead she heard a rhythmic, low sobbing coming from inside the room. The crying stopped, and a muffled voice Bettina recognized as the lieutenant's said, "She didn't know what she was doing." The drone of the sobbing began again.

Crane spoke again in a soothing tone. "I'm getting help for you as soon as I can. Here, try and drink some of this water. I'm just going to put this blanket around your shoulders. That's it, hold on tight."

Bettina waited a moment, set her shoulders to prepare herself for what she might find, and stepped through the door. Crane looked up with an irritated expression as she spoke into her phone: "Yes, I'll be here when you arrive." Crane ended the call and passed a weary hand over her face.

Bettina froze, taking in the two double beds, each one holding an open suitcase. "I won't touch anything," she said, her hands clenched at her sides.

"Just be very quiet," Crane said in a barely audible voice. "And stay where you are."

In the far corner of the room, away from the window, Barbara hunched, her head in her hands. "Oh God oh God oh God," she moaned. "It's too late." In a clotted voice she said, "I should have . . ."

Bettina noticed that the closet was open. Two sweaters hung there as if someone had just started to unpack. Nothing seemed in any disarray, but the air in the room felt turbulent all the same. Barbara looked small hunched over her knees. Bettina looked helplessly at Crane. Crane shook her head and held her hand out in a stopping motion. Then she angled her body away from Bettina and punched another number into her phone.

Barbara sat up straight, as if she heard something. Abruptly, she stood and turned toward Bettina, her arms rising in front of her like a sleep-walker. The blanket slid from her shoulders. Barbara's arms drooped as she tilted her head toward the overhead light. She turned toward the window and immediately turned away, blinking rapidly. She took a tentative step forward and swayed. For a moment Bettina thought the woman had lost her vision. A moment later her body made a quarter-turn pirouette and slowly caved in on itself, like a dancer sinking into a sitting position. Bettina didn't move. She held her breath as if hypnotized, conscious of inhabiting a moment curving so slowly through time that it arced out of view.

Crane dropped her phone and rushed toward Barbara. The action broke Bettina's trance, and she also hustled toward the falling woman. But in the moment before they reached her, Barbara collapsed on her back onto the carpet.

Crane crouched down and expertly put two fingers on the pulse at Barbara's throat. After a few seconds, the detective expelled a breath in relief.

"She's breathing just fine, but she's very pale. I think she just fainted." Bettina crouched down, placed a hand on Barbara's forehead, and called her name softly.

Barbara's eyes popped open. She looked at Crane bent over her and at Bettina's face and burst into tears.

The two women helped her into a sitting position. Bettina picked up the blanket and draped it around Barbara. "I don't think she hit her head," she said.

"I'm all right," Barbara stuttered. "But Jane . . ." Her chest heaved with effort as she cried out. With a strangled sound she lurched over to one side and vomited on the floor.

Crane hurried into the bathroom and came back with a glass of water. She handed it to Bettina, who held Barbara's head and tried to coax her to drink.

"I didn't know," Barbara said over and over again, ingesting tiny sips of the water. She groaned as if she were going to be sick again, but then she just put her head in her hands and wept.

"What? What didn't you know?" Bettina asked when it appeared as if Barbara's nausea had passed.

"I didn't know how depressed she was. She couldn't go on." Barbara clutched Bettina's hand tightly.

The air in the hotel room barely stirred. Suddenly Bettina was aware of the utter absence of Jane in the room. "What do you mean?"

"She couldn't go on," Barbara repeated.

"You mean . . . she killed herself?" Bettina asked, disbelief and dread roiling through her.

Barbara's lips trembled, her teeth clicking together. "Yes. Don't you see? She couldn't live with herself."

Crane had gone back over to the open window. Her eyes met Bettina's, and she nodded.

Before Bettina could speak, a clatter sounded on the stairs, and two EMT attendants arrived with a gurney on wheels. After adjusting the height, they lifted Barbara gently, maneuvered her onto the pallet, and strapped her in. In a matter of moments they employed a blood pressure cuff, checked her pulse and oxygen saturation, and placed a nasal cannula on her face.

"Could I have another blanket?" Barbara asked. "I'm freezing."

The male voices rumbled as they tucked the blanket around her neck. "Just relax. You're going to be just fine . . . this is just oxygen to make you more comfortable . . . are you warm enough?"

"I don't think I'll ever be warm enough again." Tears coursed down Barbara's face. One of the attendants handed her a tissue, and she simply balled it up in her fist.

They raised the cart. The attendants stopped at the door. The EMT in the rear walked over to Crane and said a few words Bettina could not hear.

"I'll be at the hospital shortly," she told him.

He nodded, resumed his position, and they wheeled Barbara away.

Crane walked over to Bettina and put her hand on her shoulder. "Joe is down with the body." She stepped over to the window, and Bettina followed. Directly below them in the back of the lodge was a small, red-brick car-parking area. There, Jane lay on her side, one leg twisted underneath her. Joe stood guard over the body, his ginger-colored hair glinting in the afternoon sun.

"She jumped?" Bettina asked, feeling queasy.

"That's what Barbara told us, that she jumped when she heard us coming up the stairs."

"But why?" The window was wide open. Bettina noticed some scratches on the windowsill. "Were they fighting?"

Crane adjusted her glasses as she looked more closely at the sill. "Barbara says no. But she told us that Jane had begun acting strangely, saying things like she'd hired the man who drugged Barbara on the trail. Then later she said she was just kidding. Do you know anything about that?"

Bettina shook her head. "Drugging the water fits with what Jane did to me this morning. It seems so long ago." Her eyes were drawn again to look down at the car park, at Jane's still body. A wave of dizziness passed over her, and she stepped back from the window. "Did you hear a scream about ten minutes or so ago? I was sure I heard something when I was coming up the stairs."

"Barbara screamed when I entered the room. I heard nothing before that. It's been approximately a quarter of an hour since. I think that's what you heard." Crane scanned the room and gave Bettina a speculative look. "Most disturbing is Jane telling Barbara that she tampered with the power steering in Alec's car. I have a call in to the station in Austin about the car. They're reexamining both the brakes and the steering. It hasn't been driven since the accident."

"The car? You mean Jane planned this way back in May?" Bettina felt the world tilt. "Jane has been calmly moderating the festival, caring for Barbara . . . yet all this time she's been hiding her role in Alec's death?"

"I'm afraid she's been hiding in plain sight." The lieutenant took a Kleenex from her jacket pocket and passed it over her forehead. "It's very hot in here."

"So what happened? Barbara obviously found out about what Jane had done."

"Yes. Jane began to let things slip—she could no longer keep what she'd done to herself. She expected that Barbara would celebrate her boldness perhaps. But of course Barbara was horrified. And afraid for her own life. My hunch is that Jane felt everything closing in around her and that she had lost her lover as well."

"And so Barbara just stood by while Jane jumped? I find that hard to believe." Bettina resisted wringing her hands by shoving them into the pockets of her cardigan.

"Apparently Jane was close to the window. Which was open. There isn't a screen." The lieutenant gestured at the gaping casement window that extended from above the kickboards halfway up the wall. Accessing the opening meant an easy step up from the carpet.

Crane continued. "They were talking about Alec. Barbara demanded a straight story about the phone call and whether Jane had interfered with Alec's car. Barbara claims she'd just gone to the sink for a glass of water for Jane. As she brought it to Jane, Jane stepped away from her and toward the window. She said that in the end Jane just gave her a sad smile and jumped."

Bettina looked at Crane helplessly. She observed two police cars, an ambulance, and a Grant County sheriff's department vehicle making the turn into the parking lot. Her chest felt tight, the pressure to speak in the few moments immense. "I guess the real question is, do you believe Barbara?" *Can any of us believe her?* she wondered.

Crane didn't move for a moment. Then she indicated the door. "We'd better go down," she said softly.

Thirty-Two

Bettina and Miriam followed the ambulance to the hospital to wait for news of Barbara. As Bettina drove, Miriam fixated on the fate of Jane. The words Bettina had uttered when she returned to the car—*she killed herself*—enveloped her brain like a curtain of fog. Her mind shut down.

They entered the hospital and sat numbly in the main waiting room on the ground floor. After about an hour, Susan Crane approached them. The afternoon had turned cool, but the hospital was freezing. Crane had put on a tan trench coat over her white blouse and black slacks. "Barbara is asking for you," she said.

The three of them walked down a long hallway, past the X-ray department, and on through a chair-lined corridor filled with patients waiting to be called up for blood tests. They rode the elevator to the third floor, filed past the nurses' station, and turned into room 351. Barbara was sitting up in bed with an IV in her arm. Her eyes were half closed. For a few moments Miriam listened to the blips and chirps of the monitors recording blood pressure and heartbeat. In her numbed state, she found the sounds soothing.

Barbara's eyes snapped open as Miriam and Bettina approached her bed. "Thank you for coming." Barbara's face looked puffy, the tendons in her neck taut as if she were trying to shout yet had no voice. She grasped Miriam's hand and gave it the barest squeeze. "Jane thought so highly of you." Her smile was painfully direct.

"I admired Jane," Miriam said simply, returning the pressure. "We knew each other only professionally, but I always enjoyed our meetings. She was a brilliant woman." Barbara's wide, dilated eyes signaled naked need. Miriam wished she had something more heartfelt to offer her.

Bettina chimed in. "We're so sorry about what has happened. Is there anything we can do?"

"Lt. Crane, could I talk to these two for a moment alone?" Barbara struggled to sit up straighter.

Crane went to the door and turned to face them. "I'll be back in ten minutes," she said and exited.

Once the door was closed, Barbara said to Bettina, "Please come closer." Her voice sounded raw, as if she were scraping the bottom of her physical reserves. "I want the two of you to know I had nothing to do with Jane's death. By the time I realized what she intended to do, it was too late . . . She kept moving away from me as I tried to get closer. I wanted to grab her and demand an explanation. I was so upset—I felt I didn't know her anymore! She stepped closer and closer to the window. I reached toward her, but she slipped past my hands. You can't imagine how strong she was . . ." Tears leaked from her eyes, but she blinked them away. She grasped Miriam's hand more strongly and reached for Bettina's.

"Of course," Bettina began. "We didn't think—"

"Oh, Barbara," Miriam said, struggling to say the right thing. "Jane—"

"No, please! Please listen! It's not just about Jane but Alec too. I haven't driven his car since the accident, not since they brought it back after the investigation. It was in terrible shape from the crash. I'm sure now that the steering was defective. In the end Jane confessed to tampering with it. But I want you to know I was not involved. I had no idea about that. Please, it's very important that you believe me." Barbara's face flushed a deep pink. Her hands began to tremble, and she breathed in shallow gasps. "I trusted Jane. I thought she cared for me. I made a terrible mistake. And Alec . . . I'd give anything to have both of them back. Anything . . ."

"Now, you must take it easy," Miriam said, stroking Barbara's arm with her other hand.

"And the money." Barbara's eyes searched their faces. "The money that Alec . . . took . . . from the university. I will see that every penny is paid back."

"Please," Miriam said, "let's not talk about that now. You have to use all your strength to get better." She whispered to Bettina, "Would you call the nurse? It seems to me that her blood pressure or blood sugar or something is very unstable."

Barbara began sobbing. "I didn't know what Jane was planning. You must believe me, please, I beg of you."

Miriam murmured, "Yes, yes, try not to worry . . . Please, you must rest now . . ."

The nurse arrived almost immediately and hooked up the blood-pressure cuff. "I'm sorry, but you'll have to leave now." She nodded at Miriam and Bettina.

"Of course," Bettina said. "We'll check in on you later," she promised Barbara.

The two were no sooner out the door than Lt. Crane joined them in the hallway. "I'm afraid Barbara's report of what Jane had told her is true— there was a leak in the power-steering fluid in Alec Martin's car. We'd impounded it for weeks after the accident, and the mileage shows it hasn't been driven since. We assume the steering failed just before the collision. It was only a matter of time. Barbara has told me Jane confessed to her that she orchestrated the leak."

"I suppose you can verify fingerprints and so forth . . ." Miriam faltered. She knew the police would soon confirm who had authored the notes they'd found. There was of course a question as to whether or not Barbara had been involved. Jane was no longer here to defend herself. To her surprise, Miriam desperately wanted Barbara to be innocent.

Susan Crane trained her clear-blue eyes on Miriam. "You and Bettina are free to go back to the others at the lodge. I'll be in touch when we're all back in Austin. Thank you for coming to the hospital. As you can see, Ms. Martin is in extreme distress. I think it meant a lot to her that you stayed with her today and tried to comfort her. I don't think she has anyone else to turn to here."

The three made their farewells, Crane rather formally shaking hands with both of them. Miriam and Bettina made their way down the corridor, but just as they reached the elevator, Crane called out. "One more thing."

Miriam had a sense of dread as the trench-coated detective came toward them, as if a resurgent Colombo were coming back to ensnare them in the events of the day.

"Dr. Held, ah . . . Miriam. You remember our discussion about the locked room?" Crane's face looked worn, exhausted really.

"Of course." That conversation had weighed heavily on Miriam, particularly her comment to the detective that if they could recreate a situation in which Jane and Barbara might reveal their intentions, they would find out the truth about Alec. She wondered if by focusing on the locked-room mystery she had somehow incited Jane to escalate her risky behavior. She pushed aside her feelings of guilt as she noticed Crane observing her closely.

Crane nodded. "Barbara and Jane's room at The Pines, unlike the locked rooms in books, didn't have only one way in and one way out. In addition to a door, it unfortunately had a very large window, and it was open. An open window raises all sorts of possibilities. For entrances . . ." She paused. ". . . and especially for exits. I don't think we imagined that would be the case."

Miriam felt small—her theoretical ramblings about the locked room now seemed quaint, a foolish whimsy. She closed her mind against the image of a body falling through space. "No, I'm afraid we, or at least I, underestimated the potential for harm."

"That often happens." The elevator doors opened. Crane moved aside to let them pass. "But it's important to realize that we did not create—or choose—that room."

Miriam was startled by this observation. She thought again about the psychological prisons we construct for ourselves, and for the first time she saw the locked room as just an extension of that notion. Perhaps in the end, she thought, we all find ourselves in the locked room we deserve.

The entourage limped through the final dinner. Patricia insisted that the remaining presenters and their guests get together as planned. Miriam felt the rightness of this decision; the day's events had been too jarring not to commemorate in some way.

After dinner the group of eight lingered over their drinks, scattered in chairs and a sofa close to the fireplace where a fire flared in the grate. Brenda joined them once the plates were cleared. She had persuaded Daphne to try her special Old Fashioned recipe, and the two of them sat off to the side, talking quietly.

Patricia clinked her reading glasses against her glass of wine to get everyone's attention. "I feel we have much to acknowledge tonight: the absence of poor Jane, the hope for a return to health for our dear Barbara, and all of our hard work this week. Does anyone want to say anything?"

Absence seemed a *very* understated way to reference a colleague's suicide, Miriam thought, but perhaps Patricia felt as overwhelmed as she did herself and simply didn't know what to say. She looked around the great room, so often during their time there dominated by Jane Auckler and her Gertrude Stein. There was indeed a large absence. The place literally did not feel the same. Without the force of personality that emanated from Jane, there was no longer the feeling of a salon, of any cohesion really. Miriam, feeling the sense of disintegration of their group, wondered what right any of them had to be there any longer.

"I do think that every death teaches us about ourselves," Daphne said, her silver hair pulled simply away from her face with a clasp so that it streamed down her back. "This one has lessons in it that we will only know over time. My first impression was that Jane was a magnificent woman. I'm saddened to learn that she betrayed Barbara and herself as well."

Miriam took in the eight sober faces seated around her. As the only one who had known Jane previously, she felt compelled to say something to mark her acquaintance's passing. She thought about how often death makes people feel closer to the deceased. Yet at other times like this one, it exposes the depth of the mystery of personality. A striking gap existed between the surface Jane had revealed to this company and her deeper layers of self. Jane the performer had been such a potent force that it was hard to reconcile that commanding presence with the crumpled body she'd seen lying on the bricks of the parking lot at The Pines. She could only imagine the horror that Barbara had felt. Was it possible that Barbara could have prevented the tragedy? Was she implicated in Jane's death? Miriam knew only that she was very glad that it was Susan Crane's job to make those kinds of deliberations and not hers.

Aloud, Miriam said, "I am devastated about Jane. She must have been in terrible pain for a very long time." Grief tightened her throat, and she realized she wouldn't be able to say very much. She kept imagining how she'd feel if it had been Vivian who had leaped through that window in despair. "Jane's death feels like such a waste of many things. Her talent and intelligence. Her productive career. Her loving relationship with Barbara. I truly hope that she has found some peace." Miriam fought an urge to flee the room. Seated next to her, Vivian put her arm around Miriam and held her tightly.

"It's hard to know what to say in the face of such a tragedy," Bettina said, her green eyes soft as they swept across the faces of her husband, Darryl and Fiona, Miriam and Vivian. "We knew so little of what motivated Jane. The stakes for her were obviously much higher than any of us realized. I'm sorry that she didn't ask for help." She took Marvin's hand.

The gathering dispersed soon after this. Daphne excused herself to go outside to walk the labyrinth under the waxing moon, while the rest of them retired to their rooms to pack and contemplate the next day's travel arrangements, comforted by their impending return home.

Thirty-Three

Back in Austin on Monday morning, Miriam bustled about her house, preparing to meet her friends at the Corner Café. As she chose a cream linen jacket from her closet to wear for her class later in the afternoon, her hand brushed the black cape she had worn for her keynote address in Silver City. The substantial gabardine seemed out of place in an Austin broiling during its warmest time of the year.

The cloak brought back the image of Barbara's black Mabel Dodge Luhan costume hanging in the storage room at Oso Grande, its simple message of "Goodbye" a stunning preview of what was to come. Initially Miriam had been certain that Jane had planted that dress and that note, as she'd clearly orchestrated the other notes that day and the events that followed. Indeed Susan Crane had confirmed that Jane's fingerprints were on all of the notes. But that particular note had the flavor of a dramatic gesture by Barbara as well. Miriam had wondered ever since she'd heard of the two women's affair if Barbara had been planning to leave Austin, perhaps move to California with Jane. Maybe she was shedding her old skin and Mabel was part of the past she had wished to jettison?

Once again she pondered how often people were attracted by attributes in others that they coveted or wanted to try on as their own. In the case of their Chautauqua, there had been a blurring of identities between the presenters and the characters they had chosen to inhabit. Perhaps Jane felt more positive, more powerful, and more charismatic by taking on Gertrude Stein's persona. Barbara, with her confidence, dramatic looks, and money, had seemed a perfect fit for the talented, charming, and willful benefactor who had been Mabel Dodge Luhan.

The two characters Jane and Barbara had embodied, Gertrude and Mabel, had been attracted to each other in history; Alice, then, rather than Alec in the recent past, had stood in their way. Alice, her lover's champion and a zealous guardian of what she saw as hers, had triumphed, keeping Gertrude and Mabel apart after she saw their attraction to each other in Italy early on. And Alec . . . his end now seemed hapless, an unchecked downward spiral. In spite of all the advantages he'd had along the way in his career, in the end no one had championed him. Miriam sighed, looking out the window to her backyard. A female cardinal was perched in the oak tree, her orange beak bright against her brownish-gray feathers. A moment later a male bird, dramatically red and black, joined her, and the two birds flew off. Without a champion or a protector, she thought, people never flourish to their full potential. Life throws too many obstacles in our way.

Miriam's chest ached as she thought about Jane and Barbara, saddened by the irony that the women who played those historic characters in the present had no chance at an enduring love. Jane's erratic behavior and eventual death made that impossible.

Alec had been sacrificed so that the two women could be together, and Jane had paid the price. But the question still remained whether or not Jane had acted alone. Miriam's conversations with Daphne seemed to indicate that there was no substantial evidence to implicate Barbara in a criminal case. Like countless people, she'd been guilty of poor judgment in the choice of both her husband and her lover. Miriam thought of her lecture, "The Locked-Room Mystery." Committing a perfect crime was almost impossible; yet some people managed it. Luck, or rather fortune, always played a part. Barbara may have finessed her way into getting rid of a disappointing husband and inheriting a fortune at the same time. Such is the way of the world.

Miriam walked out onto the breezeway that connected the house to the garage, noting how the potted impatiens and periwinkles along the low white fence had wilted in the heat. She needed to tend to them and to her own life. She breathed in the humid air, so heavy after the dry mountain air in Silver City. Yet she was happy to be back in her own yard, in her and Vivian's house with their sleek cat, Phoebe. She honestly felt like the festival had been like a voyage of weeks through exotic territories, a trip where one began as a naïve traveler and, by journey's end, emerged as a different person. She hadn't played a character as the others had, but the swirl of identities and disguises surrounding her had influenced her all the same. In time she expected to discover exactly how.

Behind the wheel of her Subaru, Miriam turned the air conditioning on full blast to combat temperatures already approaching ninety degrees. With a determined jut of her chin, she backed out of the garage and prepared to negotiate the congestion of 9:00 a.m. traffic once she moved from her side street onto Guadalupe, a major north-south artery. A new high-rise reared its half-finished façade as she crept by, waiting for a red light to turn. Ah, for the sleepy Austin of the late 1960s and '70s that she had heard so much about, already legendary in the 1980s when she had arrived . . . Now gridlock was the norm, and the reality of the "sleepy college town" existed somewhere far away.

At the café she found that their usual table was occupied. Bettina had snagged a table against the opposite wall, painted yellow, a sharp contrast with the deep-purple V-necked long-sleeved top she wore.

The two women hugged as if they'd not seen each other for weeks. "Thank goodness you're here as always," Bettina said. "I honestly don't know what I'd do without you today."

Miriam thought she saw a glaze of tears in her friend's eyes. "I'm very shaky too. And grateful to be here with you. I feel like it's a small miracle that we made it out alive."

The two women slumped in their chairs. Then Bettina straightened her shoulders as if it took some effort. "Well, I never put much faith in miracles before, but I guess I've changed my mind."

Fiona rushed up to them in green spandex tights and a matching top, her blonde hair drooping compared to its usual brisk spikes. She leaned down to hug first Bettina, then Miriam. "I just had to go to the gym this morning. So much tension. I couldn't live in this body one more minute. Really, I've been buzzing since we got back!" She plopped across from Miriam and then noticed that the surface of the table was empty. "Damn!" She turned to address Bettina. "It doesn't look like anyone's ordered anything. I'll just dash to the counter."

"I've got it covered," Bettina said, leaning over to inspect Fiona's dangly turquoise earrings. "Three lattes are on their way, yours with soy, Miriam's decaf, and mine with double shots of caffeine—and whole milk, of course."

"No Danish?" Fiona asked, her gray eyes mischievous.

"It's being heated," Bettina said. "You know, I actually lost five pounds on this trip, so I'm treating myself."

"You always have Danish no matter what," Fiona pointed out.

At that moment the barista brought their three coffees to the table with a flourish, along with a plate of peach Danish. "Hello, ladies!" She gave them a half-bow and waltzed away.

"Thank you!" Bettina called after her. The young woman was a student in Bettina's class on literature from the 1920s and had begun to dress in flapper-like tunics that complemented her slender figure. Bettina pushed up her sleeves and claimed a pastry. After the first bite, she closed her eyes and delicately removed a smear of peach from her lower lip with her tongue. "Lovely," she said.

Sipping their coffees, the three women abruptly fell into silence. Miriam realized she didn't have the energy to banter about food, usually a major preoccupation.

Bettina let out a sigh. "I feel like we need to join hands and meditate, or say a prayer about Jane. What are we going to do now that we're back and not anywhere close to the center of things? I don't suppose Barbara has called either of you." She turned to Miriam. "Or Lt. Crane?"

"Barbara most likely has her hands full dealing with the police and her affairs. And I will be very surprised if she doesn't quietly move away from Austin once Susan Crane is satisfied," Miriam said, feeling strangely bereft that she would never get to know the charismatic Barbara any better than she did now. "Once her affections had gravitated to Jane, she was clearly done with Alec. Still, in my heart of hearts I don't think Barbara knew anything about Jane tampering with Alec's car. Obviously she didn't have a hand in the attack on her own person on the trail. And yet there is no question Barbara benefited from Alec's death."

"But if every woman sick of her husband could be accused of being an accessory to murder . . ." Bettina began, shaking her head. "It boggles the mind. We just have to trust Lt. Crane to find out the truth about this one." She held up her hand to Miriam. "Please don't say it's complicated. I somehow feel we have a right to know the truth."

Miriam nodded, intending to say nothing, but she was unable to stop herself. "There is of course Jane's truth and then Barbara's truth." Bettina flashed her a warning glance, but she continued. "We just have to accept that we may never know all of Barbara's motives or actions."

"There is another way of looking at this," Bettina said in a contemplative tone, stirring her latte. "It's been bothering me that Jane told Barbara she was behind the attack on the trail. It seemed so unnecessary to do such a thing just to prove she could be Barbara's rescuer. And then I saw it another way. What if Jane admitted this to clearly implicate herself?"

Miriam nodded. "You mean that because Barbara could not have attacked herself she would not be suspected in Alec's death either?"

"Exactly. Jane had lost her bearings, but she wanted to protect Barbara. She was signaling that she was the culprit." Bettina expelled a long breath. "Maybe she knew she would be found out, that she couldn't get out of the events she'd set in motion and be free. Yet she wanted Barbara to be in the clear."

Miriam saw how Jane's destructive actions had imperiled the very person she'd wanted to protect. She had certainly failed to save herself. "Then the notes make sense too. At the time I thought they were a ridiculous risk to take. I wondered what her intention was in writing them. But what you're saying makes sense. The notes also were a way to point a finger at herself."

Bettina's forehead creased as she pushed her hair back from her face. "Maybe the notes were a call for help, and none of us recognized that. God, I—"

"Stop—you two are giving me a headache. I know you wish you could have done something. But none of us did anything because we didn't know the facts then, and we scarcely know them now." Fiona's characteristic cheer had leaked away as she'd followed the conversation. "I'm feeling very blue about all this. We had such high hopes for the festival. After the horrifying way it ended, I don't know what to do—I can't concentrate on classes, Darryl is completely stressed out with his upcoming provost interview, everything feels mundane and unimportant. And Jane . . ."

Bettina nodded, absently nibbling at the corner of a second peach pastry. "Jane is a complete enigma. It's one thing to be guilty of murder, but then to kill herself . . . I can't make it make sense."

Miriam leaned forward in her chair, suddenly uncomfortable in her own body. She was grappling with a way to articulate her feelings about

Barbara and Jane. A crucial link had been broken, and that was the simple truth. "You know, I think Jane knew that she had crossed a line with Barbara. The phone call to Alec's cell was one thing, but tampering with Alec's car was another thing entirely. Of course Barbara was horrified at the thought of her husband's murder. As soon as Jane began to confide in her, she had to distance herself from Jane, and Jane must have found that heartbreaking."

"I think you're absolutely on to something," Bettina said. "Not to mention that Barbara must have wondered that if Jane could so cold-bloodedly remove Alec, what might she do to her in time if their affair cooled? Jane had become another person. A dangerously unstable one. I just never foresaw any of it. Jane was in disguise from the moment I met her."

Fiona regarded her keenly. "She left a trail of damning actions leading to her death. We just didn't have time to put the pieces together." She ticked off her fingers one by one. "1. Jane first called Alec while he was driving and flustered him by telling him his marriage was over; 2. rigged his car to malfunction at the crucial turn so that he crashed the vehicle, resulting in his death; 3. was on the verge of being brought up on charges and had lost Barbara's sympathy because 4. she had paid someone to assault her lover; and 5. had confessed to arranging Alec's death. Men frequently commit murder or manslaughter and then kill themselves. Why is it so shocking when a woman does it?" She raised her eyes to the ceiling and then slumped in her chair. "It *is* horrible, isn't it? We knew Jane! Or thought we did. Nothing makes her jumping out that window any easier to bear."

Miriam observed that Fiona had as usual laid out a logical explanation. But in this case logic did not improve her melancholy one iota. She put a hand on Fiona's forearm. "There is so much we don't know. We have no idea of the kind of life Jane has led, the pain or trauma she has suffered in her life, the turbulence or joy of her upbringing, whether she was a resilient person by nature."

She paused, patted Fiona's arm, and brought her hand back to her coffee cup. "I can't stop thinking about what seems to me a strange coincidence. Jane, a woman of confusing motives, deceitful behavior, and self-destructive acts, chose to portray Gertrude Stein, a woman known for mentoring and championing other artists, her charm, and her love of life. It's not that they were opposites. In fact, Jane had some of those

234

qualities, and she showed them to world. But inside of herself, in the end at least, those qualities did not win out."

"You're saying she dishonored Stein?" Bettina asked.

"Not at all. Her performance was a success, and she was very knowledgeable. She wore the mask well. But inside, no. And yet she was obviously attracted to the gregarious and innovative Gertrude."

"I think we're often drawn to what we don't understand," Fiona said. "In my case, I research and write about Edith Wharton because I learn more clearly about what it was like to be a woman of her time. And, like her, I had a challenging relationship with my mother. It's also an intriguing opportunity to fill the shoes of someone who had a far more privileged and worldly life than mine." A shy smile appeared on her face. "I feel I put on a cloak of dignity when teaching an audience about her. I admire her, and I can infuse that admiration into a compelling argument that she is important to contemporary audiences. I suppose I feel some of that consequence reflects back on me. It's like a dance between me, Edith, and the audience."

"That's a wonderful way of putting it. I think the dance you describe is the basis of all scholarship as well as the public sharing of our work, whether or not it involves performance." Miriam recalled the stance of Jane as Stein, her arms out toward the audience, saying, *I always said I would not come back to America until I was a real lion. A real celebrity.* Perhaps Jane had craved notoriety. In that she had succeeded.

"I'm grateful to Patricia for giving us a venue for showing us these 'dances,' as you put it, Fiona," Bettina said. "Each of the women we saw last week accomplished great things in her life, against all kinds of obstacles. They were pioneers in a time when women had much more circumscribed lives than we do. I'm inspired by every one of them to do more and to face challenges with the grit and determination they showed. What about you, Miriam? Do you still want to talk about mysteries and write about them?"

"Funny you should say that, because if I learned anything at our festival it's that I'm tired of lecturing about locked rooms . . ."

"And no wonder!" Bettina inserted. "Has it ever occurred to you that academia is a classic locked room?"

Miriam nodded. "Let's hope we all get out alive when we're ready to leave it." She laughed. "But I don't want to just *talk* about mysteries. I want to *write* a mystery novel myself. And I plan to. In fact, I think my first title will be *The Dean's Revenge*." Miriam had a moment's light-headedness while saying this. She'd always dreamed of life as a creative writer. She'd loved her life as a professor and scholar, but she also had yearned to turn her talents in this other direction. "There, I've committed myself, haven't I?" Miriam's brown eyes looked bright in anticipation.

Fiona tapped her spoon against Bettina's cup. "And you? Are you Lily Briscoe? Will you become a painter?"

Bettina's fingers swiftly rearranged the salt and pepper shakers and the sugar bowl, moving them in circles in an approximation of a shell game. Finally she put the pepper container in the middle. "I'm going to move the tree to the middle," she said, her cheeks flushed.

"How wonderful, but what does that mean?" Miriam leaned back in her chair and regarded her old friend with affection.

"It means something different to each person, of course," Bettina said. "For me it means accepting that I'm a middle-aged academic with a fantastic family and wonderful friends. It means I can have my vision, but only if I create it. It's tremendously exciting, if I have the courage."

Bettina sat back in her chair. She picked up the pepper and shook some on the table. Then she pressed her index finger on the particles so that black flakes stuck to it. She brought it to her lips and blew the flecks into the air. "Moving the tree to the middle is life, my friends. You grasp the chance that's offered, or you push ahead against the odds. Most of all, you dare to go forward."

————————————

Acknowledgments

A very special thanks goes to my dear friend Hilda Raz, whose unerring critical eye and generous support aided in moving this novel forward. I extend many thanks also to Elise McHugh, my terrific editor at UNM Press, for her insights and enthusiasm, and to the staff at the Press, who are always a joy to work with.

I am grateful to other early readers and writers' group members for our lively exchanges around the book: Elisabeth Sharp McKetta, Sue Hallgarth, Ruth Rudner, Ellen Barber, Cindy Sylvester, Harriet Lindenberg, Tanya Brown, Phyllis Skoy, Laurie Hause, Anne Cooper, Bev Magennis, Lisa Lenard-Cook, and Lynda Miller. I wish to express appreciation to the owners and staff of the Bear Mountain Lodge in Silver City for many fine and inspiring stays in its beautiful and welcoming setting.

As always I give heartfelt thanks to my spouse, Lynda, for her many contributions, including an essential sense of humor and her perceptive reading skills. She makes so many things possible.